FIRE SCARS

Fire Scars

A Novel

JOHN B. WRIGHT

UNIVERSITY OF NEVADA PRESS | *Reno & Las Vegas*

University of Nevada Press | Reno, Nevada 89557 USA
unpress.nevada.edu

FIRST PRINTING

Cover design by David Ter-Avanesyan/Ter33Design
Cover photograph ©gettyimages/Alex Ratson

LIBRARY OF CONGRESS CATALOGING-IN-PUBLICATION DATA
Names: Wright, John B. (John Burghardt), 1950– author.
Title: Fire scars : a novel / John B. Wright.
Description: Reno ; Las Vegas : University of Nevada Press, [2023] |
Summary: "Matt Solberg is an academic who moonlights as a search-and-rescue leader.
   He is tasked with finding eleven-year-old Linda, who has gone missing after a pair of
   fires burned down her family home. After finding the girl—badly injured, but alive—Matt
   becomes convinced the fires that harmed little Linda were arson. Working with FBI
   agent Bernie Katz, Matt's investigation ultimately leads him to suspect three people:
   Tabish, a legendary smokejumper; Fleming, a ne'er-do-well hell-bent on enacting a kind
   of eco-justice in order to gain the esteem of the men he respects; and ultimately Matt's
   longtime friend and a leading expert in fire and dendrochronology, Bill Knight. As it
   turns out, while Fleming and Tabish lit the fires that set the novel's events in action, Bill
   Knight has a long-game vision not only to burn out the California transplants who are
   marring Montana but also to exact revenge on a man who, three years ago, accidently
   killed Knight's wife in a vehicle accident that he caused when he was texting and driving.
   Through the eyes of the characters in Fire Scars, John B. Wright explores what it takes
   to overcome grief, the deep fire scars each of the people who inhabit this story carry with
   them, through fast-paced, ripping action from an author who clearly understands the
   tragedy and the necessity of wildfires."—Provided by publisher.
Identifiers: LCCN 2022038155 | ISBN 9781647790967 (paperback) | ISBN 9781647790974
   (ebook)
Subjects: LCGFT: Novels.
Classification: LCC PS3623.R5398 F57 2023 | DDC 813/.6—dc23/eng/20220916
LC record available at https://lccn.loc.gov/2022038155

Mark Medoff
Writer, mentor, friend

Acknowledgments

James J. "Jim" Parsons encouraged me to convey complex geographical conflicts as human stories. George R. Stewart's novels, especially *Fire* and *Storm*, laid the foundation for all environmental novels. Judy Stone provided strong editorial guidance, helping to bring *Fire Scars* to life, as did Fred Haefele, who steered me through the plot and all matters arboreal.

In Missoula, Bob Mutch, Steve Arno, Bob Pfister, and Jim Habeck taught me a lot about ecology and fire. The works of fire expert Stephen Pyne served as bedrock. The Missoula Fire Sciences Lab, the University of Arizona Fire and Restoration Ecology Lab, and the University of Arizona Laboratory of Tree-Ring Research provided essential research reports. Norman Maclean's *Young Men and Fire* was an inspiration, as was *Fire on the Mountain* and numerous other books written by John Maclean. Any technical mistakes in this novel are entirely my own.

Bryan DiSalvatore has been a steady source of writing insight and encouragement. Paul Starrs has been an endless fount of ideas. Dave Larson remains the griot of Berkeley lore. Bob Czerniak and all my friends at New Mexico State University offered real friendship and understanding. Thanks to conservationists Bruce Bugbee and Bob Kiesling for decades of opportunities to study Montana ecosystems and help protect them.

My dad taught me about science, NASA and otherwise. My mum encouraged my adventures in writing. My sister Cathy used her economist's brain to show me how to care more deeply.

My wife Rachel Stevens taught me about love and discovering art in unexpected places. Micah the poodle reminds me to chase sticks.

Finally, my profound thanks to JoAnne Banducci, Margaret Dalrymple, and everyone at the University of Nevada Press for taking a chance on *Fire Scars*.

FIRE SCARS

1

No one was supposed to be home.

Flames were loose in the world and burning closer. Screaming fire and strangling smoke.

Edward Merchant ran down the hall of his massive log home. "Linda!" he yelled. "Get up!" He opened her bedroom door and flipped the light switch.

The eleven-year-old stirred, blinking from the sudden brightness. "What's going on?" she asked, rubbing her eyes.

"Forest fire," Merchant said, trying to sound calm. "We're leaving." He looked out a hall window. A tornado of flames twisted up from the barn. The house itself might already on fire, he couldn't be sure.

"Gotta go, *now!*" Merchant yelled.

Linda emerged from her room wearing jeans and a green jacket. The two raced down a wide staircase into the great room. An elk-horn chandelier loomed overhead, metal struts flashing red and yellow as flames climbed the outside walls and licked the sills. A window burst, shooting shards of glass into the house.

"Oh, God!" Linda shrieked, then bolted out the back door.

"Wait!" Merchant shouted. He hesitated. Two original Charlie Russell paintings hung above the mantle. It would mean just a moment's delay to take them. But then another window shattered and fire invaded the house, igniting curtains, ascending toward the ceiling.

Merchant ran out the back door into the driveway. Hard to see in the blowing smoke. "Linda!" he yelled, spinning around. "Where are you?!"

His girl was out there in this madness. Merchant checked the Range Rover. Not inside. He wheeled around, taking stock. Pillars of flame swirled from the roof. "Linda!" he screamed.

A thunderous explosion blew Merchant to the ground. The garage was a fireball, launching two vehicles ten feet in the air. "Shit!" Merchant yelled, getting to his feet. The house was fully engulfed, red flames ripping high into the smoke. Plenty of light now, but no sign of his daughter.

Scalding heat pressed in. Merchant retreated to the rimrock. His daughter had a fort somewhere out in the boulders. A ferocious howl to his left. Merchant turned and froze. A second fire surged toward him, long scythes of flame torching everything in their path. "Oh, no," he whispered. This was death. Merchant felt a calm certainty about it. The drama of the moment collapsed to awe—life ends and it ends now, for him and his daughter.

He forced himself to snap back. *Have to find Linda.*

The fire roared uphill, gaining speed. The rimrock was Merchant's only chance. A small gap appeared in the flames, then slammed shut. He couldn't go back to the house. Gone. He couldn't make it farther along the cliff. Boxed in. Fire everywhere, lunging at him.

One last look. Off in the smoke, Merchant saw the thin shape of a person. "Linda! I'm over here!"

He struggled forward, but unbearable heat forced him back. The smoke lifted and his heart sank. It wasn't a person, just a small tree with burning branches as slender as a young girl's arms.

Merchant had only one job now—survive. Live through this nightmare, then find his daughter, alive or dead. Fire closed in from all sides. He raised his arms to ward off the scorch, staggering along the rock ledge looking for a place to hide. A slot appeared.

Edward Merchant surrendered to the earth.

2

Matt Solberg was rereading *Beloved* when he got the call.

A man named Phil Becker was missing up Bear Creek Canyon in the Bitterroot Mountains. When the fifty-four-year-old hadn't returned from a scheduled hike, his wife phoned the Ravalli County Sheriff's Office, trying not to sound frantic. But she was. Her husband had just been put on blood pressure pills.

Solberg sighed in frustration: 3 p.m. on Memorial Day. Called away from his shady hammock, cold Pabst, and a ghostly good book. Staying offline to shelter himself from a world addicted to bad news.

He alerted his Five Valleys Search and Rescue team with a text message. After changing into shorts, he grabbed his pack and checked the contents: maps, compass, GPS, radio, medical supplies, food, stove, titanium pot, lighters, space blankets, whistle, signal flares, bear spray, headlamp, water filter, and two stainless steel bottles.

Tools to find lost people. In every way that people get lost.

Solberg jumped in his pickup and drove through Missoula, then south on Highway 93, eyes peeled for drunk drivers. Thirty miles later, he turned right in Victor and headed west toward the immense shoulders of the Bitterroot Mountains. The land was still green with rising hay, but year by year pastures were being lost to subdivision developments. A white-tailed doe grazed on the doomed grass. "Sorry, sweetheart," Solberg said out the window.

He pulled up to the Bear Creek Trailhead. Three people waited there, large daypacks at their feet: Jake Pengelly, Ruga Snead, and Maile Felder—"It's Maile like smiley," she'd always have to say.

Along with Solberg, this was the entire Five Valleys Search and Rescue team. Vastly smaller than most operations, but Solberg preferred it that way. Mass efforts erased evidence and cost lives.

Solberg briefed the crew on the missing man. "Any questions?"

"Does Becker have a cell phone with him?" Maile asked, cinching her daypack.

"Couldn't say. It's not in his car, but he hasn't answered any calls, so..."

"Probably no reception up these canyons," Jake said.

"Probably," Solberg said.

Ruga nodded. "And cops can't use location-tracking systems in Montana without a warrant."

"Damn right," Jake said, slapping Ruga on the shoulder.

Solberg laid a 1:62,500 topographic map across the hood of his pickup. About an inch to the mile. He used a Sharpie to divide the drainage and assigned each person a sector.

Ruga Snead, a short man with quiet confidence and loud humor, was the glue of the operation. He was held at the trailhead to coordinate search results and get horses if they were needed to bring Becker—or his body—out. He'd even call in volunteers, if it came to that.

Jake Pengelly was the finest mountain climber Solberg knew. Used his long legs to pioneer an impossible route in Blodgett Canyon—named it *A Shiver Runs Through It*. Jake would cover rocky middle elevations.

Maile Felder had backpacked the Continental Divide Trail. Solo—twice. Fit and self-possessed, she'd check out side trails along the creek.

Solberg assigned himself the high country sector—Bryan Lake. He had a hunch about where Becker was and his hunches mostly panned out. Mostly.

He eyed the crew. "Remember, his name is Phil Becker."

The team folded their maps and fanned out.

At forty-two, Matt Solberg was the elder. Six foot two, 185, with square shoulders and tapered legs honed by thousands of hard miles. A jagged, three-inch scar ran along his left cheek, the result of a fall in the Mission Mountains years before. Another scar, fainter than the first, was the legacy of a horse wreck back when he trusted horses. Yet his eyes were youthful and bright—a vibrant shade of lilac—surrounded by unblemished whites.

Solberg hiked up the trail ahead of Jake and Maile. He knew every rise and turn in the 7.8 miles from the trailhead to Bryan Lake in the Selway Bitterroot Wilderness. He'd hiked this drainage hundreds of times and had memorized it like music.

The trail zigzagged up a series of glacial steps, places where the Ice Age had dug in deep. Solberg hiked at three miles per hour, a pace he could maintain forever, it seemed. He constantly checked the trail for boot prints. Becker's wife said the lost man was wearing Vasques, size 10, well worn. All too common, but there weren't that many hikers this time of year. Tick season and the threat of Rocky Mountain spotted fever scared most people off.

At a bend, fresh tracks led uphill. Size 10s. Probably Becker.

Solberg radioed his team and kept going.

Just past 8:00 p.m., he reached Bryan Lake. Long and shallow, filling a cirque basin framed by high granite walls. Slabs of rock rose like backbones from the wine-dark water. He radioed again. "Solberg, at the lake. Got a few signs, nothing certain. Out."

Time to slow down and *see*. He carefully inspected the trail along the east side of the lake. The mat of grouse whortleberry and woodrush was only slightly damp. Yellow glacier lilies grew where the land should still be drifted in. He'd never seen the basin snow-free this early. Meant one thing—a historic fire year.

Maybe apocalyptic.

Solberg went back over what he knew from talking to the cops. Phil Becker was an experienced Appalachian Trail hiker from Pennsylvania, but he had no knowledge of the Rockies, let alone the vast Bitterroots. He carried the basics with him except for a flashlight. Told his wife he wouldn't need it—"I'll be home for dinner."

"You chose poorly," Solberg said.

Becker had hiked the previous day in Blodgett Canyon and been so inspired he told his wife he wanted to "try something rangier." And those blood pressure pills. Solberg knew that when a man has a health setback, he tries to prove he's still a lion. Often by tackling a challenge far beyond his reach.

Solberg sighed. A male easterner, bruised ego, new pills, ancient terrain, and no source of illumination. And even with Montana's legendary long spring days, it would be dark in two hours. Then came the high-elevation cold.

"Rangier," Solberg said, just to hear the word. The word didn't match Bear Creek Canyon. This was an out and back hike unless you linked up with Big Creek and made a twenty-six-mile day of it, something Becker hadn't indicated on his card at the trail register. He'd written simply, "Bryan Lake and back." To Solberg, "rangier" meant too many things. Not just a bigger hike, but massive. To range beyond the margin of the map. Range: the distance a weapon can fire or a person can reach. The habitat of an animal, beyond which it dies. Or range could just mean to search. And that's what Solberg had to do, and he had to do it quickly.

He moved through stunted trees as the forest gave way to alpine meadows. Solberg kneeled and examined a clear set of prints on the trail. Matched the description of Becker's boots. Solberg made the pass with Sky Pilot Peak rising to his right. Boot prints continued over the divide and down into Idaho. He'd guessed right: the man was trying something tough in tougher country.

He drank half a bottle of water, air chilling the sweat on his neck. Then he squawked out a message. "Sector 1. Got fresh tracks heading into the Idaho side below the pass."

Static and blatz. Finally, a voice. "Solberg, this is Pengelly. Need a hand?"

"Any sign there, Jake?"

"Zilch."

"Alright, double time it to Bryan Lake and hump over the pass. Then radio in."

"On my way. Out."

Solberg contacted Maile. "Head out and check Big Creek, he may be doing a loop."

"Good, I'll finally get in a decent run today." It was a joke, but she meant it.

Solberg moved down into the Idaho side. Still only one set of boot prints. He cupped both hands to his mouth and yelled—"Phil Becker!" Solberg tilted his head to the side like a robin listening for a worm. Just moaning wind.

Half hour later, the temperature dropped into the low 40s as the sun set below a ridgeline. Solberg put on a long-sleeved thermal shirt and fire engine–green windbreaker. He strapped on his headlamp and, after adjusting the beam, continued his inspection as if it was midday. Except it wasn't.

Solberg knew that nighttime searches were sketchy at best. Hikers "go tharn," as he called it, losing track of all reason, making horrible, often mystifying choices. Once he'd found someone less than a mile from their car, shaking from the cold, unable to process reality. Another guy had stripped down to nothing, convinced he was hot. Those were the lucky ones. Found in time.

Hypothermia—too little heat—caused dementia in the afflicted. The increasing chill made that fate seem likely for Phil Becker. Once hypothermia set in, the worst could happen.

Solberg stopped at a fork in the trail. To the right, Packbox Pass led to Big Creek and a way out. True, it was a fifteen-mile slog, but

Solberg had hiked it many times and the route was mostly downhill. To the left another trail led to up to Sand Lake, a remote side drainage. High, frigid, and fierce. Very bad place to be when you're spent and disoriented.

"Alright, Phil Becker, which way did you go?" Solberg asked.

He moved forward, carefully scanning the ground. Becker's prints weakened, then disappeared. He backtracked until he reencountered the prints, then moved forward more slowly. The signs vanished again.

Tracking dogs would be ideal in this situation—scent doesn't fade with the light. But Solberg had stopped using dogs when Emma was swept over Sweathouse Falls two years before. He'd recovered her body down in the rocks, blood still oozing from her nose, mouth, and ears. Solberg carried his friend out four miles, arms in agony, never stopping to rest. The guilt still ached in his chest. Maybe down the line another dog, but not yet. Despite the emotional and tactical logic, it was much too soon.

A quarter mile and still no prints. He retraced his route and headed up the trail to Sand Lake. In two hundred yards, he saw fresh boot tracks in a low spot.

"Damn," Solberg said. Becker had gone tharn and was in desperate trouble.

The pitch steepened, but the ground was wet and he easily followed the prints. In half an hour, Solberg cupped his hands and yelled, "Phil Becker!"

No reply. He picked up the pace and made it to the shore of Sand Lake. Light from a three-quarter moon sparkled on the water. The air was damp and cold—high 30s.

Solberg loudly blew his whistle.

He heard a moaning sound that was almost human.

"Where are you?" Solberg yelled. "Make noise and I'll find you!"

"Ova heer," came a spooky voice across the lake.

Solberg hustled toward it.

And there he was. Phil Becker lay shivering under some Labrador tea bushes, curled up in the fetal position. Hypothermic and barely alive. Solberg's job was to get him *fully* alive. He stripped off the man's sweaty T-shirt, wrapped him in a space blanket, and put a fleece cap on his head. Solberg brewed hot chocolate and fed it to

Becker like he was a sick child. Then he built two fires and placed the man between them. He brought Phil Becker back from the brink, then radioed down to Ruga Snead to send some damned horses.

Matt Solberg had searched and rescued. Sometimes things turned out that way.

3

Dr. Mathew Solberg trudged up the steps of Parsons Hall, legs heavy from yesterday's search.

The Geography Department at the University of Montana was on the second floor of a stogy former library. The facilities were barely adequate for seven faculty members, grad students, and mapping labs. "Barely adequate" also described the salaries. His colleagues mostly came from out of state and were content to consider the scenery supplemental pay. Solberg had grown up in Montana, and despite frequent world travels, he simply couldn't imagine living anywhere else. The pay was what it was.

"Morning," Solberg said, easing into the departmental office.

"Morning," Dot said back. "Hear you found the guy."

"We got lucky," Solberg said, fanning through his mail.

"That's what you always say," Dot said, a twinkle in her blue eyes.

Solberg tossed envelopes, one by one, into the trash. "Any messages?"

"One from the Helena cops," Dot said, handing him a note.

Solberg scanned it—just a name and number. "Did it sound urgent?"

"Yes, but cops sound urgent ordering pizza."

"Probably just want search training."

"Have you checked your office phone?" Dot asked.

"Mailbox is full."

"Plan on emptying it?"

"People who count can find me."

"And you're on one of your 'news fasts,' I suppose." A wry smile.

"Three-day detox."

He headed down the hall to his small office. It had a large window overlooking a grassy quad. The branch of a maple tree grew so close he could open the sash and touch soft leaves. He did that often, especially after a troubled student came during office hours.

His old wooden desk was lit by a green banker's light. A calendar pad lay on top where Solberg wrote down obligations: classes, committee meetings, due dates for articles and grant reports, search and rescue business. Beside it were neatly stacked folders, each with a green sticky note indicating its priority. A beat-up laptop was set to one side. Harvey.

Well-stocked bookcases covered three walls, the volumes arranged by subject: Biogeography, Cultural Geography, Conservation, Europe, Asia, Montana. A separate section was labeled "Fire." Solberg had fought forest fires to pay for college and his interest had evolved into scholarship.

In Montana, fire is the truth.

He fired up Harvey, plugged in a flash drive, and reviewed his lecture on Ukraine for Geography 100—World Geography. Most students only took his class to satisfy a social science requirement. That brought Solberg grim frustration he tried to live with. The students' geographic illiteracy wasn't really their fault. Subject wasn't taught in public schools anymore. He considered that existentially dangerous and kept a list of prized student bloopers in a failed attempt to make light of it.

Custard's Last Stand.

Whales is a country in the UK.

The Chinese Revolution was the Mao Mao Rebellion.

Solberg's job was to fix what he could and convince those with the geographer's gene to become a major. His specialties were a natural for some of the kids attracted to mountain towns like Missoula. Rare kids who wanted to understand the human role in changing the face of the Earth and do something about it.

He taught each one a mantra—"Geography isn't about maps, it's about ethics."

Solberg headed down the corridor to a lecture hall. About eighty kids present, more than thirty missing. Typical. He logged onto the classroom computer and projected his PowerPoint on a thirty-foot screen. The students quieted down.

"Who knows was 'Ukraine' means?" Solberg asked, standing on the stage.

Silence and squirms.

Solberg clicked into his slides. "Alright, Ukraine means 'Borderland' and Ukrainians used to be called 'Little Russians.' During the Soviet times, the place was a republic controlled by Moscow. The Crimean Peninsula was part of Mother Russia itself until Khrushchev gave it back to Ukraine in the '50s."

Glazed eyes.

Solberg kept going. "So, why is the Crimea so geographically strategic?"

The sound of silence.

"Anyone?" A pause. "Think about latitude."

Nada.

"Alright, the Russians have their main naval base at Sevastopol in Crimea. Warm water ports aren't common in Russia, right?"

Mas nada.

"The Crimea also has oil and gas resources, which often explains wars."

"Damn Bush," a kid said.

"Which one and which war?" Solberg asked.

The kid smirked and shut up.

Solberg spoke clearly. "All opinions are fine, but have facts to back them up." He needed to say that *a lot.*

"And one more thing, most of the people living in the Crimea are ethnic Russians. So, for many geographic reasons this place means a lot to Moscow."

Advanced boredom.

"Let's go at this another way. In March 2016, a thousand square miles of Alberta burned. The town of Fort McMurray nearly got wiped off the map by forest fires when it's normally cool and wet up there. Last year, the Camp Fire was the biggest in California history. Dozens of people died and the town of Paradise was destroyed. Assuming human-influenced climate change is a factor, how might Putin's invasion contribute to warming temperatures?"

He might as well have asked the students to recite the periodic table in Urdu.

"Okay," he said pointing to a sharp-eyed woman. "First things first. How did Putin's invasion of Ukraine influence the world supply of oil and gas?"

She answered right away. "Increased it."

"How and why?" Solberg asked, pacing slowly.

"Countries produced more oil and gas because they didn't want to be vulnerable like Europe. Putin tried to blackmail Ukraine and the EU into obeying him."

"Correct," Solberg said. "Then what happened in Eastern Montana and North Dakota?"

"A fracking boom," a guy said. "My cousins cashed in big."

"For how long?" Solberg asked.

The guy frowned. "Until the oil glut hit. Then they got laid off."

"Drill, baby, drill," Solberg said. "Not so simple, is it? Increased production weakened Putin, but it also caused a vast increase in consumption due to cheap prices at the pump."

"Gotta love it," a guy said. "I paid $2.30 this morning."

"Which will lead to what until prices go back up?"

"More driving and more greenhouse gas emissions," the sharp-eyed woman said.

"Bazinga," Solberg said.

A nice laugh from the students. Solberg rode the moment. "So Putin helped create a glut which may create hotter average temperatures, climate change, and more intense forest fires. Do you agree?"

"Like the fire outside Helena last night?" a kid asked. "It took out a mansion and a girl is missing."

Solberg hadn't heard of it. "Could be. But let's get back to my bigger question."

A thin guy spoke up. "President Trump says China invented the global warming hoax to weaken us."

Solberg nodded. "Do you believe he's a fair arbiter of information?"

A blank stare.

Solberg sighed and moved on. For the rest of the lecture, he tried to draw a few more thoughts out of his tired students.

When it was over, he projected a slide reading: IT'S A BIG BEAUTIFUL WORLD—GO SEE IT YOURSELF!

A decent round of applause. Several students came forward to shake his hand and say thanks. A few gave him the stink eye. The final exam was next week, but a teaching assistant would give it and a computer would score the results. Last call.

Solberg exhaled with relief. Another school year over. He grabbed Harvey and walked home. He was tired and his needs were plain: dinner, a bath, a sip of scotch, and ten hours of sleep. Solberg turned the corner onto Jackson Street and stopped. An unfamiliar car was parked in his driveway with the trunk popped. Boxes sat on the ground.

The front door of his house was wide open.

4

"Oh, Becky, it's only you," Solberg said, rushing up.

"That's right, only me," she said. His daughter carried a cardboard box to the beat-up Corolla and put it in the trunk.

Solberg followed her into the house. "I didn't know you were in town."

"I wasn't expecting you to be home," Becky said, not making eye contact.

"Alright," he said slowly. "How are you?"

"Just peachy," she said filling a box. "I drove over from Portland for a couple of days."

"Great, the guest bedroom is always made up."

"Guest, huh? No, I'm staying with a friend."

Solberg exhaled. "Is that your car?"

"Yup, just bought it. I came over to finally pick up some things Mom promised me." Becky lifted a watercolor painting off the wall.

"That was always one of your mom's favorites," Solberg said. "It's Totem Mountain, above our old place in the Bitterroot Valley. She painted it just before..."

"...she was killed," Becky said flatly.

That word again. Solberg tried to stay calm, stay the dad. "It's a beautiful painting," he said.

"But Mom promised it to *me*," Becky said, pointing at her heart.

"Then it's yours."

Becky huffed and carried the canvas toward the door.

Solberg sat in a chair on the porch. He watched Becky pace between the house and car, carrying boxes, art, and clothes; cleaning out the last vestiges of her childhood. There was an angry finality to how she moved. Getting the hell out of here once and for all. Solberg felt an old sickness in his heart. Tasted blood-metal in his mouth.

Six years before, Becky found her mother dead from an aortic rupture—an exploded heart. The sixteen-year-old called 911, then sat with the body, knowing she was dead, praying she wasn't.

Solberg was doing a search when the radio came on. "Matt, this is Sheriff Denney. I am so sorry, but your wife was taken to Hamilton Hospital and..."

"Is Judy alright?!" Matt had asked, knowing she wasn't.

"Judy has left us," Sheriff Denney had said.

In that awful moment, Solberg noticed the man's gentle phrasing and felt sorry he was the one to break the news. Weird how we react to things. After arranging for friends to be with Becky, Solberg stayed with his team until they found a lost kid.

Becky had been lost to him ever since.

Solberg stood up. "Can you at least stay for dinner?" he asked, as Becky strode by. "I'll make your favorite stir-fry chicken."

Becky ignored him. Seconds later she emerged with a guitar case. "I'm taking this," she said loudly.

It was her mother's old Martin D-18. "Sure, I haven't touched it since..."

"Good. And no, I can't stay. I'm having dinner with Brace."

Brace was her latest boyfriend. No job, surly, leech. One of a long line.

"Alright, sweetie," Solberg said softly. "But have you got time for a cup of tea?"

Becky gently laid the guitar case in the trunk and closed it. She looked over at Solberg and for a moment her guard dropped.

Solberg froze. He should rush over and hug his little girl. Apologize, for whatever she needed. Say "I'm sorry" for the existence of death, if that would help. He took a step toward her.

"Gotta go," Becky said. She jumped in the car and sped away.

Solberg watched until she turned the corner and the sound of her engine faded. "Dammit, Matt."

Solberg went inside, grabbed a Pabst from the fridge, and rolled the cold bottle against his forehead. Popping it open, he walked into the backyard and took his usual spot in a hammock hung between two maple trees. He lay back and took a sip of beer, gazing at the grassy round shape of Mount Jumbo. Fading arrowleaf balsamroots—a kind of mountain sunflower—covered the slopes. The prairie grasslands were already turning golden brown in the dry spots, weeks too soon.

Solberg allowed himself a breather. Eyes on the land, cold beer, respite from worrying. A huge meadowlark strutted around the yard like he owned the place. "Tu es mas macho, amigo," Solberg said, smiling. He took a closer look at Mount Jumbo. The brown was more widespread then he'd noticed before.

When the bird and Pabst were gone, he looked at the note his secretary had given him. It was from a cop in Helena. He punched in a number on his cell.

"Lewis and Clark County Sheriff," a woman answered.

"Matt Solberg returning Lieutenant Goebel's call."

"One moment. He's expecting you."

A three-second delay. "Dr. Solberg, thanks for calling back," Goebel said.

"It's Matt."

"Good. Matt, we have a missing person after a fire yesterday."

"What kind of fire?"

"Haven't you heard? It's all over the news."

"Been busy."

"A wildfire north of Helena took out a movie star's mansion. Guy named Edward Merchant."

"No kidding?" Merchant had won an Academy Award for Best Actor back in the early 2000s. Then he'd cranked out action pictures to cash in. Tom Cruise Lite.

"Figured you watch his movies," the cop said.

"Used to. Is Merchant missing?"

"No, just minor burns and smoke inhalation. Bad news is, Merchant's eleven-year-old daughter Linda is nowhere in sight."

"His daughter." Solberg felt flushed. "Is the local search and rescue team out looking?"

"Yes, but with no luck, and Merchant's getting pissed. Says he's heard of you. Wants you to come over."

"Because of the book?"

"Seems so."

Four years before, Solberg had written a book for a university press called *The Geography of Search and Rescue.* Sold seven hundred copies, mostly to libraries. Then a national publisher reissued it with a new title (*Not All Who Wander Are Lost: Montana Search and Rescue Tales*), a gorgeous cover photo, and blurbs that made Solberg sound like Indiana Jones. Sold twelve thousand more. He considered the whole thing bizarre.

"I'll get my team together," Solberg said.

"Just you," Goebel said. "That's the bullshit politics of it."

"Alright, but I'll bring the rest over if I need to."

"Fair enough. When can you get here?"

"Where's here?"

"I'll send the coordinates. You won't believe it."

"What do you mean?"

Goebel blew by his question. "What's your email? I'll tell you what I know."

Solberg recited his address.

"Can you come now?" Goebel asked.

"I'm no use without a night's sleep. Had a tough rescue yesterday that ran late."

"I understand. How about 8 tomorrow morning?"

"Make it 7."

"Great, see you then. Thanks, Matt." Goebel hung up.

Solberg felt exhausted. Seeing Becky always left him drained—today worse than usual. On top of that, he'd hiked twenty-four miles during the Bear Creek search and now he had to help find the lost daughter of a Hollywood star. In his experience, Hollywood types were impossible to please.

He rolled out of the hammock, went inside, and opened up Harvey to check his email. All junk except for a new message from Lieutenant Goebel. He read the latitude and longitude several times, nausea rising in his belly. Solberg accessed Google Maps to make sure he had it straight. The screen blurred as the coordinates raced into focus. The meeting location—where the actor's mansion had burned—was north of Helena above the Missouri River in a swath of dry ridges and coulees. The site of the fire was unremarkable except for one terrible fact. Its name awoke terror in the hearts of Montanans.

Mann Gulch.

Solberg stared in disbelief. "Holy shit."

5

At 4:30 the next morning Solberg drove east on Highway 200. He sipped ginger tea from his thermos, watching the sky shift from deep black to thin blue. The route was encoded in his cells. Head up the Blackfoot Valley, crest the Continental Divide at Rogers Pass, then roll into the East Front, a paradise where the Rockies rise from the plains and the sky stretches forever.

The ride gave Solberg time to ponder what was going on at Mann Gulch, but nothing made sense. The celebrities who flock to Montana rarely come during the wet gray weeks that normally pass for spring in the Northern Rockies. They favor the long sunny days of early July, when the rivers run clear and the mountaintops are still graced with snow.

Spring broke the pattern this year—cloudless and scary dry. Solberg learned from Lieutenant Goebel's email that this had lured Merchant into a spur of the moment decision to spend the Memorial Day weekend at his Montana retreat. The Academy Award winner said a rest in the mountains would recharge him after filming a movie in the swelter of Thailand. Solberg knew the myth: the pristine Big Sky remedy. Merchant had flown in his daughter Linda from Beale Academy, a pricey prep school in Massachusetts. It was a chance for them to reconnect away from paparazzi and a crumbled marriage. Merchant even sent the caretaker away.

That was the plan, anyway, but Solberg knew the dryness was a trap. When drought comes this early, so do the flames.

Solberg turned onto Beartooth Road and rolled along the eastern side of Holter Lake, a reservoir on the Missouri River created for flood control and irrigation. Fishermen launched boats at Departure

Point and parked their pickups back from the water. He headed up Willow Creek on switchbacks, then plateaued out as the sun rose.

A black slash ran up the slope. The fire had come from below, widened into a broad V, then swept uphill, incinerating everything except pockets of shrubs around rock outcrops. He'd seen it all before. Fire creates mosaics of burned and unburned ground as it forages for fuel and red-hot gasses spread the flames.

Half a mile farther and Solberg saw the ruins of a massive log home with puffs of smoke rising from the debris. Sunlight reflected off the windshields of a dozen rigs.

Solberg rolled up and was greeted with a firm handshake. "You must be Solberg. I'm Daryl Goebel." The cop glanced at his watch. "You're early to boot."

Solberg nodded. "Any sign of the girl?"

"Nothing yet," Goebel said, concerned. "Edward Merchant was treated and released from St. Peter's in Helena. Tried his best to find Linda, it appears, but he feels sick with guilt. Said he hesitated before following his daughter outside. Paintings and such. The mother is Elaine, but she's estranged from Merchant. Lots of bad blood between them, according to the L.A. cops. This place was her dream house."

"In Mann Gulch?" Solberg asked.

"She's from California," Goebel said, like it was an explanation. It was.

"Any luck contacting her?"

"She's in Europe somewhere," Goebel said.

"Convenient," Solberg said.

"Ain't it?" Goebel said, shaking his head.

Solberg looked around. "Why aren't there search dogs up here? I don't use them anymore, but with a fire, a burned body will…"

"Merchant won't allow it. Too grim. I understand his point, I guess."

"I know, but can't you just use dogs anyway?"

"Edward Merchant has juice. He's a big donor to the sheriff's campaign."

A knowing nod between the men.

Solberg scanned the terrain. "Too steep for horses. Any luck with your drone?"

"We flew it several times. Zilch. Here's a photo of the kid," Goebel said, handing it over. "She's eleven."

Solberg studied it. Linda Merchant was gangly with dark lonely eyes.

He grabbed his search pack and walked over to the charred wreckage of what was once a Hollywood actor's palace. Cops stared at the smoldering heap, arms folded. The blackened skeleton of a Range Rover slumped in the driveway; tires burned away, windows melted to stalactites.

Solberg recognized George Czerniak standing with two EMTs. The man headed up the Lewis and Clark County Search and Rescue team. He was slim and serious. His clothes were filthy with black ash and old sweat.

"Matt," Czerniak said tiredly. "Glad you made it."

"Are you?" Solberg said, with a trace of a grin.

Czerniak managed a weak smile. "If Merchant wants you, it's fine with me, especially with a kid missing."

"My team too, if needed?"

"You bet," Czerniak said.

The men shook hands.

"Anything I need to know?" Solberg asked this plainly, but he meant—*Is there anything the father isn't saying? That Lieutenant Goebel isn't sharing? That your gut knows, but you can't prove?*

Czerniak shook his head. "Matt, I've got a weird feeling about this one. There was no lightning yet the fires came so quickly that Merchant and his daughter barely had a chance. Damned suspicious."

"Fires, plural?" Solberg asked.

"You bet. One on the Willow Creek side and the other from Mann Gulch." George Czerniak let the last name hang in the air.

On August 5, 1949, fifteen smokejumpers from Missoula parachuted in to fight what they thought was a small fire in a remote coulee called Mann Gulch. It was 102 degrees that day and flames exploded uphill in the superheated air. Three thousand acres burned in ten minutes during the blowup and the men ran for their lives. Only their crew chief, an experienced hand named Wag Dodge, had the sense to light an escape fire in front of him to create a safety zone. He yelled for the others to join him, but they panicked and kept running. Two guys made the ridge and survived. The rest died, including one land-based firefighter. Thirteen strong men were turned to charred meat.

Solberg sighed. "Alright. Thanks, George, get some rest. Your crew still out?"

"Got four in the gulch, but they're rookies. Lotta turnover lately. I've got three more newbies working the Willow Creek side."

"Anything else?" Solberg asked.

Czerniak looked exhausted. "Merchant said the girl had a fort out there somewhere," he said, pointing.

Somewhere meant Mann Gulch.

6

Solberg glanced back at the house, trying to imagine where a frightened kid would run. The rimrock was formed of gray Madison limestone that had been the bed of a tropical sea millions of years ago. Solberg searched weathered crevices where rain and snow had dissolved the rock. Caves formed that way—places to hide.

A few pines and chokecherry bushes had survived the firestorm in rocky slots, but everything down in Mann Gulch was cooked to soot. Solberg paused and took in the scene. Decades before, thirteen super-fit firefighters were overrun and killed here. What chance did an eleven-year-old kid have?

Solberg followed the boot prints of previous searchers in the black ash. It was unlikely they'd missed the girl's body, but he stopped anyway and performed a terrible task. He sniffed the air for any odor of roasted human flesh. Solberg exhaled with relief when he detected none.

He pulled out an orthophoto of the area. Contour lines of elevation were overlaid across a color aerial photograph. "Alright, Linda, where's your fort?" Solberg inspected the image, trying to think like a child. Then he scanned the landscape. Sharp outcrops alternated with burned-over saddles linking Willow Creek with Mann Gulch.

This place was famous, even hallowed. Fire researchers had combed every inch, trying to make sense of the natural conditions and human errors that created the smokejumper tragedy. Norman Maclean's book *Young Men and Fire* had raised its profile to a western myth like the O.K. Corral or Billy the Kid.

Except this ground was deadlier.

The ridge narrowed as Solberg moved north, side-hilling around outcrops. No point in shouting for the girl. After a day and a half, she was either dead or incapacitated. A brief stop for a gulp of water and a piss. Steam rose from the black ash. Solberg passed a broiled rattlesnake, then another.

An hour later, the boot marks of the searchers ended at a massive block of limestone with steep slopes dropping away on both sides. This was as far as they'd come, just a mile or so from the house. Solberg shook his head in disgust. "Yup, rookies."

Czerniak had said Linda Merchant often played out here. Solberg knew that a child's geography is much larger than adults think—a natural home they commit to muscle memory. One they can navigate in the dark, maybe even in thick smoke and terrified.

Solberg carefully skirted the immense outcrop on the Willow Creek side. Slots and crevices appeared to the right. Solberg muscled his way up the slope and grabbed chokecherry branches at the base of a crack in the rock. The gap was only a foot wide, too small for even a kid. He worked the outcrop, checking every crevice, scrambling up the face whenever he suspected a crack might widen.

No sign of the girl.

Solberg slowed his mind and let the land reveal its story. A Swainson's hawk dove and grabbed a charred rattlesnake in its talons. Solberg watched it fly over a far ridge. "Blackened reptile for dinner," he said.

Then he saw it. A large unburned chokecherry bush growing at the base of a wide slot in the rimrock. A place where rain funneled down and shade reduced the drought. The outcrop had given the bush life and protected it from fire.

A refuge.

Solberg went straight for the chokecherry. Behind its branches was something man-made. Girl-made. Small chunks of gray limestone were piled up, forming a crude wall across the three-foot entrance.

A fort.

"Linda," Solberg called out. No response.

Solberg stepped over the wall and ducked into the cave. He instantly recoiled from the stench of burned flesh and hair. He squinted ahead and saw two charred sneakers, then bent sooty legs. The body wore what was left of a green jacket.

Linda Merchant.

Her arms and legs were terribly burned and the hair was mostly singed off her skull. Part of her right ear was charred. Solberg dropped his pack and kneeled down, checking for vitals at her wrist and neck. Nothing. He bent over and turned his ear to the girl's mouth. No sign of life.

Solberg calmed his breathing and listened again at the girl's lips. A faint, almost imperceptible wheezing. He felt her neck—a weak thready pulse. Linda Merchant was alive.

Solberg grabbed a bottle and dripped water onto her lips, not enough to drink—that could be lethal—just enough to rehydrate the tissue and perhaps awaken her. He left the cave, scrambled to the summit of the outcrop, and grabbed his radio. "Daryl, come in, this is Solberg. Over."

A squawk of static. "Matt. What you got?"

"The girl. Alive, but badly burned."

A brief hesitation. "Damn. Where are you?"

"On the ridge top, a mile and change northeast."

"Roger. Sending EMTs and a helicopter. Give me your GPS coordinates."

Solberg gave his position. Then he went back and sat with the unconscious girl, saying, "Linda, you're going to be alright, hang in there, help's coming," those sorts of comforting words, but he took no other actions. Gauze, antibiotic cream or anything else he applied might cause infection. The burns were that bad.

In twenty minutes, he climbed the outcrop and ignited a signal flare that spewed reddish-purple smoke. Two EMTs ran up, panting, and checked the girl. They laid an oxygen mask over her mouth. Solberg went back to the ridge and lit another signal flare for the Life Flight helicopter on its way from Helena. The pilot saw the smoke and vectored in.

There was nowhere for the helicopter to land, so the pilot hovered and lowered a stretcher. Solberg and one of the EMTs detached it from ropes in the rotor gale and carried it down the outcrop. They placed Linda on the stretcher, covered her with a thin cotton blanket, and gently strapped her in. The three men hefted her to the top of the ridge, tied on the ropes, and released Linda to the chopper, arms raised as if in prayer.

With a swirl of wind and a roar of engine, the helicopter lifted, banked, and raced toward the hospital in Helena.

Solberg had no idea if it would be in time.

7

"I'll pay you whatever you want to catch the bastards." Edward Merchant sat with his checkbook open in the hospital waiting room.

Solberg was shocked by the bluntness of the offer—and the timing. Merchant's daughter had been in the ICU since yesterday, struggling to survive. The doctors said Linda had a fifty-fifty chance, and even if she made it she'd need major skin grafts and a lengthy stay at the burn center in Seattle.

Edward Merchant was a famous actor used to buying what he wanted. The veins in his forehead bulged and his eyes were frantic.

Solberg gathered himself. "What makes you think there *are* bastards?"

Merchant huffed. "Come on. Two fires were aimed at my house. They had to be set by *somebody*."

Truth was, Solberg had never run into a more obvious case of arson. So obvious he'd lost sleep the previous night at a Super 8 trying to come up with another explanation. He couldn't. "Mr. Merchant," Solberg began.

"Call me Ed."

"Alright, Ed. That's what the police and FBI are for. You need to talk with them about who might have done this. I'm just a college professor."

"Bullshit. You kicked ass and found my girl alive."

Solberg found Merchant rude and abrasive. The kind of man who praises and insults you in the same sentence. Merchant was a youthful fifty: fit, full head of brown hair, and bright green eyes, but there was a rough edge to him. A "Don't fuck with me" vibe.

Solberg couldn't tell if the guy was actually tough or repeating lines from his movies—the hard-boiled cop, the action hero, the flawed but righteous crusader saving the world against all odds.

And there was something deeper that Solberg read as danger. "Again," he said, "I highly recommend you talk to the police and Feds. I have no authority if a crime has been committed."

Merchant wrote in his checkbook. "This is just a thank-you. There'll be a lot more if you find the pricks to blame for this."

Solberg sat back. *Blame* is a different word than *responsible*. A distinction he noticed and filed away.

Edward Merchant slid the check across the table. $50,000.

Solberg was flummoxed. His university salary wasn't much more than that. He had a young mortgage and an old pension plan. The money was tempting. "No offense, Ed, but your daughter will need that money a lot more than I do. Especially with her mother out of the picture." His last sentence was probe.

"Linda is much better off without that stupid cunt," Merchant said.

Solberg was stunned by the crudeness of the man. Any woman talked to like that just might fire back.

Merchant's eyes welled up. "I just need my daughter to be okay. To be safe. You understand?"

Solberg pushed the check back across the table. "You bet. I understand exactly what you mean."

8

Solberg went over the case during the two-hour drive home. *Who* would target Edward Merchant, *how* were the fires set, and most importantly, *why?* His estranged wife was a logical suspect, but why would she hire someone to burn down her dream house? She'd get the place in a divorce settlement. More to the point: why would a mother try to kill her own daughter? And what about Ed Merchant? Doubt nagged at Solberg—Merchant was one rough character. The grim history of Mann Gulch had added a ghastly new chapter.

Solberg braked off I-90 in Missoula and drove straight to the Fire Ecology Research Center on the University of Montana campus. The old wooden building had weathered to dark brown. He got out of his truck and walked toward it.

A sketchy guy with a crew cut and long beard came out the side door. Arms sleeved with colorful tattoos. Helter-skelter eyes, a miasma of stink trailing in his wake. Solberg didn't think much of it. Missoula was called "Zoo Town" for a reason.

He took the stairs to Dr. Bill Knight's research lab on the third floor. It was a forensics unit, but not for analyzing DNA, for studying dendrochronology—the history of trees. Bill Knight sat staring at a slab of wood through a magnifying glass. The man was sixty-five, but wiry-strong with short gray hair. Pencil-thin tree-ring cores and wedge-like cross sections of trees were neatly arranged on a table beside him.

"Solve the mystery yet?" Solberg asked.

Knight pulled away from a cross section. "Visiting an old friend," he said, smiling. There was a dorky gap between his front teeth that didn't match his courtly demeanor.

Solberg waved at the air. "Man, you need to catch a bath."

"Students who drop by are not always fastidious," Knight said.

"I passed him on the way in," Solberg said.

Knight hesitated a beat, then held up the magnifier. "You're out of practice; tell me what you see." Always a teacher, a mentor: the professor of forest secrets. Solberg called him the Good Doctor, but never to his face.

Solberg sat down and studied the tree rings. Concentric circles moved out from the core like ripples in a pond. He knew the basic story well. Wide rings meant wet years or release from shade when overstory trees fell. Thin rings meant drought or crowded stands.

"I'd say this ponderosa pine is about three hundred years old. Maybe from one of your sites on the west side of the Bitterroot Valley, judging from the pattern."

"Perhaps," Knight said, giving nothing away. "But what does the pattern show?"

"This tree started slow with a dense packing of rings in the heartwood. Then it produced wide rings during the moisture of the Little Ice Age. Late 1700s, I'd venture, just before Lewis and Clark."

"And long before the ursine shill," Knight huffed.

Solberg smiled. "Yes, way before Smokey Bear."

"Go on," Knight said, deadpan.

"The rings show cycles of wet and dry years, like always. The 1930s drought is obvious. Wet in early '80s. Not sure, but I swear I can see the snowy winter of 1996–97. Drier since then. The last rings barely stand out."

"Which means what?" Knight asked.

"Very dry conditions, like we're getting lately. Or the forest thickening up and starving the tree of moisture. Did I pass the quiz?" Solberg asked.

"Not yet," Knight said.

"No rest for the wicked," Solberg said, grinning.

"Tell me the fire history," Knight said. "That's what matters."

Solberg inspected curving brown wounds along the edge of the cross section. Each was a marker of flames burning past the tree, but not killing it. A legacy of wounded flesh. They're called "fire scars."

Solberg did a quick assessment. "Looks like eight fires were hot enough to scorch the tree, but not hot enough to kill it. Then the fire scars end about 130 years ago."

"Same old story, isn't it, Matt?" Knight said, sighing.

Solberg leaned back. "Let me guess. Last burn was in the 1880s."

"Yes, 1886," Knight said. "Cattle grazed off the grass and cleansing fires ended."

"Then the forests thickened and the pine beetles came," Solberg said.

"And the people," Knight said.

"Careful," Solberg joked. "Some of those people were my ancestors."

Knight showed a gap-toothed grin. "Let's find the liniment."

Solberg took a chair as the Good Doctor pulled a bottle of Laphroaig scotch from his desk drawer. A MacArthur "genius award" plaque hung crookedly on the wall behind him. The photo of Molly, Knight's dead wife, was missing, a discolored square where it once reigned. Bill Knight made strong pours into two glasses—neat—and set the whisky bottle close by. Silence as the men sipped Laphroaig. The sacrament of scotch.

Solberg was baffled by the timing of the Mann Gulch burn. In summer, forest fires get started by lightning, campfires, chainsaws, any number of things. This had happened in the spring. "Who sets fires in May?" Solberg asked quietly. "It's hardly prime time."

Knight smiled slightly. "You're working the Mann Gulch fire."

"Yes."

"I'm glad it's you," Knight said.

Solberg sat back, confused.

"As you suggest, it's very strange," Knight said. "Rarer than rare for fires to happen this early. Even in country as dry as Mann Gulch."

"It would take someone with experience to pull this off," Solberg said.

"Obviously," Knight said. "The results were excellent."

"If you think like an arsonist," Solberg said, brow furrowed.

"Yes, if destruction is your metric," Knight said matter-of-factly.

"And with Merchant's success in show business, there could be lots of people who might want to fuck with him. And they'd have the money to hire a pro."

"Hollywood is a fetid morass," Knight said.

Solberg leaned forward. "Cops say the mansion was built for Merchant's soon to be ex-wife."

"Lowers the chances she's involved, doesn't it?"

"I agree," Solberg said. "Unless she's rabidly pissed and not thinking clearly."

"Cops talk to her?" Knight asked.

"She's overseas. Has been for months."

"Nothing suspicious there, right?" Knight rubbed his temples wearily. "But what if Merchant had the fire set to destroy the place his wife loved? Causing pain is a popular choice in divorces."

"He and his daughter were staying there. Why would Merchant do it?"

"Maybe the arsonists he hired screwed up the date. Most criminals aren't in Mensa."

"I don't see it," Solberg said. "Ed Merchant was genuinely shocked when I talked to him."

"Ed, huh?" Knight said. "Just remember, Merchant is an actor. He can fake genuine."

"He did have a weird edge. Shit, I bet this mystery goes viral in no time."

Knight nodded. "Already has. It's being covered by everyone from local Montana TV stations to U.S. networks to the BBC. An irresistible story. Movie star with an injured daughter and a failing marriage. The mystique of Montana and the terror of arson."

"But there are lots of motivations for arson."

"Yes, but terror is the most gratifying side effect," Knight said.

"Because it destroys peace of mind."

"Precisely," Knight said. "Houses can be rebuilt. Minds can be ruined. If you want to inflict real pain on someone, arson is a logical choice."

"Remind me to never cross you," Solberg said, smiling.

"You never would, Matt. Alright, where did the fires start?" Knight asked.

Solberg leaned forward. "A Helena cop named Goebel emailed me this morning. One ignition was above Willow Creek on a steep side slope, the other was at the base of Mann Gulch and easily accessible."

"Probably two arsonists, given those locations."

Solberg nodded. "One who was fit enough to deal with tough terrain and one who wasn't."

"One young and one old," Knight said.

"Or a leader and a follower," Solberg said, leaning forward, then back.

Knight gave a cryptic smile. "What about the ecosystems?"

"Both fires were set in grasslands with encroaching pines. I checked with the National Weather Service. There was no lightning that night, so it was definitely arson."

"Accelerant?" Knight asked, eyes on the ceiling.

"Couldn't say. I didn't have any gear so I didn't inspect the sites."

Knight looked back at Solberg, displeased. "You have to keep up or this won't be very interesting." The Good Doctor's usual game. Knight eyed him. "Did this cop tell you anything useful about the possible culprit?"

"He did."

"Imagine that," Knight said.

"Goebel said he'd collected strange things from each site."

"And exactly *how* did he contaminate the crime scenes?" Knight asked.

"He found what he called 'some weird shit' partially melted by the flames," Solberg said. "I saw the images and told him they were pyrometric cones."

Knight seemed bemused by that information. Pyrometric cones are ceramic gizmos that potters use to monitor heat in a kiln. Each type reacts to temperature differently. If the kiln is too hot, the cones melt to puddles, too cool and they stay unchanged. Cones are a kind of thermometer for firing ceramic art.

Knight shrugged. "I tried using cones to measure heat intensities in prescribed burns, but they were erratic. Gave up on them. So, pray tell, why were they put there?"

"Not sure. Goebel sent me digital photos of the things exactly as he found them." Solberg called up two pictures on his phone and handed it to Knight. They showed scatters of burned cones, four inches in size, arranged in three rows.

"These should be analyzed by a ceramic artist," Solberg said.

"No need," Knight said. "Your arsonist has a sense of humor. Send me the images."

Solberg took his phone back and emailed the photos to Knight. Soon they were looking at the pictures on twin thirty-inch computer screens.

"*Now* what do you see?" Knight asked.

Solberg studied the images. Some cones had melted into rough circular blobs. Others retained a linear shape. No obvious letters or figures. No directional arrows or township and range patterns. They didn't indicate much of anything, as far as he could tell. "I don't get it," Solberg said, sitting back.

Knight tapped a pencil on his desk in alternating speeds.

Dot, dot, dot.
Dash, dash, dash.
Dot, dot, dot.

Solberg looked shocked. "SOS?"

"Morse Code distress signal," Knight said, shaking his head. "Oh so original. Now let's decode the other site."

The second pattern of melted cones—the one in Mann Gulch—was both simpler and more disguised.

Dash, dash.
Dash.
Dash, dash.

Knight quickly translated the letters.

M
T
M

"Mean anything to you?" Solberg asked.

"Yes, but work the problem," Knight said.

Solberg mulled. The Good Doctor studied his face.

"Mary Tyler Moore," Solberg said, smiling. "Wait a minute, MTM was an eco-raider group back in the '90s called the Montana Tree Monkeys. They spray-painted MTM on the logging trucks and bulldozers they ruined by putting bleach in the gas tanks."

"And they spray-painted those letters on trees they'd driven metal spikes into."

"To scare off loggers," Solberg said. "Could it really be them?"

Knight smiled slightly. "You never know, but the Tree Monkeys were just pissed-off college kids. Hell, the FBI even interviewed me for having some of them in my classes. Feds figured I was a criminal mastermind for *talking* about the eco-radical movement. Morons."

"Feds or kids?" Solberg asked.

"Both."

"The FBI put a few of them in prison, right?" Solberg said.

"Yes," Knight said, "but only for three-year pulls. And if the group is reborn, why the silly little code? It was never their style."

"Maybe they found a new one," Solberg said.

"Or someone co-opted their old one," Knight said.

Solberg was frustrated. "Why would a long-dead eco-terror group suddenly target an actor and nearly kill his daughter? It doesn't add up."

Knight sat back. "Unless it wasn't them at all."

"So we're back to square one?"

"Matt, there's nothing fancy going on here, just a single question. Who holds the biggest grudge against Edward Merchant?"

"Or, alternatively, who holds a grudge against people *like* him?" Solberg asked.

"Rich big shots," Knight said. "Well done, Matt."

"But that doesn't narrow the field. Lots of Montanans hate the wealthy newcomers and talk about running them off."

Knight nodded. "But so far it's just big talk, isn't it?"

"Maybe someone just got bigger," Solberg said.

Knight smiled. "Fire is such a lovely monster."

9

Solberg walked across campus in the cooling air. Talking with the Good Doctor was always a challenge. The Socratic method with the answers obscured. Today more than usual. Knight always spoke of fire in scientific terms. *Lovely* or *monster* never came up.

Solberg called Lieutenant Goebel in Helena and told him about the SOS and MTM codes. Goebel sounded justifiably skeptical, but said he'd call the FBI to see if there was anything linking the Montana Tree Monkeys or other eco-sabotage groups to Edward Merchant. He said Bernie Katz at the Bureau was already chasing the estranged-wife angle. No need for Solberg to do anything more for now.

He felt bone tired. The strain of the past week's rescues, his daughter's visit, and the Laphroaig were all taking effect. Home would be restful—the calming sound of Rattlesnake Creek and the perfume of cottonwood trees. But Matt Solberg needed company and the idea of the Grizzly Bar felt like wisdom.

The campus was deserted as he headed downhill to the Clark Fork River and walked west on a path beside the water. The river was dropping fast as the meager snowpack melted out early. Gravel bars were already visible.

Solberg crossed the Clark Fork on a walkway slung under the Madison Street Bridge. On the north bank he grabbed his cell phone and dialed a familiar number. "Hey, Bo, it's Matt."

"Hey, stranger," Bo said. "How the hell are you?"

"Long story," Solberg said. "Can I buy you a drink?"

"Let me guess, the Griz Bar?"

"As God intended," Solberg said.

"Yes, she did." Click.

Minutes later, Matt Solberg entered the front door of the Grizzly Bar. It was a long narrow place with an antique wooden backbar and dingy walls covered with photos of local sports teams and star players. A pantheon of slow white guys. The lighting was as bright as an operating room, something the owner Ned Lutey said reduced fistfights. The Griz was a hundred-year-old bar famous for cheap beer and the best burgers in Montana.

"Hey, Solberg, you fucking academic." It was Barkey Boyd's usual greeting.

Solberg smiled and sat down on a stool across from Barkey. The man was short and mustached—going bald. Four other carpenters and tradesman were gathered around him at the far end of the counter, a place they called the Flight Deck. Tired guys drinking the nicks and pains away. Nods, smiles, and obscene greetings were exchanged as a glass of Pabst Blue Ribbon beer was poured for Solberg from a plastic pitcher.

"Hey, Matt," Barkey said. "What do you call a North Dakotan with a pig under one arm and a chicken under the other?"

"No idea," Solberg said, grinning.

"A bisexual," Barkey said.

The group burst out laughing, Solberg included. It felt good to be off duty. Solberg bought a fresh pitcher of PBR, shared it, and listened as the men talked about fishing, construction, and "fuckin' Californians." People from that state were as popular as anthrax in Montana. They were blamed for everything from high real estate prices (true) to wolf reintroduction (mostly not true) to lousy pay (complicated).

"Say, Matt," a carpenter said, "how's that kid over in Helena?"

"Linda Merchant will probably make it, but she's badly burned."

"A damn shame," Barkey said. "You okay?" There was real concern in his eyes.

"Just worn out," Solberg said.

Every head turned toward the door as Bao Xiong—"Bo" to everybody—walked into the bar. She was forty-six, five foot two, and slim with long, basalt-black hair and warm brown eyes. When she smiled, you breathed better. Or you ached.

Bo walked over and gently touched Solberg on the shoulder. "Hi, Barkey. Hey, guys."

The men mumbled greetings. Bo intimidated men without meaning to. She was a professor in the Geography Department with Solberg. Born in Laos and raised in Missoula. Exotic no matter what she did. Brilliant no matter how much she wanted to be regular. Bo always tried to put the men of the Griz at ease. It wasn't a stretch; she liked them. Respected that they worked hard at something and were good at it.

"Say, Barkey," Bo said. "How did the North Dakotan die from drinking milk?"

Barkey played along—knew 'em all. "No idea, Bo."

"Cow fell on him."

A kind round of laughs.

As the bar filled, Solberg and Bo found a corner table and sat down. Bo sipped a Gray Goose martini, *very* dry, with a twist. Fancy for the place, but everyone went along. It was only 6 and the Grizzly Bar was still quiet enough to hold a conversation. By 8, kids would take over and crank up the jukebox. For now it was a pub.

Solberg felt calmer around Bo. The muscles in his back relaxed and he leaned forward to hear whatever she had to say.

"I read the news about the Merchant girl," she said. "Are you alright?"

Matt sipped beer and said nothing.

"That bad, huh?" Bo said.

"Something you never want to see." Matt's eyes welled up with tears. He forced the emotion down.

Bo reached across the table and rested her small hand on his big one.

"The poor kid must have been terrified," he said, eyes on Bo. "I can only imagine."

"But you found her, Matt," she said, massaging his hand.

He nodded half-heartedly. They drank in silence for a while.

"Becky showed up at the house the other day," Matt said.

"She staying with you?" Bo asked, although she knew the answer.

"Grabbed her last possessions and drove off like her tail was on fire. Sorry, bad choice of words."

34

"It's okay," Bo said. "Maybe one day Becky will stop blaming you for her mom's death."

"Maybe I will too," Matt said.

Bo started to say something and stopped.

Solberg settled his tab, adding a $10 tip. Ned Lutey rapped his knuckles on the bar as a thank-you.

Matt and Bo walked down East Front Street, passed the Stockman's Bar, took a right on Higgins, and climbed down the stairs to Caras Park. A wedding reception was in full swing under a huge canopy. "That's My Daughter in the Water" played as the bride and groom danced in an explosion of cell-phone flashes.

They walked for an hour along the Clark Fork River without speaking until moonlight danced on the riffles and the liquor wore off. Bo took Matt's hand and led him to her blue house beside the water. They went in the backyard and lay together in the hammock listening to the river. Matt hugged Bo close. She kissed his neck, then whispered in his ear.

They went inside and made love slowly, like it mattered, which it did. When they finished, Matt Solberg held Bo Xiong in his arms and cried.

10

The meth flashed and exploded in Rod Martin's face. He screamed, breathing in flames through his cotton mask. His lungs were instantly destroyed by the toxic mixture of combusted acetone, alcohol, ether, and propane. The man stumbled out of the trailer house and fell to the ground on fire.

Charlene Martin was knocked flat by the concussion. She jumped up and ran to her husband. He writhed in agony, making crude mammal sounds. She kicked dirt on him to put out the flames, but it was no use. The volatiles were in charge now.

She sprinted to the pickup and grabbed a fire extinguisher. By the time she turned back, the trailer was an inferno. Charlene choked on the rancid smoke and circled around to reach her husband. A surge of heat pushed her back, retching from the stench of burning chemicals.

"Oh, my God!" she screamed. Charlene wheeled around and frantically looked for her ten-year-old daughter. "Dakota!"

"Mom!" came the girl's voice. She was just returning home on her bike. "What happened?!"

"Get in the truck now," Charlene said.

"But where's Daddy?" the girl asked.

"Just get in!"

The girl obeyed and the woman jumped into the driver's side. "Shit!" Charlene yelled.

Keys were in the burning trailer. There was no other vehicle. Charlene Martin grabbed a .45 revolver from under the seat and got out of the truck in shock. *Was this really happening?* Her husband was dying and she couldn't reach him. What little she owned was burning up right in front of her.

Charlene took her daughter's hand and together they ran through the pines. Even in her methed-up state, she knew they couldn't use the road. The fire department and cops would find them for sure.

A look back. The trailer house was a pyre, the poisoned flames spreading into the forest.

11

Matt Solberg crossed the Bitterroot River on the Eastside Highway and turned up Threemile Creek Road. Police cars, fire trucks, and a water tanker were parked near the smoking wreckage of what had been a trailer house. He pulled up and parked.

The ground beside the blackened trailer was littered with plastic bottle, acetone cans, broken beakers, antifreeze jugs, and reddish-stained coffee filters. Meth lab trash.

Volunteers from the rural fire department hit the fire with long water hoses and shovels. Seemed contained. If it wasn't, flames would feast on timber and fatten into a crown fire. Solberg was certain that slurry bombers stood ready at the Aerial Fire Depot in Missoula.

His search team—Maile Felder, Jake Pengelly, and Ruga Snead—were already on site talking to firefighters. Sheriff Spike Denney walked up.

"What have we got?" Solberg asked.

"A good start," Sheriff Denney said.

"What do you mean?" Solberg asked.

"One dead drug cooker and the other afoot in bad country."

Solberg scowled.

Denney took the hint. "Shame is, the woman took her daughter along."

"Who we looking for?" Solberg asked.

"Charlene Martin. Thirty-two. Popped twice for minor drug offences. Her husband, Rod Martin, thirty-seven, is the deceased. Had quite a record, even did a stretch in Deerlodge for peddling heavy weight. When the meth lab blew, the guy lit up like a torch."

"Vivid," Solberg said.

Denney took the hint again. "The victim had no chance, which is typical of these things. The pickup over yonder was their only vehicle. So Charlene's up there somewhere with her ten-year-old kid," he said, pointing to the Sapphire Mountains. "Girl's name is Dakota."

What Denney hadn't mentioned was the woman's mental state. Shock, terror, loss. Or the girl's. While the sheriff could dismiss Charlene Martin as a "meth cooker," Solberg saw her as a lost person.

Denney also hadn't mentioned if the woman had a gun.

"Alright," Solberg said to his team. "Let's get to work." He divided the topo map into sectors and made assignments. Denney matched each of Matt's crew with an armed deputy, then retreated to his "command post"—an old police car. The teams were about to fan out when the news came in over the radio.

"No need, Matt," Denney yelled. "Dispatcher just got a call from Henry Smoot. They turned themselves in over at the Triple-R Ranch on Grayhorse Creek. Henry's got a gun on them until we get there."

Solberg felt relieved and sad. There was no need for a search, but the woman's life was ruined. He'd never met her, but he knew people like her—an addict with a history of physical abuse. And now facing a long prison sentence, Charlene Martin would become an institutional woman. One with no hope of ever having a meaningful life.

And the girl. Unless a family member claimed her, Dakota Martin was lost forever.

"Okay, guys," Solberg said, folding his map. "Guess that's it."

The dull boom of a gunshot echoed in from the direction of Grayhorse Creek.

Denney grabbed his radio. "This is the sheriff. I heard gunfire. Anyone close to Henry Smoot's place? Over."

At that exact moment, Deputy Tommy Barnes pulled up at the Smoot ranch house. He squawked back: "This is Barnes. I heard the radio traffic and I'm on scene. Send backup."

Sheriff Denney sent two patrol cars racing away.

Deputy Barnes drew his .40 caliber Glock and moved quickly toward the Smoot house. He heard screaming inside and took position to one side of the front door, pistol raised. "This is the police! Henry, you alright?" The screaming was awful: a girl's feral wail.

Barnes flipped the knob and kicked the door open. He took a quick look, saw a body on the floor, and rushed inside, gun held straight out with both hands. "Police! Nobody move!"

Dakota Martin was shrieking. Her mother lay on floor in a hash of blood and flesh, her face shredded by a shotgun blast.

"I had to," Henry Smoot said, dazed. "I took her revolver off her but then she started acting crazy and grabbed it back. I swear it, Tommy." Smoot gripped a Remington 870 shotgun.

"Lay the weapon down, Henry," the deputy said evenly. The man snapped out of it and did as he was told. The deputy radioed the sheriff. "Send an ambulance and a female officer over here. The vic is—" he hesitated and looked at Dakota. "The woman is 10-55."

"Sweet Jesus!" Spike Denney said. "And the girl?"

Dakota sent a scream across the world.

"Never mind, Tommy. I hear. On our way. Out."

"I need to come," Solberg said to the sheriff.

"No, there might be more armed meth heads out there."

"Doesn't matter, I should be there."

"Crime scenes are no place for civilians," the sheriff said.

Solberg grabbed the sheriff's arm. "I need to help the girl!"

Jake stepped between the men and eased Solberg away. Sheriff Denney gave Jake a look—*What the hell is wrong with this guy?*

Denney got in his cruiser and roared off, lights and siren on. The other cops followed close behind, going fifty in tandem down the road.

Solberg watched them leave, eyes wide, breathing hard. Maile touched him on the shoulder. His muscles shuddered.

Ruga tried a joke. "Damn, Matt, remind me to never piss off a Norwegian." No one laughed.

Jake took over. "Alright, guys, time to go home."

Maile and Ruga eyed Solberg, trudged to their rigs, and drove away.

Jake hung close. "Matt, got a minute?" He pointed to his white Chevy pickup. The men climbed inside and Jake poured Solberg a cup of ginger tea. "Your favorite."

Matt took a sip. "Blew it, didn't I?"

"Everyone's got the heebie-jeebies, Matt. It's just a matter of voltage."

Solberg did not smile.

They watched the fire crew make headway on the burn. They'd have it out shortly. If it had happened two weeks from now—a conflagration.

Jake turned back. "What the fuck, Matt? You can't lay your hands on a cop."

"I know. I'm just so tired of…" Solberg stopped and drank some tea.

"Tired of what?" Jake asked.

Solberg shrugged. "I'm just overworked, I guess."

Jake knew better. He was with Matt the day his wife died. When the team made finally made it to the Solberg house, Becky would only talk to Jake and only cry with Maile. She never even looked at her dad. And now, six years later, Becky Solberg was still enraged and far away.

Jake took a sip of tea. "Sorry I wasn't at Mann Gulch to help. You saw some awful stuff that day and now this girl is…"

"Mann Gulch wasn't your call. For some reason, they only wanted me."

"You know the reason."

Solberg shrugged.

Jake nodded. "It's one that scares the hell out of me."

"And what's that?" Solberg asked.

"You're willing to risk everything for people you don't know."

12

The FBI Resident Agency in downtown Missoula was a two-story brick building on West Front Street next to the Stockman's Bar. One-stop shopping.

Solberg came to share what he knew about the Merchant fire in Mann Gulch. He did consulting jobs for the Bureau as a "landscape forensics consultant"—someone with a deep knowledge of Montana's physical and cultural geography. His search and rescue work provided a natural link. The resident agency handled a diverse case load: counterterrorism, cyber crime, civil rights, major thefts, kidnappings, drugs, white-collar scams, and smuggling along the U.S.-Canada border. Experts like Solberg with specific, even arcane, expertise were tapped as needed and budgets allowed.

Solberg sat in front of Special Agent Bernie Katz, watching him pore over a file. The man was fifty-something and doughy, with thinning hair and wild eyebrows. Solberg had met Bernie when he transferred in from Newark three years before. Helped him with a lost child case that turned into a kidnapping. When Bernie and his agents were stumped, Solberg accurately guessed where the father was holed up. Ever since, Bernie had increasingly relied on Solberg's local knowledge. The line between consultant and investigator began to blur.

Katz also brought in Dr. Bill Knight for fire cases—arson, a crime on the rise.

Matt started the conversation. "You guys close out that meth fire yet?"

Katz broke out of a frown. "Yeah. Well, soon. The damn fools basically killed themselves. Girl is with protective services. They're trying to scare up a decent relative willing to take her."

"Any luck?" Solberg asked.

Katz's scowl returned. "The tree doesn't grow far from the apple."

Solberg knew exactly what he meant. Beneath Montana's gorgeous veneer lived thousands of marginal characters doing their best to get by. And sometimes their best turned out to be cooking meth. Kids were often swept away in the wreckage.

Bernie leafed through a file, closed it, and looked up. "Alright,

Mann Gulch. Merchant's wife is the logical choice for those fires. She had the motive and money."

"So you're sold on her?" Solberg asked.

"Hell, no," Bernie said, sagging. "It's too simple."

"Why do things have to be complicated?"

"Because they just are," Bernie said.

Solberg sat back.

Bernie leaned forward. "The cops gave me your Morse code theory about Mann Gulch. Why should I believe you?" He locked his eyes on Solberg, eyebrows twitching. When frustrated, FBI Special Agent Bernie Katz was as intense as a badger.

"Not sure you should believe me," Solberg said. "But who lays out ceramic cones just in time to be melted unless they set the fires?"

"They could have been there for years."

"Forensics?" Solberg asked.

Bernie nodded. "Underway in Salt Lake."

"Alright, for now let's use logic," Solberg said. "Do you think that pyrometric cones—these heat-sensitive ceramic gadgets—just happened to be sitting in tidy rows in the path of two simultaneous fires? And why did the cones have different melting temperatures to form different shapes? I think it's a message."

"I know, SOS and MTM, the Montana Tree Monkeys," Bernie grunted. "I've seen the photographs Deputy Goebel sent over. But so far we have nothing that links Merchant with eco-radical groups. No sign he pissed them off with his politics or movies. Those cones are probably false leads, but amateurs aren't usually bright enough to come up with shit like that."

"Or Calvinist enough," Solberg said.

Bernie smiled. "Deception requires a work ethic."

"Especially on steep ground," Solberg said.

Bernie shook his head. "I'm still pissed at Goebel for picking up those clues. A contaminated crime scene is big trouble during a trial, assuming we catch the bastards."

"Goebel couldn't control the sites for long," Solberg said. "Willow Creek is used by dirt bikers, and tourist boats go to Mann Gulch every day. Maybe he shouldn't have picked them up, but at least we have the photos."

"Yeah, yeah." Bernie had a habit of tapping the face of his watch with his right index finger. Sent a message—*You're wasting my time; tell me something I can use.*

Solberg intentionally slowed down. "Alright Bernie, let's go back over what we know. Eyewitnesses spotted the fires at roughly the same time. The topography forms two chutes leading up to Merchant's house—Willow Creek and Mann Gulch. There were no lightning storms, so arson is a good theory. And anyone using Google Maps could see Merchant was a sitting duck on that ridge top. You just have to figure out who has a major beef against this guy."

"Oh, is that all?" Bernie fumed. Then calmed down. "Damned Google Maps. I'm no good at that thing."

"Not much need back in New Jersey?"

"In Jersey, it's all exits."

"Must be why you keep me around."

"I need a *yeshuvnik*."

"A what?"

"A rube," Bernie said. "But one with brains. Keep going."

Solberg chuckled. "Anyway, conditions in Mann Gulch are dry. But the fires were still set in May when there's usually enough moisture in the ground to stop their spread. That's the part I don't understand. If they want to burn down Merchant's place, why not wait until summer?"

"Who the hell's 'they'?" Bernie said, scowling.

"I haven't a clue," Solberg said.

Bernie Katz sipped coffee.

"ATF involved?" Solberg asked.

"Shit, no. I don't need a bigger media circus than I've got. Some putz from ESPN even called me wanting an interview."

"ESPN?"

"Apparently Merchant made a baseball movie years ago."

Solberg nodded. "A comedy. Nobody laughed."

"Movie stars," Bernie said, scratching his head. "Alright, if you don't know who set the fires, then how did they do it? The scene give you any sense of the arsonist?"

"Had to be two people, given the terrain," Solberg said.

"I already know that," Bernie said. "By arsonist, I mean head perp, the asshole who planned this. No way one guy could set a fire at Willow Creek, drive over to Holter Lake, take a boat to Mann Gulch, set another fire, motor back, and disappear without being seen. I had a fit young agent re-create that scenario. Took her three hours. So it was two crews—and therefore a conspiracy."

Solberg had forgotten Bernie Katz's talent for breaking down the logistics of a crime. A mistake he vowed never to repeat.

Bernie sat back. "Let me ask you something. This eco-terrorist theory sounds bizarre, but they've done similar things before. You run in environmental circles. Could some of those kooks be behind it?"

The question and Bernie's tone struck a deep nerve in Solberg. He hated that people (like him) who studied Nature and worked for its protection were reduced to stereotypes or scapegoats. Climate change, habitat protection, Superfund cleanups—didn't matter. Too often conservationists were portrayed as irrational, unpatriotic, and dangerous.

Solberg spoke in measured tones. "It's possible but not probable that this was eco-terrorism. You weren't living here, but monkey wrenching peaked decades ago in the West and even then it was more talked about than done. Edward Abbey and that pipe dream."

"Who?"

"Dead writer. Good one."

Bernie shrugged.

Solberg went on. "But none of that explains Merchant as a target. To me this whole MTM message smells like bullshit. 'Wacko wind-kissers hating capitalism.' And that SOS message? I mean really. No, there's something else going on. Maybe it's geography."

"Mann Gulch?" Bernie asked.

"When a guy builds a house on history, he makes enemies."

"What kind of enemies?"

"The exact people who would never do this," Solberg said.

"Spare me the Zen riddle," Bernie said.

"Smokejumpers," Solberg said, hating that he had to.

Bernie sat up straight. "Smokejumpers? They *put out* fires."

"Yes, but Mann Gulch is special to them because of the 1949 tragedy. Or maybe Merchant pissed off fire scientists who see that landscape as a laboratory."

"All of them?" Bernie asked, eying Solberg.

"Yes," he said.

"Even Bill Knight?" Bernie asked.

"Yes, but he'd never succumb to anger."

"Why?"

"Because anger is about losing control," Solberg said. "Knight *never* loses control."

Bernie wrote that down. "Okay, let's keep things simple for now. Who hates Edward Merchant enough to commit arson? So far we've got an absent wife, firefighters, scientists, and old hippies."

"Plus anybody opposed to land development," Solberg said.

"Young hippies," Bernie said, scowling.

"Look, Merchant's a Hollywood star with a surly rep. Might be a *few* more people pissed at him than that."

Bernie tossed a wad of paper toward a barrel and missed. "It's Chinatown Jake."

Solberg stood up. "We done?"

"No. When can you go to Mann Gulch and have another look?"

Solberg had secretly wanted—no, needed—to sort out the Merchant fire. He'd lost too much sleep thinking about Linda. The girl was in pain and far from home. Still lost.

"Haven't you guys already fully checked the place out?" Solberg asked.

"Yes," Bernie said.

"But you're not happy with results?"

"I just want a second opinion. A *yeshuvnik* opinion." Bernie grinned.

Solberg smiled. "Okay, I'll head over tomorrow, but I need to bring someone."

"Bill Knight," Bernie said.

Solberg tilted his head. "I swear the Good Doctor can read a fire's hungry little mind."

13

Solberg and Bill Knight took a ferry from the Holter Lake dock to the mouth of Mann Gulch. Neither man paid attention to the spectacular canyon walls rising up from the Missouri River. The Gates of the Mountains. In 1804, Lewis and Clark named this remote place where the Missouri slices through the Rockies.

The pilot snugged the boat into willows and the men scrambled ashore. The pilot would be back in four hours, giving them ample time to examine the ground and get Knight's take on the cause of the fire. They'd already checked out the Willow Creek burn and concluded it was a crude case of arson, probably just gasoline and a match. To be sure, they took soil samples for processing back at the University of Montana.

Solberg and Knight paused before heading uphill. Each, in his own way, spent a moment remembering the thirteen fire fighters who had died here in 1949.

Knight looked frustrated. "Gotta piss for the tenth time today." He turned away and took a dribbling leak.

Solberg figured it was age, something that waited for him just over the horizon.

They entered the gulch using crude trails worn into the land by visitors. Mann Gulch was a draw for necro-tourists—people pawing over the sites of famous deaths. Elvis's Graceland, Jim Morrison's apartment building in Paris, the Dakota in New York where John Lennon was murdered. Mann Gulch carried its own extreme lesson, but not about drugs, booze, or guns. About fire.

At first the grass and scattered pines were unburned. Yellow arrow-leaf balsamroots and purple lupines were already past their prime. The men gained elevation and saw only blackness above them. Mann Gulch had been fully embraced by fire.

"Damn," Solberg said. "Hard to believe it happened again."

Knight took a picture, then lowered his camera. "Why shouldn't it? Same ecosystem, same fire regime. Apparently, there's been enough time to produce sufficient fuel loads."

"Except it was May, not August, warm, not hot, and arson."

Knight frowned. "That house was an atrocity." There was a flint-sharp edge to his words.

Solberg let it go. He felt the same.

In ten minutes they reached the edge of the burn. From a single point of ignition, blackness spread out in a widening V leading uphill. As in 1949, everything upslope was combusted.

"As expected," Knight said.

"You mean the behavior?" Solberg asked.

"Fire moved as I thought it would," Knight said.

Solberg looked at the terrain. "Heat drew the flames uphill, just like in '49."

"Yes," Knight said. "Simple physics."

Solberg snapped photos while Knight took soil samples, deposited them in plastic bottles, and wrote numbers on each. In an hour, they paused for water.

"It's the same modality as Willow Creek," Knight said, raising his bottle.

Solberg watched him drink. Bill Knight's detached manner was legendary. This consummate scientist investigated fires like he was conducting an autopsy.

Until three years ago, that is, when Knight's wife, Molly, was killed in a car wreck. Then cracks showed in his façade. He spent more time alone. Under stress, he was short-tempered. Some days, there was gunmetal darkness in his eyes. Work became his shrinking world.

They scoured the ignition site looking for clues. "This ground looks just like Willow Creek," Knight said. "No tree struck by lightning, no campfire ring, no glass bottle to focus sunlight on dry grass, and..."

"...no incendiary device, fireworks, or flares," Solberg said. "But the FBI guys tramped all over this place. Evidence could be gone."

Knight disagreed. "This fire was very simple, which makes it clever."

"What do you mean?" Solberg asked.

"Hide in plain sight," said the Good Doctor. "Nothing distinctive."

"Except for those pyrometric cones," Solberg added.

"Yes, unless they're trying to fool you."

"Me?"

"Us," Knight said.

A mile later their boots and pant legs were black with ash. No cones or other evidence appeared. They passed a cross erected where a smokejumper named James Harrison had died. A bright twenty-year-old from Missoula just getting started in life. The stone marker was superficially stained by the fire. Rain—if it ever came—would wash it clean. Other crosses appeared: Joseph Sylvia, a Marine from

Plymouth, Massachusetts who fought in World War II. So many losses—sons, brothers, cousins, fathers.

The slope steepened dramatically. Knight was out front, stopping occasionally to take photos and make notes. They stood to catch their breath a few hundred feet below the rimrock.

"This is the place," Knight said.

"You sure?" Solberg asked.

"Positive. This is where Wag Dodge set his escape fire back in '49."

"You think if the other guys had listened to him, they would have survived the blowup?"

"Norman Maclean thought so," Knight said. "I traipsed all over this drainage with Norman when he was researching his book."

Solberg nodded. "*Young Men and Fire.*"

"Or old. Take the lead, Matt."

Solberg chose a diagonal toward the rimrock. The going was steep and hot through a blanket of slippery black ash.

A notch in the rim opened up. Solberg crested out and stood on the limestone ledge. A minute later, Knight stood beside him, panting. As they removed their packs a breeze cooled their back sweat. They studied the view. Mann Gulch was a palette of blackness: charcoal, jet, raven, onyx.

"By next spring, this place will green up beautifully," Knight said. "The fire released nutrients to refresh the grass. Cleaned things up, is all. Nothing wrong with that."

Solberg looked north to a rimrock where Linda Merchant had barely clung to life. "Except when there is."

14

"We got another one!" Bernie Katz yelled.

"Another what, Bernie?" Solberg gripped the phone.

"Another millionaire's house burned down. This time east of Missoula. Guy's name is Richard Walker."

Solberg had never heard of him.

"You still there?" Katz asked.

"Anyone missing?"

"No, this isn't a search and rescue bit."

"Then why the hell are you calling me?"

"Because of your tender disposition. Look, I know you're tired, but I need you and Bill Knight to help me check out this new fire. Maybe it was set by the same punks that burned down the Merchant place. What did you guys find yesterday?"

"Lab tests are underway, but it looks like a simple case of arson."

"That they tried to make appear complicated with those ceramic gadgets," Bernie said.

"Maybe. Any messages left at this new fire?"

"No groovy potter's cones found to my knowledge. But so far all I have is the Granite County sheriff's word for it. I'll be there in half an hour. Can you meet me?"

Solberg almost cursed. "Alright, where is it?"

"Three miles up Powder Creek, north of Bearmouth. You know it?"

"Powder has two meanings up there—dry snow and gunplay."

"Sounds right. Will you call Knight?"

"Yes, but it'll take Bill an hour longer than me."

"Just get him there." Bernie hung up.

Solberg shook his head. Bernie was being thorough in checking out the burn, but why not just use Bill Knight? Solberg could hold his own, but the Good Doctor was the final arbiter of anything to do with fire. What was *he* there to investigate? The whole business felt weird.

Solberg left a message for Knight and headed to Bearmouth.

Six bends up Powder Creek he saw a wide swath of black ash. It stood in stark contrast to the golden grasslands on either side. Columns of smoke rose from the backcountry, but nothing major as these things go.

Twenty hotshot firefighters stood up ahead slugging water. Their yellow Nomex fire shirts were filthy with coal-colored grime. Their work had gone well and Air Attack from the Missoula Fire Depot was on the scene. A helicopter sloshed water on the blaze. A DC-10 slurry bomber groaned overhead, releasing an orange sluice of fire retardant just over the ridgeline.

Solberg parked and felt his shoulders relax. Then he saw the charred hulk that had once been Richard Walker's home. *It had happened again.* Solberg walked to a communications center set up in a truck, where Bernie Katz was bearing down on the fire's Incident Commander. From the look on the man's face, he wasn't used to such behavior.

Bernie turned and saw Solberg. "You finally made it."

"What have we got?" Solberg asked.

"Arson. Again."

"Don't overwhelm me with facts, Bernie."

"Follow me."

They walked to the edge of the road. Bernie squatted and winced. "Haven't moved it," he said, pointing to the ground.

Solberg sank into a comfortable crouch. "Cigarette butt."

"We pay you too much. Look closer."

"You mind?" Solberg said, pulling tweezers from his shirt pocket.

Bernie nodded. "Just pick it up, check it out, and put it down. I want Knight to work this scene. If he ever gets here."

Solberg felt confused. *Again, why am I here if Knight is coming?* He inspected the butt, turning it so he could see all the way around the filter. Then he set it back down. "Trace of lipstick," Solberg said matter-of-factly. "No sign it was recently burned."

"A lie," Bernie said under his breath.

"What?"

"Not you, the butt. It's a goddamned lie. A bush-league clue dropped by someone to make it look like the ignition source."

"Seems like it."

Bernie Katz shook his head. "Another rich-prick arson case. Just what I need."

A white Dodge Ram pulled up. Bill Knight slowly emerged from the cab carrying a daypack and one trekking pole. He paused to look at the burned-over land.

Bernie brushed by Solberg and extended his hand. "Glad you could make it, Dr. Knight."

Dr. Knight, Solberg thought. *Why is Bernie being so formal?*

"Mr. Katz," Knight said, shaking the agent's outstretched hand. He looked amused as he turned to Solberg. "Handsome burn. Any ideas?"

"It's your fire," Solberg said.

Knight nodded like a king.

The three men walked to the ignition site. Bernie showed Knight the cigarette butt then collected it for evaluation by FBI forensics in Salt Lake. Knight gave a gap-toothed grin then went to work, placing soil samples in plastic bottles. He moved slowly without urgency, missing no detail, studying the fire-front like Darwin searching for a Galapagos finch.

Knight snapped close-up photos of the land surface. With the line fully surveyed, he moved into the burned swath and bent over at the waist, eyeing the ground, poking at it with his trekking pole. Knight moved in a perfect grid search pattern. His boot prints showed the mathematical precision of it.

Bernie Katz and Matt Solberg watched this astonishing display of focus.

"Kind of Aspergery, isn't he?" Bernie asked.

Solberg was caught off-guard. "Not really."

"Why don't you think so?" Bernie asked seriously, interested in Solberg's response.

"I've known Bill for more than twenty years. He's just singular."

"You mean strange."

"Like most geniuses, I suppose. But he's not exactly on the spectrum. Bill loved his late wife Molly with all his heart. Throws himself into work as a remedy for grief."

"How'd she die?" Bernie asked.

"Car wreck three years ago. Figured you knew that."

"I did. He changed after that?"

Bernie was handling him, Solberg recognized. Being cop-ish.

"As I said, he works more and cares less about what people think of him. Molly kept him grounded and her death was a blindside hit."

Bernie spoke softly. "I'm sure you know all about that, Matt."

A breeze wafted by. Then a voice boomed out of the radio. "Command 1, we found a body," it said, the speaker out of breath.

"Command 1. Repeat and explain," the Incident Commander said.

"This is Dawson. We're a mile northeast of base. Just moved into some unburned trees and found him. Guy is—was—about sixty. No life signs."

The Incident Commander held his edge. "I'm sending a helicopter. Make purple smoke."

"Roger that. But sweet Jesus…"

"Was the victim burned?"

"No, that's the weird part."

"Explain, Bobby."

"He looks perfect, except for his shoes."

15

Solberg stood on a small deck built on his roof. A widow's walk. The view of Mount Jumbo, Sentinel, the Rattlesnakes, and Lolo Peak had a grapefruit cast. Burnt orange and pink. This smoke wasn't from Powder Creek; that burn was east of town and put out. It was pouring in from grass fires in the Palouse Prairie region of Idaho and Washington. Missoula was downwind and when the crud came this early, a nasty fire season was in store. Nothing could stop it but drenching rain, and that miracle was not in the forecast.

"Crap," Solberg said.

The Season of Smoke. That's what some Native people call summer in Montana. And here it was, early by the calendar but arriving as unstoppably as a meteor. Solberg knew that low-intensity fire was as necessary as water for life to thrive in the Rockies. With each burn, slumbering fertility is released and forests are reborn. The king is dead; long live the king. But in recent decades, fires had become bigger and more destructive.

Climate change had turned summer into sorrow.

Solberg meditated angrily for twenty minutes, then poured a cup of coffee and checked his email. A short message from his daughter Becky. She needed $1,000 to repair her recently bought car. No personal details or plans to visit—just a cold-hearted ask.

He walked outside and smashed his coffee mug against a tree. "Dammit!" A neighbor pretended not to notice his outburst as Solberg meticulously picked up every shard and hosed down the tree. Then he walked to campus, trying to calm down.

At 9:55 Solberg walked in through the Good Doctor's unlocked office door. Long wooden tables formed a work area in the center. Stacks of reports, journal articles, and grant applications were neatly laid out, and marked with blue sticky tabs. Another table supported an elaborate microscope and computer setup. Tree wedges and slotted boards full of tree-ring cores were left out to save time. Solberg ran his fingers over the fire scars on a large wedge. One end of the lab was crowded with plastic bins full of God-knows-what. A large black-and-white analog clock ticked on the wall.

"Matt," said Bill Knight from behind him. "Sorry I kept you waiting. I was in the can."

The clock read exactly 10:00.

Solberg smiled at his punctuality. "No worries. Just having a look around."

Discomfort flickered on Knight's face, then a gap-toothed smile. "Sit," he said, pointing to an overstuffed chair in front of his desk.

Solberg sat. "Bernie Katz call you about the guy who died up Powder Creek?"

"Heart attack," Knight said with no emotion. "As far as they know, anyway. His name was Carl Bristow and his wife doesn't want an autopsy. Katz might, depending."

"Depending on the cause of the fire. What's your report going to say?"

"First, tell me what *you* saw," Knight said.

"I saw a ham-fisted case of arson. The cigarette butt was either a ruse or irrelevant litter. The arsonist probably used dry grass and walked along the slope setting the fire."

"You're exactly right, Matt. And Bristow did it."

Solberg was shocked. "Wasn't he just a neighbor caught in the flames?"

"No way," Knight said. He clicked on his computer and turned the screen toward Matt. "Here's an FBI picture taken outside the burn path," Knight said, pointing. "It shows footprints in the soil with a much deeper impression at the heel than the toes."

"Bizarre-looking thing," Solberg said.

Knight nodded. "Now, here's their photo of the former Carl Bristow."

Solberg grimaced.

"Notice anything strange?" Knight asked.

Solberg refocused on the image. Carl Bristow lay on his side like he was napping in the woods. Blue jeans, checked shirt, untouched face, and no burns on the body. Solberg looked closer. The man wore Converse sneakers with the toe box cut away. His black-stockinged feet extended a few inches beyond the sole. "Tried to cover his tracks, didn't he?" Solberg said.

"Indeed," Knight said. "People do that. Flop around in shoes too big or squeeze into ones too small. Doesn't fool anybody for long."

"FBI forensics?" Solberg asked.

"Bernie says his hands were covered with gasoline residue. Bristow's the guy."

"What was his axe against Walker?" Solberg asked.

"*Missoulian* says Walker closed a road into the backcountry and it caused a dustup between them. The gate blocked hunting access and firewood gathering. But I suspect a lot more was going on."

"Like what?"

"Not sure, but Walker is quoted as saying he'll never rebuild in Montana. Called us 'redneck terrorists,'" Bernie said, reading a note.

"He can never set foot in a Montana bar again," Solberg said.

"Imagine our despair."

Bill Knight shut down the computer and rested his hands across his chest. "But who's to say what Carl Bristow had in mind? That's Bernie Katz's job and therefore partly yours."

"You give me too much credit."

"Not too much credit for a *yeshuvnik*." Knight smiled slightly.

"Can't believe Katz shared that with you."

"Bernie is fascinated with what I do," Knight said, shaking his head with amazement.

"Not sure I'd want the FBI fascinated with me."

"Ah, Bernie's harmless."

"What the fuck?" Solberg said, slapping the armrest.

Knight sat up straight. "Where did that come from?"

"Never dismiss the power of the FBI. They can turn anyone's life upside down because they goddamn feel like it. Did it to *you* back in the '90s."

"That old eco-raider bit?" Knight said. "MTM, as you so nicely recalled. The Bureau just asked me a few questions back then because some of those MTM idiots were registered for my classes. No big deal. Besides, I do fire analysis for the Bureau now."

Solberg sighed.

"What got into you?" Knight asked.

"Sorry, I had a shitheel morning."

"What happened?"

"Heard from Becky. One of her sucker-punch emails."

"Too early for the liniment, I suppose."

"Way too early, but thanks."

The old clock ticked.

"You took down Molly's picture," Solberg said, pointing at an empty space on the wall.

Knight turned. "Yes, it's finally time to move."

"Move?"

"Move on," Knight said.

"I can't believe it's been three years."

"Her death seemed unreal until recently." Knight sagged in his chair.

Solberg allowed him a moment. "What changed?"

Knight deflected the question. "What changed it for you after Judy died?"

"I had a daughter to raise. Not that it's working out so well."

"Becky's a good kid. She'll come back to you."

"Maybe."

Knight leaned forward. "You didn't kill Judy, no matter what your girl thinks. Or *you* think. It was an undiagnosed heart condition."

"A broken heart," Solberg said.

"Poetic, but inaccurate. She loved you."

"And Molly loved you."

Knight showed his gap-toothed smile. "For reasons not yet in evidence."

Solberg smiled, then shook his head. "I can't believe that Michael Slaton still comes to the Bitterroot every summer."

The muscles in Knight's jaw clenched.

"You ever see Slaton?" Solberg asked.

"Sometimes, driving around the valley in his red Escalade."

"Must be tough to take."

"I want to crash my rig into him. Make him feel the agony Molly did."

"But you don't."

"Course not," Knight said.

"Have you spoken to him?"

"That wouldn't go well."

Solberg slowly shook his head. "Slaton never paid a price, did he?"

Bill Knight sat back. "Karma takes time."

"And we're not in charge of that, are we?" Solberg said.

"Damn shame."

16

Solberg tried to work in his university office, but couldn't focus. Karma wasn't a concept Bill ever talked about. Too much Krishna, not enough Kant. But it was a relief to see him moving on from Molly's death. The two men shared the kind of connection you never want.

Solberg mailed Becky $750 to repair her car. She'd have to come up with the other $250 herself. A soft attempt at tough love.

Back when Becky was in high school, she barely talked to him except to scream accusations. How he'd killed her mother by being away and cared for strangers more than his family. She had a gift for stabbing at Solberg's soul. He *was* away a lot. That *did* cause tension in his marriage. In the two years Solberg and Becky lived together after the tragedy they weren't a family—they were barely roommates. Since she'd moved away for college in Portland, he'd reached out to her countless times, with little success. Gave her whatever she needed, often more than was good for her. Neither approach worked. He was out of ideas for reconciling. A failure that only deepened his guilt.

Solberg walked across the footbridge over the Clark Fork River and back into the Lower Rattlesnake neighborhood. His mind calmed as he moved from place to place. A geographer's way of coping.

He'd lived in the Lower Rattlesnake when he was in college, renting a place on Cherry Street with some buddies. The nickname of the house remains unrepeatable in polite company. Days defined by epic amounts of hiking, climbing, beer, weed, and sexual Pilates.

But then he'd found Geography as a major, studied with monastic focus, and invented a life.

Solberg walked through the familiar maple-shaded streets. The creek made a quiet burbling sound, its flow weakened until rain and snow would revive it in the fall. The houses he passed had been built a century before, back when Missoula was a small sawmill town. The designs were simple, the sizes modest. Clapboard structures with front porches framed by lilac bushes. Shady backyards with tall pines and privacy. Walking distance to downtown for a beer, Mount Jumbo for a hike, and the creek for a cooling plunge. True, many houses had been remodeled, Solberg's included, but these changes did nothing to weaken their integrity. And he liked his neighbors: forklift drivers, small-business owners, mechanics, retirees, and college kids. But Solberg knew that in time anything could happen to the Lower Rattlesnake.

A red squirrel stared at him from a branch. "Impermanence is a sovereign bastard," he told it.

Solberg opened his unlocked front door, drew a glass of cold water, and sat at the kitchen table. Sweat trickled down the back of his neck as he took a long drink. He closed his eyes and exhaled a slow, deep breath. Home.

His cell rang loudly. "*Dammit.*" It was FBI Agent Bernie Katz. Solberg let it ring, deciding whether to answer. He'd had enough drama. But then he picked up and spoke casually. "Hey, Bernie, how are you?"

"Passable," he said. "I need you to come over. Got something on the Mann Gulch fire."

"Can't we do this on the phone?"

"No."

Solberg held his temper. "Alright, I'll be right there."

Ten minutes later, Solberg strode into the FBI Resident Agency. "Sit down," Bernie said.

Solberg looked around—no chairs. "You pulling a Vince Lombardi on me?"

"Mavis!" Bernie yelled.

A strong woman hefted two chairs into the office and placed them in front of the desk. Solberg sat down and waited. Bernie's desk was a midden of files, letters, and reports. The man fanned through the mess, found a folder, and opened it. "Have a look," he said, handing it to Solberg.

"Me? I have no authority to..."

"I'm giving you access because you have a right to know. You found that poor burned-up girl. Just don't get blabby about what you're about to see."

Solberg nodded and took the folder. Inside were printed copies of dozens of messages between Edward Merchant and a woman named Blanca Chacón. Personal emails. Love emails. But as the dates progressed, the tone grew hateful. In a message dated about two months earlier, Blanca was enraged by Merchant's pulling back from "all the promises you made." She complained bitterly about "being thrown away like trash."

Solberg felt creepy reading the emails; a voyeur to a twisted relationship. As he read, he saw Merchant's mean streak emerge. When Blanca confronted him about breaking it off, Merchant turned into a royal prick. "Fuck you! I *never* promised you this would last," he wrote. "You came into this relationship with your eyes wide open, chica."

Solberg accessed his basic Spanish. *Chica*—girl. A diminutive, not always one of endearment.

"Pinche culero!" she wrote back, matching rage for rage. "You can't just toss me away like a street whore! I raised Linda and I love her. I am much more than a nanny to her and you know it. You won't get away with this. I live in East Los! There are some very dangerous people around here!"

There was more, but Solberg got the point and closed the folder. "I guess we have a motive," he said.

"Oh, yeah," Bernie said, eyebrows celebrating.

Solberg sighed. "Merchant's a real schmuck. Having an affair with the nanny then ditching her. What a cliché."

"Full bore," Bernie said. "Promised to marry her, yadda, yadda. If I had a beer for every time I've heard that, I'd be shitfaced in Panama."

Solberg chuckled. "But how did you get all these emails...?" He stopped himself. He was talking to the FBI. "Alright, but why did they correspond by email? Surely they knew these messages would be found."

"Rule of the sub-hundred," Bernie said matter-of-factly.

"What the hell's that?"

"Median IQ is always 100, so half the population has an IQ less than that. They're a head cold away from being Forrest Gump. I say Edward Merchant, Mr. Big-Time Hollywood Actor, is a total dumbshit."

"Or massively arrogant," Solberg said.

"Or both," Bernie said, frowning. "And his last movie really sucked. I want my 10 bucks back."

They sat for a minute, thinking. Traffic moved by out on West Front Street.

"Okay, Bernie, why don't you just do your federal cop thing and round her up, or whatever you call it. I'm no use here."

Katz waved his hand. "Agents in L.A. will pick her up tonight for questioning. Not sure what they'll learn."

"Why?"

Bernie sat back. "Chacón has a strong motive to set the fire, but she lives a thousand miles away. She has some money from her affair with a rich guy, but there's no record of recent air travel to Montana. No rough associations we know of, despite her big talk. But people in her world are very tight-lipped around cops."

"For good reason," Solberg said. "Blanca may not have a record, but she could know some bad guys. Ones who are good at evading the law."

"How the hell would you know that?" Bernie huffed.

"I teach Cultural Geography. East Los Angeles is a great neighborhood with a tough underbelly."

"That gives Chacón motive *and* opportunity," Bernie said.

"And once again, the means, thanks to Merchant," Solberg said.

"You're starting to think like a cop."

"Thanks, I guess," Solberg said.

Bernie plowed on. "From the tone of these emails, she would have killed Merchant with a ball peen hammer if she had the chance. But, I'm not sure she would have put the girl in harm's way. I've read those messages ten times. She really loves Linda. Dammit, an angry mistress is just too easy an answer."

"Again, why do they have to be hard?" Solberg asked.

"Because they *just are*," Bernie said.

Solberg sat back. "What if Chacón didn't know the girl was at the house that night? What if she thought only Ed Merchant was home?"

"Or, more likely, the guys she hired didn't know the girl was there," Bernie said, folding his hands.

Solberg thought for a while. "Setting fires sounds easy. But you've got to understand plants, terrain, wind direction, lots of things."

Bernie nodded. "And L.A. guys aren't exactly forest rangers."

"But they live next to chaparral vegetation that burns all the time. Hard not to notice how fire spreads into houses. All you've got to do is find out who set the spark."

"No shit," Bernie said. "But I'm still looking into Merchant's soon to be ex-wife. The Agency can't officially track her, but we know she's going from spa to spa in Europe. But that doesn't rule out that *she* hired people to set the fires."

"This is getting really fucked up," Solberg said.

"Welcome to my world," Bernie said, setting the Merchant folder to the side.

Solberg crossed his legs. "What about poor Carl Bristow? Did he really burn down Richard Walker's house over a gated road? Sounds unbelievable."

"No, we found out it was more than that," Bernie said. "Bristow never got over his son's death from an IED in Afghanistan. Kid was a decorated Marine."

"Oh, no," Solberg said. A respectful moment passed. "But why did Bristow set a fire? And how is that connected to losing his son?"

"Grief makes people do crazy things."

Solberg considered that; he and Bill Knight still grieved their dead wives. Matt coped by finding lost people and spending time with Bo Xiong. Knight coped by grinding on data sets, seeking solace in reliable numbers.

Bernie moved on. "From interviews with his neighbors, we learned that Bristow was also royally pissed off about Walker's wealth. 'Rich pricks ruining Montana,' that old chestnut. He also didn't care for

Walker's liberal antiwar politics, how he ran his ground, you name it. Walker ended up standing for all that Carl Bristow came to loathe. He needed payback for his son's death and the only WMD he had was fire."

"Shit," Solberg said, shaking his head. "The man actually burned out a neighbor. Maybe he was a copycat inspired by the Merchant fire in Mann Gulch."

Bernie nodded. "Or maybe Bristow went after Edward Merchant too."

"Why would he? Other than being rich guys, they have nothing in common."

"You're probably right. Dick Walker was the trigger. Carl Bristow had lost so much of his life he threw the rest away."

Katz poured a cup of coffee, sat back, and took slow sips.

Solberg grew impatient. "You need anything else from me?"

"Yes. I need you to keep working on the Merchant case."

"Why?" Solberg asked. "The fire analysis is done."

"Not sure. I just want you to spend as much time with Bill Knight as you can get away with."

"Get away with?" Solberg repeated, shocked.

Bernie shrugged. "Just an expression. Like you said, this man knows all there is to know about fire."

Agent Bernie Katz tapped the face of his watch with a finger. "I'm interested in him."

17

The Solstice. Dr. Bill Knight respected its mathematical elegance. On June 21, summer began when the noon sun stood overhead at 23.5 degrees north along the Tropic of Cancer. The beaches of Mazatlán, the deserts of Mali, and the rainforests of Myanmar all received the vertical bake. The Bitterroot Valley sits at 46.5 degrees. Therefore, at noon the sun angle was 67 degrees and summer heat slammed the Rockies. The longest day.

On the Solstice, it was Knight's custom to backpack alone into the Bitterroots as far as the snowpack allowed. Take a break from school, research, and worrisome students. This year, one student in particular: a bearded, foul-scented guy named Fleming. The guy Matt Solberg had smelled and complained about at Knight's office.

The Good Doctor was concerned about lessons he'd given Fleming. First was his usual spiel about how the woods needed to burn to stay healthy. "High-frequency, low-intensity events. A wise and ancient disturbance regime." Fire Ecology 101.

But Fleming was a rapt audience who wanted more. Sure, he was an unwashed cretin, but that just made him a perfect host for Knight's fury. Knight had even given the kid suggestions about where a forest fire might "do the most good." It was a fantasy, a projection—no more than that. All fire ecologists have a secret list of places that *ought* to burn. But deep down, Knight knew he was toying with a troubled soul. Arson only requires anger, gasoline, and a match. Each time Fleming left his office, Knight felt remorse for tempting that crude trinity.

He hiked on for five more miles up Sheafman Creek all the way to a glacial lake without stepping on snow. Only the highest, shadiest areas retained any white.

Knight stashed his pack and headed toward the flat-topped summit of Castle Crag. He'd climbed this peak a dozen times with Molly, following her swaying lengths of sorrel hair, burnished and blending, lifting like spider webs on currents of air, settling back as perfect and soft as a soul.

He made the summit. Gray granite peaks glowed in all directions: Totem, Sky Pilot, Canyon. An expansive space opened above the green fields of the Bitterroot Valley, the blue mass of the Sapphire Mountains rising beyond. From this height the crowding of cars, bars, and houses faded away.

At that moment, it was like looking back in time, before the valley was part of the big world. Back when he and Molly canoed from Bell Crossing to Stevensville Bridge naming every ranch, tracing their brands in the water with paddles, knowing with pure certainty this would always be true.

The pattern of development ripped Knight back to the present. A contagion of houses was exposed in window shine and roof reflection, in subdivision fence lines and knapweed fields, in the raw ragged texture of a brutalized world.

Bill Knight exhaled. He turned west and looked across the Selway Bitterroot Wilderness. Millions of wild acres spread out before him when you added the River of No Return, Gospel Hump, and Sawtooth. A sacred province of rocks where bears are king.

Knight turned back and looked down at what was left of the Bitterroot Valley. "It's all spiled, I reckon," he said. "The whole caboodle." Knight had memorized key lines from Bud Guthrie's masterpiece, *The Big Sky*. The book was vital to him—prescient and sad.

He made a small campfire inside a ring of white granodiorite rocks and gazed at the storytelling flames. It was a primal pastime, he would argue, one of the few things we still shared with Lucy, Ardi, and our anthropoid cousins before them. The coals pulsed back and forth from light to dark—cryptography he'd never solved.

A rising wind whirled the Great Bear into position above Kootenai Crags. Tonight was unusually warm, with moist Pacific air tempting a chance of rain. A bank of clouds quickly formed over the Bitterroots, blacking out the stars.

The first flash of lightning came from the north. Knight studied his illuminated watch. Thunder trudged in eighteen seconds later—it was near Victor. Then a closer bolt of lightning and a mere second before the boom. The lookout on St. Mary's Peak was wide awake now, the tower's lightning rod singing with electricity.

Heavy wind flowed down the glacial canyons, changing pitch with each bend. Sheafman was narrow and short. It made a high tone like a child blowing across the top of a full bottle of Coke. Mill Creek and Fred Burr Canyons reached all the way to the Idaho line. They fetched deeper sounds.

Knight smiled. Everything was as it should be.

Lightning and thunder exploded overhead. "Shit!" he yelled, nearly levitating from adrenaline. Knight burst out laughing as the rumble decayed. It felt good in his belly. First time in a while. The strike was extremely close and he smelled something burnt. Logic told him to stay safe among the rocks, but his heart wanted to be part of the drama, like John Muir riding a whirlwind spruce. Knight laced his boots and climbed the south canyon slope. Flashes showed him the way. Thunder was constant now, echoing and building, fading and rumbling back. Yet he felt no rain. A dry lightning storm.

Fire weather—and weeks too soon.

A red glow appeared up ahead. Knight backtracked to the lake, crossed a logjam over the outlet creek, and bushwhacked through the forest. The glow brightened. He scrambled across boulder fields until he saw the burning tree. It was a direct hit. Lightning had ripped off the top of an alpine larch and flung it thirty feet downhill. Fire burned in the heartwood of the standing wreck, flaming sap oozing down the trunk in a curving sash.

Knight approached in awe. Something unimaginably ancient—fire—had been delivered to the Earth. He sat next to the burning tree, watched, and waited. The flames burned with a frustrating tameness. No abating or advancing. He knew this was the nature of most high-country strikes. A tree might burn for weeks without spreading its sermon to the forest.

Knight raised his hands to the burning tree. Then he turned and warmed his back, feeling muscles loosen and relax. Dr. Bill Knight measured the space between fire and ground. It was only six feet, the height of a man.

18

Solberg paced in his backyard, working the problem. Bernie Katz "was interested" in Dr. Bill Knight. Meaning he suspected the man was an arsonist. That was absurd, but Katz was a bulldozer who seldom dug in the wrong place. Motives, clues, and logic took a back seat to the man's Jersey instincts. And while he'd closed the Bristow and meth lab cases, the Merchant fire in Mann Gulch was still in play.

Calliope hummingbirds hovered, drinking from a red feeder. "Bill Knight isn't setting fires, right?" Solberg said to them. The hummers happily slurped sugar water. "You are wise, my wee beasties."

Bo Xiong walked into the backyard carrying a large bag of takeout. "Bless you," Matt said.

"You okay?" she asked, setting the bag on the picnic table.

"Better now," Matt said. They hugged until Bo broke the embrace.

Matt opened the wine while Bo served fried wontons, steamed rice, and pad thai onto square white plates. "Yum," she said. The sun was still up, but getting low. Matt dispensed healthy pours of pinot grigio into stemless glasses.

Bo lifted her wine. "What should we drink to?"

"Till 4 in the morning," Matt said, clinking his glass with hers.

Bo laughed and dove into her pad thai. Matt went straight for the wontons, dousing them with sweet vinegar. An hour and two glasses later, they were finished.

"Feel better?" Bo asked.

"Body, not mind."

"FBI stuff?" Bo asked.

"And then some."

"Meet me in my office," Bo said, motioning to the hammock.

Matt went first, then Bo slid in. He cradled her with his right arm.

Mount Jumbo turned gold in the early evening light as the smoke thinned and cooler air flowed down the valley. Squirrels scurried up the cinnamon-bark trunks of ponderosa pines, twitching their bushy tails with pleasure. Ravens flew overhead so close you could hear the rush of wind under their wings. "Commuters," Matt said, looking up. "Heading home to the Rattlesnake Wilderness."

"Ravens have such a weird life," Bo said. "Spend their days at the dump and their nights in heaven."

"Sounds like me," Matt whispered. He kissed Bo gently on the cheek.

Bo turned toward him. "You don't have to work for the FBI, you know?"

"Yeah, I know," Matt said. "But Linda Merchant needs my help."

"A lost girl," Bo said.

"I know, like Becky."

Bo nodded.

"Not exactly a psychological riddle, is it?" Matt said.

"No, but that simplicity *is* a riddle."

"You're onto me."

"It will take me a lifetime to be onto you," Bo said.

Matt felt thrilled and terrified by the idea.

Wave after wave of ravens flew overhead, swooshing their wings toward the wilderness. "A storytelling of ravens," Bo said.

"No, a conspiracy of ravens," Matt countered.

"It depends."

"On what?"

"The day," Bo said.

"Then you won't like my collective noun for *Homo sapiens*," Matt said.

"Which is?" Bo asked.

"A disappointment of humans."

Bo laughed. "Clever, but pretty cynical."

"Kind of like me?"

"Minus the pretty part," Bo said.

They snuggled closer in the hammock. Breathing in and out, swaying in the dusk.

Matt turned to Bo. "Bill Knight is really hurting."

"How?"

"Grief finally hit over his wife's death. He says he's moving on, but I'm not sure."

Bo squeezed Matt's arm.

"And to make matters worse," Solberg said, "Bernie Katz is grasping at straws on the Mann Gulch fire."

"Explain," Bo said.

"One of those straws is Bill Knight."

"That's illogical," Bo said, scrunching her forehead. "Bill's odd, but not that odd. He loves Mann Gulch, but not enough to hurt Edward Merchant. Or his daughter."

"The hummingbirds agree."

Bo smiled. "If Michael Slaton's house burned down, I'd suspect Knight too. But Slaton's place is untouched, right?"

Matt kissed Bo. "I love you and your brain."

"We're a package deal," she said.

They huddled closer. Matt surrendered to her warmth.

"Can I ask you a question?" Bo said.

"Of course."

"Sometimes I wonder..." She stopped short.

"What?" Matt asked.

"Never mind, you've had a tough couple of weeks."

"Come on, tell me."

"Alright. Sometimes I wonder if you're ready for this."

"I love our nights together," Matt said.

"You know I'm talking about more than that."

Matt tilted his head in agreement.

"Okay," Bo said. "Here's the problem. When you're hurting, I get the call. When you're not, the phone goes dead. It's like you're always making up your mind about me. About how far you want to let me in."

Matt stared at nothing. "I failed at this once, you know."

"Judy's heart failed, not you."

Matt grimaced.

"I'm so sorry," Bo said. "That came out really harsh."

"It did, but you *do* have a right to want more from me."

Bo looked into his eyes. "More doesn't mean all the time or forever, Matt. It just means clarity. You understand?"

Matt exhaled heavily.

She hugged him close.

A single raven *whooshed* overhead.

"I don't want to lose you," Matt whispered.

"I'm not lost," Bo whispered back.

19

Cyr, Montana exploded in flames. Matt and Bo ate breakfast, glued to the radio coverage.

At 2 this afternoon a fire was spotted by truckers on Interstate 90, at Cyr, a rural area thirty miles west of Missoula. They alerted the authorities, who sent in the Lolo Hotshots. That firefighting crew is now battling the blaze with support from Aerial Attack slurry bombers operating out of the Missoula Fire Depot. Early reports indicate that the fire began along Fish Creek Road and quickly spread upslope in dry grass, brush, and thick timber. Incident Commander Bruce McLeod is here with me.

REPORTER: What's the status of this new fire?

McLEOD: There are now twenty hotshots on the ground. Two air tankers from Missoula are dropping retardant and a helicopter is dropping water on the flames.

REPORTER: What are conditions like out there?

McLEOD: Things are extremely dry, but we got lucky by having light winds. Right now the fire is only 20 percent contained, but we're making progress.

REPORTER: Have any homes been lost?

McLEOD: Yes, two.

REPORTER: Has anyone been hurt?

McLEOD: Too early to say.

Matt's ringing phone interrupted the broadcast. He had half expected it would. "Solberg," he said, setting down his coffee.

"Matt, this is Mineral County sheriff Roy Cousy. There's an old woman missing in the Cyr fire. Can you pull your search and rescue team together?"

"You bet, Roy. Where should we gather?"

"Cyr Bridge access site on the Clark Fork. We've set up shop there. Firefighters are spread out on the Beauchamp Ranch."

"Good thing old Baptiste isn't alive to see that," Solberg said.

"They'd have buckshot in their ass for sure," the sheriff agreed. "When can you make it?"

"Forty minutes. All of us in an hour."

"Thanks. But Matt, there's something you should know. This one's personal."

"What do you mean?"

"The missing woman is my cousin Lucy."

Solberg felt a jolt. "Make it thirty minutes." He sent a group text to his search team. Then he threw on hiking clothes, laced his boots, and grabbed his search and rescue pack.

Bo watched him prepare. They went outside and she hugged Matt. "If you die, I'll kill you," she whispered.

20

Twenty-nine minutes later, Solberg arrived at Cyr Bridge on the Clark Fork River. This was the beginning of the Alberton Gorge; a legendary stretch of whitewater smoke obscured the low northern ridges of the Bitterroot Mountains. The light was golden and diffuse. The sun a blood orange.

Sheriff Roy Cousy opened the door of Solberg's pickup. "I should write you up for speeding," he joked, tilting his cowboy hat back. "Thanks for coming, Matt."

"You bet. Tell me what you know."

"The missing woman's name is Lucille Beauchamp. My cousin Lucy. She's seventy-seven, but strong as an ox. Lives in the family's old ranch house on Fish Creek and leases her grazing land to a family nearby. She rides everyday along Fish Creek or up Silver Canyon. There's no sign of Lucy and her three horses are gone, but the saddles are still in the barn. She probably turned the horses loose to fend for themselves. I sent two deputies out to search for Lucy and they came up empty. Then I called you."

Solberg nodded and stared at the brown sky. Too smoky for drones.

The sheriff looked up and nodded. "Drones are as useless as a glass hammer."

Solberg smiled. "As soon as my crew arrives, we'll go find her."

"From your mouth to God's ear," the sheriff said, patting Solberg on the back.

On cue, Jake Pengelly and Maile Felder pulled in. Three minutes later, the whole team gathered at Solberg's truck. After he briefed them, Solberg laid a topo map across the hood, took out a marker, and gridded the area. "Ruga, you work these forests east of the creek and up to the mountains. Keep your eyes peeled and your radio on. This fire could get frisky and do it fast. Jake, you head up Silver Canyon and sweep the drainage. Maile, you search the area from the river up Fish Creek to the Pardee Bridge," he said, pointing. "I'll take the upper grid, starting just past the Big Pine campground and work my way downstream to Maile. Clear?"

"Clear as gin," Ruga said, smiling.

"Remember," Solberg said, "her name is Lucy Beauchamp."

Everyone sped off to their assigned starting points. Solberg drove slowly up Fish Creek Road, window down, eying the bottomland. He stopped at two ranches to ask if anyone had seen Lucy. No luck.

Solberg paused at Big Pine—194 feet tall, loftiest ponderosa in the state. "Stay strong, dear friend." Then he pulled over about five miles from Lucy Beauchamp's ranch. The outer perimeter of the search. She might be fit, but she was seventy-seven and likely on foot.

He lashed his pack and methodically walked transects downstream through cottonwoods and pines along the west bank of Fish Creek. He checked the willows at the water's edge—no sign of human or horse prints. It was unlikely Lucy had crossed the creek. Despite the drought, the flow was a bit too strong for an older person to wade.

Fish Creek meandered back and forth down the canyon. Solberg side-hilled where the mountains pressed down tight. There were horse tracks in several places, but none looked fresh, and no human footprints at all.

After two hours he radioed in. "This is Solberg. Upper creek is clear so far. I'm three miles from the bridge. Over."

Nothing. He tried again—static and dead air—and no cell phone coverage. Solberg drank half a liter of water and devoured an energy bar.

He crisscrossed the bottomland, scaring up dozens of white-tailed deer. "Sorry, ladies."

After two more hours, Solberg's gut told him Lucy wasn't there. From what Sheriff Cousy said, she was very experienced outdoors. Lucy wouldn't have slugged her way this far south just to find a place to wait out the fire.

Despite all that, Solberg kept going. Once in a while his intuition was wrong. Like the time in the Mission Range when he swore no ten-year-old boy could possibly have made it up to Lucifer Lake. When a tribal cop found the kid, he was in a diabetic coma. Or that December day when he overlooked a side canyon in the Rattlesnake Mountains and a dementia victim died of exposure.

Solberg thought of Beckett's inspirational line—*Try again, fail again, fail better.* "Samuel, you're full of shit."

The day wore on with no success. Just past 6, Solberg straggled up to the Pardee Bridge. Maile Felder sat on a flat rock, casually soaking her feet in Fish Creek. "Hey there," she said, smiling. "I was about to start a search for *you.*"

"Radio and cell wouldn't work in the canyon. You find Lucy?"

"You bet. I stumbled on her two hours ago a couple of miles

down from here. She's fine, just exhausted. Already back home. Her horses too."

Solberg took off his boots and socks, sat beside Maile, and dunked his feet.

Maile chuckled. "She's pretty cheesed off by the search. Said she didn't need our help. 'I'm just tendin' my stock, little girl' is the G-rated version of what she came up with. About all she needs now are water, food, and a good night's sleep."

"How was she when you found her?" Solberg asked.

"Squirrelly. No food all day and she knew enough not to drink the creek. Called it 'trots-water.'"

Solberg smiled. "Giardia doesn't have the same ring."

The creek flowed through a gallery of cottonwoods and willows. Hard to believe how dry the forests were ten feet upslope of the water.

"We had a good day," Solberg said, bumping Maile's shoulder with his.

"We needed one," Maile said, wiggling her toes in the water.

"How's the fire going?" Solberg asked.

"Slurry bombers are nailing it. Helicopter bucket drops are easy with the river this close, and the lack of wind is helping. It'll be fully contained in a few days. No smokejumpers were even called in."

"Anybody hurt?"

"Nope and the Forest Circus even managed to save most of the houses. Not that people out here respect that outfit."

Solberg felt content. Lucy Beauchamp was safe and sound. Days like this were the reason he did search and rescue work. To bring out the living. Today, at least, everything had worked out okay.

21

Maile gave Solberg a ride back to his truck and headed down the gravel Fish Creek Road. He followed, hanging back to not eat her dust. Twenty minutes later, they pulled up to the Beauchamp ranch house. It was a half-log, half-frame contraption with crooked windows and a large front porch.

Jake and Ruga were there to greet them. "How's the fishing up there, Matt?" Ruga asked, smiling.

"Sorry, guys. Radio and phone wouldn't work. Everybody okay?" Grins all around.

"Good job today," Solberg said. "Alright, you know the drill." They gathered in a circle, arms over each other's shoulders. A minute of silence.

When they separated, Maile reared back and yelled, "Yabba dabba do!" Everyone laughed, including tired firefighters getting a meal. Normally, his crew stayed all business. But today, Solberg figured, *let 'em hoot.*

Jake Pengelly chimed in. "First round's on me. What do you say, Charlie B's in an hour?"

The team headed toward Missoula and beer. Solberg stayed behind. He never drank with his team members unless he ran into someone by accident. Even Jake Pengelly. Kept his distance to stay in charge.

Sheriff Roy Cousy emerged from the house. The men shook hands.

"Jesus, Matt. Thanks for finding Lucy. I was worried sick."

"Thank Maile Felder. She found her, not me."

"But it's *your* crew. Come inside and meet my cousin."

Solberg hesitated. People show a wide range of emotions after being rescued. Some are gushy and overly grateful. Others are embarrassed or pissed off. Somehow it was *his* fault they got lost in the first place.

"Alright," Solberg said. "But just for a minute."

Cousy smiled. They crossed the porch and walked into the Beauchamp place. A rail-thin, sunburned woman with long white hair sat on a wrinkled leather couch. Her skin matched it. Lucy finished a tall glass of water with an EMT watching her.

An emptied dinner plate rested on an antique metal safe with its door gone and boxes of cartridges and shells stacked inside. The stone fireplace had a .50 caliber Sharps rifle mounted above the mantle and a pump-action Winchester scattergun leaning against the flue. The furniture had been homemade a century ago—darkened shaved logs. Elk-antler lights above and scuffed wooden floors below, splattered with decades of chewing tobacco.

The décor was "Buckshot Revival."

"Lucy," the sheriff said, "this is Dr. Matt Solberg. He was in charge of the Five Valleys Search and Rescue team today."

"A pleasure to meet you, ma'am," Solberg said, tipping his green baseball cap. "Just call me Matt."

The woman scanned Solberg for defects and found plenty. "What gives a flannel-mouth kid like you the damn right to cross my land?"

"Well, we were invited by..." Solberg began.

"I didn't invite you, nor want you. I was doin' just fine. Findin' some bed ground for my horses is all. Then a bunch of government peckerwoods start runnin' around and..."

"Now Lucy," Sheriff Cousy said, interrupting her screed. "Matt and the rest are volunteers. They're not government."

"Like you, Roy?" Lucy gave him a blistering glare, then calmed down. "Well, just the same, they had no earthly right. This is *my* place. My dad, old Baptiste, left me the whole shiteree when he died years ago. I know the first name of every badger on this place and..."

"I knew Baptiste," Solberg said, brightening.

Lucy eyed him suspiciously. "If you did, why are you smilin'?"

It was a fair question. Baptiste Beauchamp was once the meanest son of a bitch in Mineral County. The competition was fierce, but he prevailed. He stole saddles, made raw land deals, poached timber, and shot rock salt at passing cars when the mood struck.

Solberg told his story. "I met Baptiste when I had a summer job at the Diamond Match sawmill in Superior," Solberg said. "Ran into him at the Four Aces Bar from time to time. He told me stories about his dad, Remy, horse-packing supplies to the timber and mining camps over in Idaho. About Andrew Garcia's tales from his mountain man days back in the late 1800s."

"He did, did he?" Lucy said. "Alright, would you call Baptiste a handsome man?" Lucy eyed Solberg, slowly rubbing her tongue against her cracked lower lip.

He was trapped. Tell the truth or hedge? "Ah, he was kind of regular, as I recall."

"Bullshit!" she snapped. "He was as ugly as a dime's worth of dog meat."

"I was just trying to..." Solberg began.

Lucy cut him off. "Then tell me this, what did Baptiste always wear around his neck?"

Solberg blanked for a second, then responded. "A griz claw hanging from a silver chain."

Lucy smiled and twenty-years fell off her leathery face. "That's the right damn answer. You really did know the coot. What was your name again?"

"Solberg."

"You a Jew?" she asked, forehead creased.

"Norwegian."

"Alright, then. Not that being a Jew is a bad thing. Old Baptiste taught me that they're the chosen people. For exactly what, I don't know, other than runnin' banks and taking shit from Krauts and A-rabs."

Sheriff Roy Cousy rolled his eyes. "Well, Lucy, you've had a big day and we better go. You get some rest."

Lucy suddenly looked tired. She turned to Solberg. "Come by sometime and I'll spin the tales myself. My dad was a bangtail liar. Oh, and bring that Millie girl along if you want. Or whatever her name is. The one I cussed out. She ain't no trouble."

"You bet, Lucy," Solberg said, tipping his cap.

When they got outside, Cousy looked amused. "She *never* asks *anybody* to 'come by sometime.' Not sure how you did it, but thanks. She's isolated out here and I worry she'll die alone."

"No way around it, Roy." It was the truth, but softened just enough.

22

After leaving Lucy Beauchamp's place, Solberg drove east on a washboard road, accelerating to smooth out the ride. Time to go home and take a shower. Drink a Pabst or two. Spend time with Bo, if it wasn't too soon. Take her words to heart and call her on a *good* day. Lucy Beauchamp's rescue made it one.

Just ahead he saw Bill Knight's white Ram pickup parked beside some green Forest Service rigs. Knight was inspecting the ground beside the road. Agency officials stood back, watching.

Solberg pulled over and walked up. "Hey, Bill, guess you got the call."

Knight nodded and went back to work. He was precise and unemotional, moving like a heron stalking a fish: pausing, freezing, then moving on.

Solberg made small talk with the Forest Service people. Ten minutes later, a Ford sedan pulled up. It had U.S. government plates and the charisma of a cinder block. Bernie Katz emerged from the driver's side. A tall, muscular guy wearing a black all-business suit rose up from the passenger's seat. He wore sunglasses and a blank but somehow surly expression. Two young agents hung back.

"Hey, Bernie," Solberg said.

"Matt, this is Special Agent Ezra Benson from the Salt Lake Field Office. I've told him all about you."

"A scary thought," Solberg said, extending his hand. Benson's grip was firm but gave nothing away.

"I heard about the rescue," Bernie said to Solberg. "Nice job."

"Oh, the woman just strayed a bit. Maile found her. What brings you out here?"

Bernie's eyes checked with Benson, who gave a slight headshake *no*.

"We're just checking in," Bernie said. Agency secrets were being withheld.

"Fair enough," Solberg said. "It looks like Knight is finishing up over there. Nice to meet you, Agent Benson." The man was a marble statue.

Bill Knight moved out of the ashes, carrying clear plastic bags full of evidence. Soil and pieces of broken mirrors.

Solberg motioned at the FBI agents with his head. "What's with the Men in Black?"

The movie reference meant nothing to Dr. Bill Knight.

Solberg shrugged. "Any idea what caused the fire?"

"Garbage bag bomb,"

"I thought they were a myth."

Knight set his pack and evidence bags in the passenger's seat of his pickup. He leaned against the back panel, facing away from the FBI.

"Why the intrigue?" Solberg asked.

"Most FBI agents are Eagle Scouts trained to lie under oath. I work with them, but I don't trust them."

"Fair enough. How does a garbage bag bomb work?"

Knight spoke low and clear. "You take a black garbage bag and fill it with rags soaked in kerosene. Any volatile will do, but kerosene works best. Seal the top with twine so air can't escape. Lay it in dry grass at night when no one is around. Ideally on a south-facing slope. When the sun comes up the next day, it slowly heats the kerosene fumes inside the bag. The flash point is reached at 130 degrees Fahrenheit. At that threshold, the volatile material vaporizes to form an ignitable mixture. When it climbs to 428 degrees inside the bag, you reach the auto-ignition temperature. Spontaneous combustion. The fire starts while the arsonist is a hundred miles away with a dozen witnesses around."

"Sounds foolproof," Solberg said, shaking his head.

"Except only fools try it," Knight said. "The conditions required are so specific that an external heat source is usually needed. Things like broken glass or a mirror to focus the sun's rays on the bag. Even then, you can't be certain it will start a fire. But in this case, it did. I found chunks of mirrors scattered beside what's left of the bag."

"Clever. Investigators like you will know its arson, but not who was responsible, given the time delay."

"Yes, but it lacks elegance," Knight said. His voice had an edge. Was it condemnation or disdain?

Solberg looked over at Bernie. The Mormon statue beside him had not broken character. Benson stood with his arms folded, head turned in Bill Knight's direction, eyes obscured by obsidian-dark sunglasses.

Special Agent Ezra Benson was working a case.

23

Matt Solberg took an escalator down into the terminal of Seattle-Tacoma International Airport. Towering glass walls let in natural light. An old airplane hung from the ceiling near an abstract metal sculpture. A guy in a suit held a sign: DR. MATT SOLBERG.

"I'm Solberg," Matt said, offering his hand.

The guy ignored it. "Mr. Merchant sent me to take you to the hospital," he said in a monotone. "You bring a bag?"

"No need. I'm flying back later today."

They got in a limo and headed north on I-5. Solberg glanced at his watch: 9:37 a.m. As they passed the Seahawks and Mariners stadiums, the deep blue expanse of Puget Sound opened to the west. Ferryboats steamed in all directions on the choppy water. The driver took an exit and dropped Solberg at the front door of a sprawling hospital complex. "Here's my number," the driver said, handing Solberg a card. "Mr. Merchant hired me for the day. I'll park nearby. Call when you need me."

Solberg got out of the limo feeling self-conscious. The driver rolled away.

A large sign identified the building as Harborview Medical Center. Solberg went inside through electronic sliding doors.

"Dr. Solberg?" asked a woman.

He turned and saw a stunning blond of indeterminate age and recent nose. "Hi, my name's Astrid. I work for Mr. Merchant."

"Matt," Solberg said, shaking her hand.

"Let me take you to Linda's room," Astrid said. "She really wants to talk to you. Here, put this on." Astrid handed him a surgical mask and strapped one on herself.

They entered an elevator and got out on the fourth floor—the burn center. Strange medical smells and the low hiss of air being vented in and out. Astrid pointed at a door and stood back. Solberg walked into a room where a girl sat in bed being attended to by a nurse.

He stopped dead. A third of the girl's face was red gristle. Most of her right ear was burned away. The nurse was applying white cream to her charred hands and arms.

"Ah, I'm Matt Solberg here to see Linda Merchant."

Somehow the girl managed a smile. "I'm Linda. Are you the man who saved me?" There was a sweetness in her voice that broke your heart.

"I'm the one who *found* you," Solberg said. "The doctors and nurses saved you."

Linda nodded seriously.

The nurse finished applying ointment and carefully wrapped fresh bandages around Linda's wounds. The girl cringed and closed her eyes. Solberg said nothing, giving her time.

Who could do this to a kid? He thought of Becky, his only child:

76

twenty-two, but forever a little girl in his heart. He'd called her a few days ago and offered to fly down to Portland after his time here.

"Not sure what we'd talk about," Becky had said.

"Then we can just hang out," Matt had said.

"Nope, Brace got us tickets to a Metallica concert."

"Okay," Matt had said, too cheerfully. "Another time real soon."

"Maybe." Then Becky had hung up. No "See ya, Dad." She never used that word anymore.

Becky Solberg had vanished from his life. A failed search.

The nurse gathered her supplies and left the hospital room. Linda held up her bandaged arms. "Dr. Robinson says I should play the Mummy in a movie."

Solberg was surprised by her sense of humor. "He's right. You'd make a great Mummy. Which version do you like? The one with Boris Karloff?"

"Never heard of him. I like the movies with Brenden Fraser and Rachel Weisz."

Solberg drew a blank.

"You know, the ones with Arnold Vosloo," Linda said, like that cleared things up.

"I'm sorry, I don't know that actor."

"He played High Priest Imhotep. The really scary guy who changes shape."

"Sorry, I haven't been to the movies lately."

"*The Mummy* came out in 1999, way before I was born."

Solberg laughed. "Impressive. You sure know your movie history."

Linda smiled. "I met the cast at a studio thing. My dad knows tons of people."

"Where *is* your dad? I expected he'd be here with you."

The smile fell from Linda's face. "He's in L.A."

"What? You're here all by yourself?"

"No. Astrid's here. She's new, but really nice."

"But I came here to see both of you," Solberg said, disgusted.

"My dad was here until yesterday. Then he flew down to Malibu to get the house ready for me."

"I thought you were getting more treatment here?"

"I am, but Dr. Robinson says I can take a short break before the skin grafts. There will be a nurse at home '24-7,' as my dad says."

At least someone will be there full-time, Solberg thought.

Linda Merchant sat in bed like a child soldier. Injured, in pain, and abandoned. He felt like sweeping the kid up and taking her home to Missoula. Home to Bo.

"How are you doing?" Solberg asked, leaning in.

Linda fidgeted with a bandage. "Okay."

"That fire must have been really scary," Solberg said, trying to get the girl talking.

Glazed eyes.

"Have you talked to anyone about that night? It might help to say what you're feeling."

"How would you know what I'm feeling?" she said, staring at nothing.

"You're right. I can't." Solberg sat back, giving the girl room.

Linda's eyes went to the open door, her emotions rising.

"You want that closed?" Solberg asked.

A nod. Solberg closed the door and sat down.

"Are you a dad?" Linda asked, sounding very young.

"Yes. I have a daughter. She's grown now."

"What's her name?"

"Becky."

"Did you send her away to school?"

"No, she lived with me until college."

"Would you ever leave her alone in this place?"

"Never."

"Really?"

"Not in a million years."

Linda burst into tears. "Then why did my dad do those things? He never asks me about the fire. I thought I was going to die that night! And now I'm a monster!" The girl cried inconsolably for a long time. Gradually the weeping subsided.

"Good for you, Linda," Solberg whispered. He handed the girl a box of tissues from a bedside table. "But you've got one thing completely wrong."

Linda looked confused.

"You're not a monster," Solberg said. "You're beautiful and brave."

"Really?" Linda's eyes had a spark again.

"Yes."

"But my ear is ruined."

"The doctors will build you another one."

"As good as new?"

"Cute enough to have all the boys flirt with you."

A hint of a grin. She wiped her eyes and blew her nose. "Do you really think I'm brave?"

"Yes. Surviving that fire was amazing. Most people would have given up."

Linda drank in the praise. Looked like she didn't receive much.

"My dad survived too, but he isn't brave at all."

"Why would you say that?"

"Because he didn't find me, you did."

"He tried, I guarantee it."

"He did?"

"Yes." There was no need to say her dad hesitated before racing after her that night. "What's he up to these days?" Solberg asked.

"He shoots in a couple of months. Another dumb explosion movie."

"Who will take care of you when he's away?"

Linda frowned. "Astrid, now that Blanca isn't around. My mom is gone too."

Blanca Chacón, Solberg thought. *Stay steady and bring the conversation back to her.* "I'm sorry your mom isn't here, Linda. She should be."

The girl looked grateful for the plain talk.

"Do you know where your mom is?" Solberg asked.

"She's in Europe somewhere. You know, boyfriends and fancy spas. But she emailed me a big gift certificate to Macy's."

Solberg's disgust was palpable. "So your dad and mom aren't together anymore?"

Linda acted nonchalant. "No, they hate each other."

"That sounds really hard," Solberg said.

Linda looked right at him. "It's better this way. My mom is a space shot."

Solberg saw a premature wisdom in her eyes. "Tell me about Blanca."

Linda visibly relaxed at the sound of her name. "She was my nanny and lived with us in the Malibu house."

"Do you like her?"

"Blanca's the best. We played games when I was little. She always made sure I had fun and stayed safe. And I love her Mexican food. Dad was away most of the time, so Blanca was kind of my..." She stopped short.

"Kind of your mom?"

"Yeah," Linda said. "Especially after my real mom stopped living with us." She hesitated. "I wish Blanca was here."

"She sounds great. Why did she go away?"

Linda shook her head. "I'm not supposed to say."

"Alright." Solberg waited a while. A nurse ducked his head in the door, checking on the girl, then hurried away.

After a few minutes, Linda's need to talk won out. "My dad and Blanca fought a lot."

"What did they fight about?" Solberg asked, crossing his legs.

"Blanca wanted to be my new mom. At first Dad was happy about that. But after Blanca had her family over for visits, he got weird. Like they weren't good enough or something. Dad even called one of her cousins a thief when he misplaced his wallet."

Linda picked at one of her bandages, tears welling in her eyes. Solberg sat back.

"It was awful," she whispered. "Blanca did nothing wrong, but Dad treated her worse and worse. One night, they had a huge fight and he told Blanca to go away forever. She yelled awful stuff she didn't mean."

"Like what?" Solberg was whispering too.

Linda's injured faced twitched. "That she would hurt my dad."

"Hurt him how?"

Linda wiped tears from her eyes. "She didn't say, but she was really scary."

"But you don't think she meant it?" Solberg asked.

Linda shrugged. "Blanca is usually so nice. She was my only friend." Her words hung in the air. Suddenly, the girl looked exhausted.

"It's time for me to go," Solberg said, glancing at his watch. "Will anyone but Astrid be here to look in on you? I can stay as long as..."

"It's okay, I have Dr. Robinson too. He's super nice."

Solberg took out a business card and wrote his cell phone number on the back. "Here," he said handing it to the girl. "Call or email me anytime you want."

Linda's eyes softened. "Thank you for finding me."

Solberg gently hugged her. "I'll find you again."

24

Bill Knight walked a sector of the Cyr burn he'd classified as "Extreme Fire Risk." The land was scorched beyond recognition.

A grubby shadow followed close behind. Fleming. They walked slowly through a skeleton forest, puffs of black ash rising with each footfall.

"This fire was impure," Knight said, pointing.

"What do you mean?" Fleming asked, his face a blank.

"Nature's hand was forced but, just as I predicted, everything was combusted."

"So we were right?" Fleming asked.

Knight felt pride and scorn. "No, I was right. But this fire was confused. See those two burned-out houses? Who lived there?"

"Rich pricks," Fleming said.

Knight spoke softly. "No, they were ordinary people."

"A house is a house," Fleming said, frowning.

Knight sighed. "That's the riddle, isn't it? But the ecosystem here was nothing special. Just beat-up stands used as a woodlot."

"So it shouldn't have burned?"

Knight's mind went back to the dry summer of 1977, viewing the scene like a flashback in a movie. His firefighting crew was stretched thin across too much ground. Knight hacked away at a burning log with a Pulaski, a hand tool with an axe on one end and a hoe on the other. A firebrand blew overhead and landed on the deck of an unfinished mansion being built in prime elk calving ground.

Virtuous habitat.

He ran over to kick the burning branch off the deck and save the home. That was his job. But fifty feet away he stopped, scanning in all directions. No one around.

Bill Knight stood back and watched.

The flame began as a seed of fire. Then a crimson slash meandered up the plywood walls until, with a loud *whoomp,* the fire gained life. It raced along the eaves, then flowed through unglassed windows into the framing grid and roof trusses. Soon curtains of flame blew from the windows until the roof burned through and the structure collapsed into a pyre, fireballs leaping fifty feet into the smoke.

He never told a soul what he'd done. Or what he'd learned.

The Good Doctor came back to the present and turned to Fleming. "Are all houses wrong?"

"You called them a contagion," Fleming said.

Knight grimaced. "I did, but is that ethical?"

Fleming was caught flat-footed. His usual stance.

Knight looked around the charred landscape. "A man without ethics is a wild beast loosed upon the world. Camus said that."

"Cam who?"

Knight nearly smiled. "In the right place, houses are a place of sanctuary and love."

"I've never seen that," Fleming said, spitting into the ashes.

"I have," Knight said.

Fleming shrugged. "But what about houses built in the wrong place?"

Bill Knight angrily kicked a blackened log. "In the wrong place, houses are just fuel."

25

Solberg lay in his hammock reading *Flight Behavior.* Monarch butterflies carry a clear warning. Earth's climate is rapidly changing. We are changing it. The process is wicked, and the results are devastating.

Solberg's phone buzzed. It was a text from Bernie Katz: "Al and Vic's 5:30." Bernie never got in touch this way. Something was up.

Solberg walked out of the Lower Rattlesnake and passed a row of large red metal Xs—a public art piece at the north end of Higgins

Avenue near the railroad depot. Soon he eased into Al and Vic's Bar, a dive famous for magisterial pours of hard liquor.

Solberg got a shot of Bushmills and walked over to where Bernie Katz stood holding a drink.

"Matt," Bernie grunted. He said nothing more but slugged his shot, went to the bar, and ordered another double Maker's Mark. He walked slowly back to Solberg, as if he didn't want to reach him.

Solberg gently rolled the whiskey around in his glass and waited.

"Matt, I gotta ask you something tough," Bernie said softly. "Do you trust Bill Knight?"

Solberg felt a jolt. An FBI agent was meeting offline, asking about his friend in a way that conveyed a full charge of suspicion.

Bernie slugged what was left of his Maker's and motioned to the door. Solberg set his unfinished glass on top of a keno machine and joined Bernie outside.

They turned left past the upscale James Bar and a yoga studio to reach a vacant lot next to the Poverello Center—a large Victorian house where homeless people got a meal and a bed. Several down-on-their-luck guys sifted away when they spotted Katz. The man oozed cop-ness.

"Why all the cloak and dagger shit?" Solberg asked. "We've danced around this before."

Bernie nodded. "I got tired of dancing." He pulled a piece of paper from his suit coat. "Read," he said, handing it to Solberg.

FBI INTERNAL MEMO

Date: February 12, 1995

Re: Summary of environmental terrorism investigation

Subject: Dr. William Knight, School of Forestry,
University of Montana

Findings: Based on the testimony of several students (kept anonymous here), the Agency believes that Knight is the head of a tree-spiking ring responsible for several injuries at the Bonner sawmill. The group is called the Montana Tree Monkeys. Knight is known to lecture on the methods, strategies, and aims of eco-terrorist groups—in particular, on how to drive spikes into merchantable trees. The strategy is to instill terror in loggers in the woods and men pulling the green chain at sawmills. His radical goals are to stop logging in the National Forests and reintroduce wildfire. He is also widely known to strongly oppose land development in Montana.

We questioned the suspect on three occasions and he claimed no connection to the crimes. But he was arrogant and evasive. At present our investigation has not built a sufficient case on Knight to charge him. The Lead Agency recommends that his actions continue to be monitored. Knight is extremely intelligent and may have pulled back from criminal activity when confronted. He may pursue eco-terrorist acts in the future.

We continue to define Dr. William Knight as a person of interest.

Solberg finished reading. "Whoa."

"So you've never heard of this case?" Bernie asked, moving closer.

"Everybody in Missoula's heard of it, Bernie. I was student at the U back then and it caused a helluva stir. The Bureau even hauled off some assholes for tree-spiking and sabotaging logging trucks. But I didn't know you guys thought Bill Knight was a real suspect."

"He never mentioned it?"

"Said you just asked him a few questions."

"No, the Bureau did a full investigation. Doesn't it seem strange he never told you that?"

Solberg nodded. "It does. But Knight teaches classes on the environment. I took several from him years ago. We discussed eco-terrorism and no one in the room supported it."

"Or admitted they did," Bernie said.

Solberg was pissed. "Bill Knight was a professor doing his *job*. The *Missoulian* even ran a series back then explaining how tree-spiking works! Practically published a manual on it, for Christ's sake!" He was shouting without realizing it.

"Keep going," Bernie said. "Not sure the city council over there heard you."

Solberg turned around. A dozen homeless men watched from the Poverello Center. "Sorry, didn't mean to be their after-dinner theater."

Bernie lowered his voice. "You know that I've been suspicious of Knight, and this memo explains why."

"I don't believe it," Solberg said.

Bernie talked plainly. "I realize he's your friend, but could Dr. Bill Knight be setting forest fires?"

Solberg's face flushed. "That's crazy, Bernie."

"That's a non-answer answer."

Solberg shook his head. "Bill Knight's been a big help to you at Powder Creek and Cyr. And he had no motive to set those fires."

"As far as we know," Bernie said. "But what about Mann Gulch? You said the place was a laboratory to him. Did Merchant's house make Knight angry enough to do this?"

Solberg held back what Bill said—*That house was an atrocity.*

"Bernie, most Montanans hated that place. It hardly makes Knight stand out."

"But he does stand out. And most Montanans aren't linked to the Montana Tree Monkeys."

"Oh, come on. That's weak bullshit and you know it. Are you getting pressured by that Ezra Benson character from the Salt Lake office?"

"It's partly that. Benson's left town but he's still leaning on me pretty hard about the Merchant mess. Really wants it solved."

"So do I," Solberg said. "For Linda Merchant's sake. But blaming Bill Knight for Mann Gulch is a ridiculous reach."

"Maybe," Bernie said quietly. "The Montana Tree Monkeys lead could be a lame dodge by someone trying to throw us off the trail."

"You're finally making sense," Solberg said.

"Or it could be a smart dodge by somebody trying to make the arsonist look stupid. Someone clever like Bill Knight."

"What about Ed Merchant's pissed-off wife?"

"We've checked her out. She's all booster, no payload."

"Shortest crayon in the box?"

"Yup. But she's selfish enough to know that the fire would reduce the size of her divorce settlement. From what I hear, money makes this girl go 'round."

"So you're back to Knight by default?"

Bernie opened his hands in front of him. "I had to ask."

"Why?"

"Because the only other suspect is Blanca Chacón. She fits the profile, but otherwise doesn't fit at all. How in hell would she know anything about fire cones and the Montana Tree Monkeys?"

"I agree, unless she worked with someone local."

"*Oy.* You got any ideas?"

"I'm too tired for ideas." Solberg pointed to the James Bar. "Let's finish this night off properly."

Bernie nodded. "Why not?"

They walked to the door of the James. A Hunter Thompson quote about "weird heroes" adorned the outside wall.

"But you said it was 'partly' pressure from Salt Lake," Solberg said. "What else makes you suspicious of Knight?"

Bernie Katz smiled. "Jewish genes. I'm a little suspicious of everyone."

26

Montana's forest fires bedded down overnight. But as the sun gained strength, two dozen lightning-caused burns woke up, covering Missoula with soul-crushing smoke. People talked of little else but fires and dread of more. The disasters of past years were recited like epitaphs on gravestones.

> *1910–The Big Burn*
> *1988–Yellowstone Torched*
> *2000–Bitterroots Overrun*
> *2007–Firestorm*
> *2017–The Summer of Smoke*

Everyone worried that this year might beat them all.

Solberg got a text from Bill Knight to meet him at the Missoula Fire Sciences Laboratory. He drove past the airport and parked at a 1950s-era government building. The Fire Lab was part of the Rocky Mountain Research Station managed by the U.S. Forest Service. Scientists stationed there studied fire processes, fuel dynamics, smoke dispersion, fire management strategies, and hazard risk. Their work saved lives.

After checking in, Solberg walked down a narrow corridor lined with colorful research posters. He passed offices where women and men stared at data-filled computer screens. Every room was stuffed with file cabinets, reports, and scientific gear.

Solberg entered a conference room where Bill Knight stood holding a rolled-up map. "Dr. Knight, I presume," Solberg said.

"Matt," he said.

"What have you got?" Solberg asked, pointing at the map.

"The Rosetta Stone." Knight was known for cryptic comebacks, but this one was clear.

"How bad a fire season we in for?" Solberg asked.

"Maybe not as catastrophic as 1910, but don't count on it," Knight said.

The mention of that year sent a pain down Solberg's spine. Three million acres burned in two days when spot fires coalesced into a firestorm. Flames leapt rivers driven by hurricane-force winds. Firebrands landed miles away, sparking new ignitions. Wallace, Idaho was incinerated. Four towns in Mineral County were wiped out: Taft, Haugen, Saltese, and DeBorgia. Rescue trains saved most of the residents. Thousands of firefighters, many of them immigrants and poorly trained city men, could do little but try to survive. Dozens died in agony. Historians call the event "the Big Burn."

"What's the pattern of risk?" Solberg asked.

Knight unrolled the map and took pebbles from his pocket to weigh down the corners. "I prepared this for the emergency-preparedness folks and county commissioners, but they're not taking it seriously."

"Why are you sharing it with me?" Solberg asked.

Knight stared out the window. "Because evil is waiting out there." There was a pause, and then the Good Doctor snapped back and ran his index finger over the map as if he hadn't spoken the solemn words. "The fuel loads are greatest in the west side of the Bitterroot Valley from Lolo to Darby. And the Blue Mountain region is primed for tremendous crown fires." Knight's finger paused on the map. "Especially here—Murphy Creek. Those people won't stand a chance." He swallowed hard. "I found the same conditions in the Garnets and Sapphires, but those ranges have far fewer houses."

Solberg's forehead creased. "What do houses have to do with it?"

"More houses mean more people to get careless and cause fires."

His answer didn't ring true. In the West, 70 percent of acres burned are caused by lightning. That fact should have been obvious to someone like Knight.

"Lightning is usually the driver, Bill," Solberg said. "Why are you...?"

"Gray Thompson at Oregon State just published an article in *Science* saying that in hot, hyper-arid conditions caused by climate change, human-caused ignitions rise exponentially. Especially as we build more houses in the forest."

Solberg glanced at the abstract. Plausible.

"So," Knight said, drawing him back. "The pattern is clear. Years of drought and a century of fire suppression loaded the gun. Now all we need is something to pull the trigger."

"Or someone," Solberg said.

The men studied the map. Fire risk was color-coded.

GREEN–*low*
YELLOW–*moderate*
ORANGE–*high*
RED–*extreme*

Only valley bottoms and high, north-facing slopes were colored green. The rest of the map was a swirl of treacherous orange and red.

Solberg bent over and looked at sections covering the Bitterroot Mountains. A shroud of high-risk red draped down from the summits, covering sixty miles of bench lands. "Piney woods people are sweating pretty good right now," he said.

"Building houses there is recklessly unwise," Knight said. "Newcomers build in the trees seeking privacy. They make their own little world and..."

"...now comes their wake-up call," Solberg finished.

"I hope it doesn't come to that," Knight said under his breath.

The two men stared at the fire risk map.

"All that contested shade," Knight said softly.

"Contested?" Solberg asked.

"Elk, ranchers, houses. A chain of claims from habitat to cattle to California mansions. It's the story of the West in one view."

"Why single out Californians?" Solberg asked. "Lots of people are moving in."

"Seems logical, given what I've found," Knight said.

Solberg had no reason to doubt his finding. Lots of reasons to wonder why he sought it.

"I talked to Bernie Katz the other day," Solberg said.

"How's old Bernie doing?" Knight asked, rolling up his map.

"He showed me an FBI memo from 1995. Seems they did more than ask you a few questions about the Montana Tree Monkeys."

Knight flashed a gap-toothed grin. "Yes, they actually tried to build a case against me for eco-sabotage. Those charges were foolish."

"And untrue?"

"Of course they were untrue," Knight said calmly.

"Okay," Solberg said, "but why didn't you tell me about the investigation?"

"Didn't think it mattered. I've spent my career calling for sensible forest management. I investigate fires for the Bureau now. I'm a scientist, not a random criminal."

"You're never random. But you should have told me."

Knight sighed. "Sorry."

"But did you know the FBI has monitored you ever since?"

Knight scowled. "I'm not surprised. Logical thinkers are always feared. Copernicus, Galileo, Descartes, Newton, Darwin, Mumma."

Solberg was impressed that Mumma was on the Good Doctor's list. Back in the early '90s that honorable man was forced out of the Forest Service for not cutting enough Montana timber to please the politicians back East. He refused to break the Clean Water Act, the Endangered Species Act, the Multiple Use Sustained Yield Act—the foundational laws of the agency. Solberg considered John Mumma a hero. In that moment, the very idea of the Good Doctor setting fires felt ludicrous.

"Got time for a sip later?" Solberg asked.

"Sorry," Knight said, rolling up his map. "I've got plans."

27

Dry lightning storms bombarded the Bitterroot Mountains overnight. The sky built thunderheads that lied. No rain fell, only virga—thin veils of moisture that evaporate before coming to earth. The clouds' only harvest were lightning bolts that started a dozen new fires within fifty miles of Missoula.

Solberg slept poorly during the storm. Every time he dozed off, flashes and thunder woke him up, sparking a loop of fear. Drought, fuel, lightning, houses, death.

At first light, he sat at the kitchen table drinking coffee and reading the National Interagency Fire Center "Situation Reports" online. Under "Lost Horse Fire," he read: "Bitterroot Mountains, forty acres in size and hemmed in by rock faces and talus slopes. The terrain was inaccessible on foot and too jagged for smokejumpers, so helicopters dropped water and air tankers sloshed fire retardant on the flames. The Bitterroot Hotshots were monitoring it, and while the burn was o percent contained, it posed no threat to structures or people."

This information calmed Solberg's nerves. He fanned through the website and stopped short on another page, headed "Blue Mountain Fire." The report read: "It appears likely that lightning ignited three fires in tinder-dry forests just west of Missoula. However, arson has not been ruled out."

These areas were colored bright red on Bill Knight's map—highest fire danger.

Murphy Creek was the worst off. The place was in the exact situation Bill Knight warned about. Scores of homes were built in a narrow canyon with a puny stream and thick forests dying from climate change–induced drought. Solberg reflected with dread on what he knew—aridity turns tree sap into tar with the flammability of gasoline.

He dug into the Incident Report. A thousand acres were aflame so far. Four twenty-person hotshot crews deployed by the Region 1 Interagency complex at Fort Missoula. No containment achieved and mandatory evacuations in force. Residents of Murphy Creek were trapped and running for their lives. Just as Bill Knight had predicted. "Holy crap," Solberg said.

The only positive news about the fire was its location. The Missoula Fire Depot was only three miles away. Slurry bombers could drop retardant and refill quickly. But if the wind came up, flames would be fanned into a maelstrom. Quick response would meet quicker blowups.

While he was online, Solberg received five texts: from an Incident Commander asking where Bill Knight was, three reporters, and a writer working on a piece for the *New Yorker.*

He called Knight twice. No answer. He texted the Commander—*Bill Knight is missing.*

"Where the hell are you, Bill?" Solberg asked out loud. He blew off the other texts.

Solberg ate a turkey sandwich on his rooftop deck. Continents of smoke loomed over the Bitterroot Mountains. The Lost Horse fire was too far south to see, but he'd hiked that canyon many times and knew it would probably burn uphill into granite cliffs and quietly whimper away.

By mid-afternoon, the Blue Mountain fire had grown into something loud. The radio said that fifteen houses had been destroyed and hundreds more were threatened.

Solberg drove to the base of McCauley Butte and hiked up to gain a vantage point. Slurry bombers groaned overhead, pounding hundred-foot flames with load after load of retardant. Helicopters made frequent runs to the Clark Fork River, filled their dangling buckets, spun, bee-lined, and dumped tons of water onto the massive fire front.

Solberg made another unanswered call to Bill Knight. There were easy explanations: he was out of range or he'd forgotten his phone in the truck. But still…

Solberg's cell rang. "Matt, this is Sheriff Haroldson. You handy?"

"I'm on top of McCauley Butte watching the shit."

"A family is missing up Murphy Creek. My deputy said they wouldn't leave this morning and now there's no sign of them. Can you come?"

Solberg had zero interest in sending his crew into that war zone. "You sure the family didn't make it out?" he asked.

"Not 100 percent sure, but close enough," the sheriff said. "My guys and the firefighters are coming up empty. Friends haven't seen them and we're getting no response from the cells of the couple or their two teenagers. I suspect the family is up in that mess."

Solberg held the phone away from his face and swore. "Dammit!"

"You still there?" Haroldson shouted.

"Yeah, I'm here," Solberg said, bringing the phone back to his ear. "I'll get my crew together. Where should we meet you?"

"Blue Mountain trailhead. Forest Service has set up shop there."

"I'll be there in fifteen minutes. My crew, as quick as they can."

28

The Blue Mountain trailhead looked like a military camp. Green Forest Service pickups were parked next to red Internationals used to carry firefighters. A hundred people moved about with purpose, wearing yellow fire shirts and hard hats. Solberg found Missoula County sheriff Hank Haroldson in the commotion. Six foot three, red beard, Viking.

"You made it," said Haroldson. He quickly briefed Matt on the situation. "Where's the rest of your crew?"

On cue, Jake, Maile, and Ruga drove up. Haroldson nodded his approval.

The search and rescue team gathered around a Forest Service pickup. Solberg spread a map out on the hood. "The family we're going to find are the Petersons. Dad is Roy, mom is Alice, kids are Roy Jr. and McKenna. Their place is here," he said, circling the last house up Murphy Creek. "The canyon narrows to forty yards. There are no caves, at least according to this topo map. Only two ways in and out. The easy way is down-valley to the Bitterroot River. The hard way is up a funky dirt road that leads into the Blue Mountain Recreation Area."

"Any connections to Deep Creek or Sleeman Gulch?" Jake asked.

"Rough ones," Solberg said. "Take a dirt bike or ATV."

"They got any of those?" Maile asked.

"Don't know. I want the three of you to cover the Blue Mountain side. Tons of rough side roads to check. I'll search the narrows along Murphy Creek working my way up to you. Clear?"

As usual, no questions.

Sheriff Haroldson eyed the team. "No one dies today."

No reaction. They knew their job.

Ten minutes later, Solberg drove up Murphy Creek Road. The stream was only five feet wide and being gulped by willows, Rocky

Mountain maples, alders, chokecherries, and cottonwoods. Wood frame houses, log cabins, and barns crowded the valley bottom, separated by small pastures cut by cross fences. Angus cows and mixed-breed horses hunkered down in the bushes, eyes wide with fear.

The fire had raced in from the southwest, driven by thirty-mile-per-hour winds, jumped the canyon, and was now devouring three more houses. Solberg accelerated past the fire engines and hose crews. Nothing he could do.

He parked near a steel gate where the road ended and left the keys in the ignition. Someone might need to move the truck. Beyond lay a narrow track into the woods.

A large crow sat on a fence. Solberg smiled. "I loved you in *It's a Wonderful Life*. Which way did they go, Jimmy?"

The bird tilted his head and stared.

Solberg's smile vanished as he looked around. Down-valley was a lethal patchwork of flames. But up-valley was worse: the main fire-belching mass of what the Incident Commander now called the Blue Mountain Complex. Three burns had collided and morphed into a beast.

Solberg went to the creek, dipped his green baseball cap, and put it back on. A refreshing drench of water poured down his face. The effect wouldn't last long on this high-'90s day.

He headed over to check the Peterson place. It was, to put the best light on it, a "homemade house." The structure was a warren of rough timbers and jury-rigged windows with a singlewide trailer sutured to one end. A green metal roof covered the whole contraption. Solberg nodded in respect. Metal roofs are wise.

He tapped on the front door and walked inside. Everything was in basic order. No sign of quickly grabbed possessions, no laundry on the floor or unwashed dishes. The boy's room had Seattle Seahawk memorabilia on the walls. The girl's reminded him of Becky's from years before—lavender music boxes and glass figurines.

Life interrupted.

Solberg went out to the barn. The door was open and he smelled gasoline. Fresh tracks from a four-wheeler led onto the dirt driveway. Solberg kneeled and took a close-up picture of the treads with his cell phone. He grabbed his radio and called in. "This is Solberg at the Peterson house. Recent ATV use. Will follow up. Over."

A squelch of static. "Matt, this is Maile. Got it. What should we do?"

"Stay with the plan. I think they're on a four-wheeler, possibly heading your way."

"Our way? Not sure that's wise. Out."

Solberg followed the tracks until they entered a confusion of tire marks on the dirt road. He scanned right. No ATV tracks heading toward the river. To the left, broken snowberry stems. The Petersons had managed to drive around the iron gate. Solberg squatted and inspected the roadway. Two linear impressions in the cheatgrass about four feet apart—standard wheelbase of four-wheelers. He compared the tracks to the picture in his phone. The Petersons had made a run for it.

It was six miles to the divide, three more to the Blue Mountain lookout tower. Smoke plumes in that direction made it an unappealing option. Might have been less treacherous when the Petersons fled, so Jake, Maile, and Ruga's positions were crucial. But the terrain presented more options than searchers: Deep Creek, Martin Creek, Petty Creek, and the entire ridgeline of the Grave Creek Range.

You're a real genius, Matt.

A larger crew would really help. But there were a hundred fire-fighters out there and any one of them might find the Petersons before his team did.

The wind got stronger as the fire breathed in air and spit it side-ways. Visibility was down to a hundred yards and falling. The Blue Mountain Complex was in charge now.

Solberg drained his water bottle, then made a trip to the creek to filter more. A quick leak in the bushes—too dark. He drank another bottle of water and refilled it. Then, eyes on the ground, he followed the treads, checking for signs that the Petersons had headed off-trail.

Whoomps all around as trees crowned out. Firebrands the size of baseball bats blew overhead, driven by forty-mile-per-hour winds. One landed ten feet away and Solberg stomped it out with his boot. Flames flashed above the trees, advancing the fire front at a terrifying speed.

Time to turn around, Matt. Then he thought of McKenna Peterson and found he was picturing his own girl—Becky. Solberg kept going.

Ten minutes later, a radio check-in. "This is Solberg. Any sign up your way?"

A belch of static, then Maile's voice. "Matt, things are very dodgy up here. Crazy-strong winds. Lolo Hotshots say we should bug out. Over."

"Then get the hell out of there!"

"Now?" she asked.

"Now!"

"What about you?"

"I'm fine," he lied. "Gonna check Road 17806 a while longer."

Maile paused then decided. "We're heading over to reel you in."

"No!" Solberg shouted. "Get back to the fire camp at the trailhead. I'll see you shortly."

"Are you bullshitting me, Matt?"

"No more than usual. Out."

Solberg stowed the radio in his pack and headed higher. A bull elk ran right at him down the road. Solberg stepped aside as the terrified animal raced by. "Good idea, Bubba."

He hiked uphill with the wind blasting smoke and ash into his eyes. He rubbed them clear with a kerchief. The treads of the four-wheeler looked fresher. But the flames were much too close, cracking and snapping as trees surrendered. The heat felt like a kiln. "This is officially stupid," Solberg said. He'd search up to the next switchback and then head back. He'd lie down in what was left of the creek if he got trapped.

At a sharp turn, the four-wheeler tracks veered onto an even rougher road through the burning forest. Solberg followed it, picking up his pace. Flames rushed at him from three directions. A swarm of sparks burst overhead, spraying him with fire. "Shit!" Solberg yelled, swatting burning debris off his body.

The Petersons were on their own.

Solberg did a quick scan. Retreat was now impossible—a gale of flames sealed the road behind him. Uphill was no better—forests exploding. Nearby, slabs of shale pressed down tight. There were prospector digs, but too small to hide in. He thought of Ed Pulaski, who survived the 1910 Big Burn in a mineshaft. Matt Solberg needed one—*now*. Openings in the rock to his left. Too little, much too little. Then a wide seam, but still no good. A burning tree crashed to his right. Then another.

Up ahead, he saw a four-wheeler and hustled toward it.

"Over here!" A man crouched at the mouth of a mineshaft, waving his arms.

"You Peterson?" Solberg asked, running up.

"How did you know that?" the man asked, stunned.

"I'm with Five Valleys Search and Rescue. Got room?"

"You bet," Peterson said.

Solberg bent down and squinted into the shaft. A woman and two teenagers, a boy and a girl, huddled together. He sat in the dirt beside them. The seeker and the sought.

Tree trunks thundered to the ground and blood-red light exploded across the blackened walls.

Peterson spoke calmly. "And he gathered them together into a place called Armageddon."

The land was a lake of fire, as if Earth had been thrown into the sun. The air ignited and howled in grief. Solberg heard a death song. Feral, magnificent, hideous. *Nothing will survive.*

The girl wailed into her mother's chest. The boy gripped his father and they prayed. "Yea, though I walk through the valley of the shadow of death…"

A flaming tree crashed across the entrance, spraying them with scalding cinders. "Let's ease on back," Solberg said, trying to sound calm.

Peterson moved his family deeper. The shaft quickly filled with hot smoke. They wouldn't burn to death, they'd suffocate. Everyone coughed and hacked. The smoke got thicker and hotter.

Solberg thought of Bo and Becky. *His* family. He mouthed a Buddhist prayer.

The five refugees survived for a minute. Two minutes. Then the smoke thinned as the fire front moved by. Death had passed by this day.

Solberg scuttled toward the entrance. The fallen tree was smoking, its bark burned off, its body bleeding hot sap. He looked outside.

A black moon of blowing hot ashes. Then he looked back into the shaft. "We're safe now."

The mother cried and kissed her children. Peterson shook Solberg's hand. "Thank you, sir."

"Not necessary," Solberg said. "You saved *me*."

"But you came looking for us in this misery," Peterson said. "What's your name, anyway?"

"Matt Solberg."

"I'll remember that," Peterson said, slowly nodding his head.

29

Bo let Matt sleep in past noon. When he woke, Solberg remembered only vaguely how he'd gotten home the night before. But he recalled Bo's anger about the risk he'd taken. And the hugs and curses from Maile, Jake, and Ruga when he straggled back to the Forest Service fire camp.

Solberg had broken his second commandment: "Don't be a moron."

But the Petersons were safe. They would probably have been safe without him, but he'd made sure, bringing them all the way down Murphy Creek to the waiting arms of weeping relatives. He'd ridden crossways on the back of the four-wheeler with the girl, McKenna, hugging him tight.

Solberg had smoke-ravaged lungs, so this was a day to rest. He creaked out of bed and Bo handed him a mug of coffee, smiling with relief that he was okay. After a long shower, Matt sat at the kitchen table and ate a mountain of eggs and home fries smothered in green chili.

"Want more?" Bo asked.

"I'll explode," Matt said. "But give me an hour."

"I'll make a pot of pho for later," Bo said.

"Hmong comfort food."

"With fresh garlic bread." That relieved smile again.

"Hmong-Italian comfort food," Matt said. "Add some lutefisk and you win the trifecta."

"Lutefisk is gross," Bo said, crinkling her nose. "It smells like..."

"Fishy toe jam," Matt said.

"If they had toes. But why do you like it?"

"Never said I did. Lutefisk is a Norwegian tradition, so we choke it down out of pride. Especially at Christmas. It's our way of feeling Christ's pain."

Bo laughed, then scoured the fridge and pantry collecting pho ingredients.

Matt fired up Harvey. The online Situation Report for the Blue Mountain Complex said, "Lightning is now believed responsible." Solberg tried to buy that. Arson would lead to questions he didn't want to ask.

A loud knock at the front door. Solberg gimped over and opened it. "The one and only Bill Knight," he said, smiling.

"Hey, Matt, I heard about the search. You okay?"

"Medium rare," Matt said. "Come on in."

Knight took a seat at the kitchen table. "Hi, Bo. Sorry to barge in like this."

"No trouble," she said. "Would you like some coffee?"

"No, thanks. I just need to talk with Matt."

Bo felt the brush-off and headed to the backyard to read.

Knight opened a notebook. "How was it out there?"

"Evil," Matt said.

"Don't anthropomorphize," Knight said, making a note.

"It was extreme. Three fires joined up and meant business. Just like you predicted, the fuel loads were immense and the pace of spread was exceptional. Brutal winds kept building and the sound of the thing... well..."

"Go on, what did the fire sound like?"

"Like Godzilla waking up."

Knight didn't laugh. "Be specific. Was it a roar, a moan? Describe it."

"Why?"

"Because sound indicates heat, fuels, terrain. Part of my modeling."

Solberg's face twitched. "It sounded like a fiend. A violent entity of some kind. The most terrifying thing I've ever heard. Sorry, I anthropomorphized again."

"You have that one coming," Knight said. "Besides, fear provides useful data."

"How is fear relevant?"

"It predicts how people react after a forest fire. Do they stay or leave?"

"No one would stay after experiencing what we did."

Knight made a long note.

"Hey, where were you yesterday?" Solberg asked.

"Checking the Lost Horse burn. Out of cell range, I guess."

"Why weren't you at Blue Mountain?" Solberg asked.

"Figured I'd wait until things calmed down. Care to join me and go see the results?"

"What you call results, I call a nightmare."

"I warned them, Matt. I really did."

"It was spooky how your prediction came true." Solberg eyed him closely.

Knight turned away. "Alright, go get some rest."

"Part of my plan."

Knight left the house and drove away.

Bo came back inside. "Thoughtful of Bill to check in on you."

"I guess," Matt said. "Sorry he blew you off."

"It's just his way."

"Maybe," Matt said. He went in the bedroom and collapsed into a nap.

When Matt woke up at 4, it was 98 degrees. He and Bo walked over to soak in Rattlesnake Creek. Despite the hot summer, the water was still refreshing; born high in the Rattlesnake Wilderness, flowing as clear as Stolichnaya.

Matt lowered his face into the creek, eyes open. The bed was covered with flat green, red, and tan rocks deposited in a snakeskin pattern. Legend had it that Lewis and Clark named Rattlesnake Creek for this effect. It was a story Solberg chose to believe. In his heart, though, he saw these rocks as ambassadors from deep time. Everything else in life might change, but these artifacts made of hardened mud felt like eternity in his fingers.

Matt and Bo walked home and ate bowls of pho with garlic bread dunked in. When Matt finished the dishes, Bo kissed him, then headed off to her air-conditioned office at the university.

Solberg sat in the living room for hours, rechecking the fires online.

The Lost Horse blaze had crawled into the wilderness, so more Bitterroot hotshots were moved over to the Blue Mountain Complex—same basic terrain as the 1910 Big Burn. Unthinkable losses could happen on ground like that. But the fire had "only destroyed twenty-two houses." The big subdivisions had escaped for now.

30

Independence Day was born gray. Smoke soon bent the light to burnt copper. By 3:00, the sky was a fume. By 4:30, the temperature hit 106 degrees—a record: 20 degrees above normal. The ashy air burned your lungs. Drunks careened. Dogs defected.

To make matters worse, Matt's holiday text to his daughter went poorly. "Sorry you can't be here for the July 4th party on the North Side," he wrote. "You always loved the pig roast."

"I'm a vegetarian now," Becky replied. "But the money you sent helps. Brace has stuff to deal with."

Her boyfriend, the specimen known only as Brace, always seemed to have stuff to deal with. But at least Becky offered thanks. It was much better than her usual silence.

Out on Jackson Street, things were loud. Kids shot bottle rockets and set off strings of Black Cat firecrackers.

Matt Solberg and Bo Xiong decided to lie low. There would be no backpacking trip, lakeside camping, or river float. Despite the horrible smoke, tourists and Montanans would compete for every square inch of unburned paradise. Missoula always emptied out on the Fourth of July—this year more than usual—so the search for peace began in your own backyard.

And that's exactly where Matt and Bo hunkered down, waiting out the heat, taking another short walk to Rattlesnake Creek for a cooling plunge, then lying in Matt's hammock shaded by Norway maples. They napped together until their breathing synched up like mated cats.

Matt woke up first. Bo felt small and vulnerable in his arms. He knew better. In 1975, her parents fled Laos at the point of a gun, carrying baby Bo in their arms. Hmongs were seen as Yankee collaborators by the Laotian and Vietnamese Communists who took power following the defeat of the United States. Like many Hmongs, Bo's parents followed their military leaders to safety in Montana. The mountains sort of reminded them of home. In time, a chain of migrants formed until Missoula had a sizeable Hmong exile community.

Bo Xiong was raised in Missoula, went to Hellgate High, got her PhD in Geography at Penn State, and spoke English with a Montana twang. She was as American as the Stars and Stripes, born from a collision of love and violence.

Bo woke up and stretched. "How long have I been out?"

"Half hour," Matt said. He kissed her once on each eye.

Bo returned that kindness.

"Say, you still want to go to the North Side party?" Matt asked, snuggling close.

"I suppose, but it's a medieval mess out there."

31

At 7:00, Bo and Matt drove into the North Side neighborhood and parked on Emerson Street. Matt grabbed a bottle of cab and Bo carried a cucumber salad to a modest green house. The North Side Fourth of July party was a legend in Missoula, a rite of passage for elder hippies, their kids, and grandkids.

Fifty people were scattered in groups, laughing and talking. Kids sprawled on a trampoline and panting dogs weaved about. A keg of beer rested in an ice-filled cattle trough with a stack of red plastic cups beside it. The Youngbloods played in the background—*Try to love one another right now.*

Matt and Bo placed their contributions on the buffet table and poured drinks. A draft and a cab. Handshakes and hugs from old friends they rarely saw. Life intervenes.

A wiry man with a gray ponytail came over. "Matt, glad you made it." A brief man-hug. "And the amazing Bo." He kissed her on the cheek. "Now the party can start."

Bo smiled and meant it.

"Good to see you, Spence," Solberg said. "Food ready?"

"Dogs are gathering, so the butchers must have knives in their hands."

A cooked pig was spread-eagled on a large table set off to one side. Dripping grease was lapped by slippery mutts.

A square-shouldered man named Rob Tabish cut up the carcass near a pit where the poor beast had roasted overnight. Tabish was in his sixties, but still exuded brute force. He and his buddy Jim Steele wore Uncle Sam hats and thick aprons, their faces dripping sweat. They skillfully pared pig from bone and handed it off to a rarely washed guy of about thirty who laid the meat on platters.

Solberg's radar pinged. Meat-boy wore a crew cut, long beard, and beered-up smile. His arms were covered in multicolored tattoos. A lumbersexual—no shortage had ever been reported in Missoula. But this guy looked familiar. Might be the same student he saw coming out of Bill Knight's lab a few weeks ago. The one who left a foul miasma behind. But this guy didn't look like a student at all.

Solberg was acquainted with the butchers—Tabish and Steele. Hard not to be. Plaques honoring them hung at the Smokejumpers Center out by the airport—each had made more than two hundred jumps to fight fires. In the Northern Rockies, they were actual heroes.

Everyone lined up at a long plastic table, heaping pork, potatoes, beans, veggies, and homemade bread onto thick paper plates. Bo filled up on salad and laughed with friends. Contented sounds filled the yard as people sat, ate, and drank. The background music moved on to Crosby, Stills, Nash, and Young—*Our house is a very, very, very fine house.*

Matt filled his plate then walked toward Hank Weaver. The short solid man was a community organizer who had tackled a long string of fights in his career: affordable housing, health care, unions. He'd succeeded in getting the city to build a footbridge over the railroad tracks connecting the North Side with downtown Missoula. A legit deal—although there were rumors that said otherwise.

"So, Hank, what are you up to these days?" Solberg asked, sitting down.

Weaver smiled broadly. "Building a better America." He said this every time they talked. It broke the ice, but revealed nothing.

"You still working on the minimum wage bill?" Solberg asked.

Weaver snorted. "Right-wing PAC money slayed the thing before it had a chance."

"Sorry. Fifteen bucks an hour isn't out of line, especially phased in like you proposed."

"I'll be damned," Weaver said. "Didn't think an FBI shill like you would give a shit."

"Not FBI, search and rescue. Sometimes they overlap."

"Not J. Edgar Hoover, Davy Crockett," Weaver said, deadpan.

"Minus the hat."

Weaver stared at Solberg suspiciously. "What do you want, Matt?"

Solberg set his plate on the ground and leaned forward. "I'm sure you've heard about the recent fires in Mann Gulch."

"Yup."

"I'm trying to figure out who set them. You remember the Montana Tree Monkeys?"

Weaver chewed pork. "Saboteurs for bunnies as I recall."

"You heard anything about them being resurrected?"

Weaver smiled cynically. "Shit Matt, you work for the FBI. Why would I tell you any fucking thing even if I knew?"

"Fair enough," Solberg said. "But this one cuts across all that. Linda Merchant almost died because somebody set fires targeting her bedroom. I say that's bullshit whatever your politics."

Weaver conceded the point with a tilt of his head.

"Come on, Hank, are the Tree Monkeys back in business?" Solberg asked.

Weaver got twitchy. He looked around the gathering of his oldest friends—Rob Tabish, Jim Steele, important others. "I have no particular idea," he said, stirring his food.

Solberg suspected it wasn't true. Just the wrong setting for such a question. Maybe later, one on one, Weaver would tell him what he knew. He had in the past, some of the time. "Alright, Hank. I'm just trying to bring the Merchant kid some justice."

Weaver nervously tapped his foot on the ground. "How's she doing?" he asked.

"Linda's face, arms, and legs have third-degree burns. She's in Seattle for skin grafts."

Weaver looked stricken.

"I know," Solberg said. "Pretty fucked-up deal."

Hank Weaver nodded.

The host, Spence, and his wife Janice stood on the deck facing the crowd. "Hey, everybody," he announced. "It's time to start the Fourth of July festivities. Find a chair and cozy up to your sweetheart."

"That's right," Janice said. "Like always, we're going to start off with a reading of the Declaration of Independence. This year the honor goes to legendary smokejumper and bullshit artist Rob Tabish. Alright, Rob, let'r rip."

Tabish emerged from the kitchen wearing a white powdered wig. The crowd erupted with laughter and hoots. "Tabish for president!" someone yelled.

The man paused for effect. "If nominated, I will decline. If elected, I shall flee to Mexico."

More laughter.

The rarely washed guy lifted his right arm, fist formed. Some of his tattoos were Chinese characters.

"Alright, you pinko sacks of shit, listen up!" Tabish boomed.

The crowd laughed, then quieted down. Tabish read in a loud, dramatic voice. "When in the course of human events, it becomes necessary for one people to dissolve the political bands which have connected them with another and to assume among the powers of the *earth*..."

A cheer from the crowd.

"We hold these truths to be self-evident, that all men (*and women*) are created equal, that they are endowed by their Creator with certain unalienable Rights, that among these are Life, Liberty and the pursuit of *happiness*..."

A bigger cheer.

"That whenever any form of Government becomes destructive to these ends, it is the Right of the People to alter or *abolish it!*" Tabish raised his hand and flipped off the sky.

A crescendo of howls and raised beer cups. Rob Tabish faced the crowd and roared like a grizzly.

His tattooed admirer held up a lighter and flicked on the flame.

"Be careful!" Tabish yelled, grinning. "It's fire season out there!"

32

People were playing hide-and-seek in the trees. Rob Tabish, Bo, Hank Weaver, Bernie Katz, even Bill Knight. The forest was on fire, but still deep green. Solberg never found a soul.

He woke up a sweaty wreck. It took a hot shower with Lava soap to wash off the dream.

Solberg got dressed and sipped Evening in Missoula tea, checking Harvey for news. Three hundred and twenty more houses had been destroyed across the state, but still no fatalities. A relief, but the fires were spreading at terrifying speeds.

He climbed up to his widow's walk and glassed the mountains to the south. Hard to see in the crud, but a fire near Stevensville was making a run for it. Solberg saw desperation in the flying of slurry bomber pilots. Their drop altitudes were dangerously low, a sign of a last-ditch assault to save property.

His cell phone rang and Solberg checked the number. Unknown. "Matt Solberg," he said, all business.

"Hi, this is Linda Merchant."

"Linda," Solberg said, surprised. "Is everything alright?"

A pause. "Um, yeah. I'm fine."

The girl was far from fine. "Are you getting new skin grafts?"

"Yes, the doctors are doing my face now."

"Good," Solberg said, a bit too cheerily. "You'll be beautiful again before you know it."

Linda giggled. "Hey, good news! Blanca is back!"

Blanca Chacón, Solberg thought, *the wildcard.* "Really? That's great. I know how much you like her."

"She and my dad got back together. Isn't that cool?"

"Wow," Solberg said. The news was a jolt given how the woman's anger had scared Linda. "And they're getting along now?"

"They are. Dad even bought her a Mercedes. Bought two more for her cousins, including the guy he called a thief. It's amazing."

Solberg instantly upgraded Blanca Chacón as a suspect in the Mann Gulch fires.

"Well," Linda said. "I just wanted you to know I'm doing better."

"I'm so glad to hear that," Solberg said.

"Thanks, and I really appreciate your emails. Sorry I didn't answer them all."

"It's alright, you've been busy."

Linda paused before speaking. "Can I call you again?"

"Anytime you want. And now that I have your number, I can check in on you."

Solberg could almost hear the kid smiling.

"Great," Linda said. She suddenly got shy. "I guess I should go now."

"I'm proud of you, Linda."

"Thank you, Dr. Solberg."

"Call me Matt, okay?"

"Okay. Well, bye, Matt."

It was a relief to hear the kid sounding upbeat, but Linda Merchant's struggles were just beginning. Pain from skin grafts, scars for the rest of her life. Solberg tried to take solace in the fact that she *had* a life.

But her call meant Blanca Chacón was now back in the mix. Those expensive cars sounded like a payoff, but what was Merchant buying? Silence about Mann Gulch? Had Blanca's cousins set the fires for her? But why would Merchant reconcile and reward them if he knew that was true?

Solberg rubbed his temples. Mann Gulch was a bigger mystery than ever.

Then there was Bill Knight. Bernie Katz was still sniffing around the man, but it made no sense to consider the Good Doctor a suspect. He had no connection to Merchant, and the Tree Monkeys lead sounded like bullshit. Knight had shared his fire risk maps with the authorities and even checked in after the Blue Mountain rescue. That was not the profile of someone hiding a dark secret.

But Bill Knight had predicted the *exact* areas that burned at Blue Mountain. And he said worrisome things. Fire *results*—like Blue Mountain was an experiment. Said he *warned* people in Murphy Creek. Called Merchant's house in Mann Gulch *disgraceful*.

Solberg pushed his doubts aside. Bill was a blunt and provocative man. If you took what he said wrong, you'd get him wrong.

Matt's sense of the Mann Gulch fires—and now the Blue Mountain

Complex—was as unclear as the sky. Maybe Hank Weaver would come clean with whatever he knew about the Montana Tree Monkeys or whoever else the arsonists might be. It wasn't much, but it was all he had.

Solberg needed to stir the pot.

33

Sometimes the pot gets stirred for you.

Solberg's cell phone rang early the next day. "Matt, it's Hank Weaver. Meet me at Denny's. Got some shit to tell you."

Solberg was caught off guard. "When?"

"Now. I just ordered their famous Grand Slam Grease Bucket."

Solberg glanced at his watch: 6:17 a.m. "I'll be there in fifteen minutes."

"Alright, but don't dally," Weaver said.

Solberg grabbed his wallet. Traffic was light on the Highway 93 strip: chain restaurants, discount stores, and a pointless mall. He hoped Weaver knew something useful about the Merchant fire. But Weaver could be playing him by passing on information he gleaned from Solberg to whoever did the crime. It was hard to get a clear read on that man.

Solberg entered Denny's. Weaver sat in a far booth, back turned to the door. The booths around him were empty.

"Hank," Solberg said, drawing close. True to his word, Weaver was polishing off a hubcap-sized heap of sausage, eggs, bacon, and home fries.

"Have a seat," Weaver said, chewing a mouthful. "Vile shit, but oh, so tasty."

"I didn't figure you for a place like this," Solberg said, sitting down.

"You know me, Matt. A man of the people." He looked around the room and took a gulp of coffee. "Besides, nobody I know is likely to see us talking here."

A waitress came to the table. "What can I get you?" she asked Solberg.

"Just coffee, thanks."

She hurried away.

"Alright," Solberg said. "What's on your mind?"

"Linda Merchant," Weaver said, lowering his voice. "Might be able to help you there."

Solberg leaned forward, elbows on the table.

Weaver scanned the room before speaking. "I know you figure me for a leftneck fool, correct?"

"Not at all."

"Then how do you figure me?" Weaver clearly relished having Solberg need something from him. He slowly mopped up grease with a wedge of toast, waiting for an answer.

The waitress returned with a cup of coffee and set it on the table. Solberg nodded his thanks.

"Come on, time is money," Weaver said with a smug smile.

Solberg countered with the truth. "Alright. I agree with a lot of what you do. You may be locked in a time warp, but your politics are not as alien to me as you think. Remember, I went to Berkeley."

"So did Oppenheimer and he built the fucking bomb."

"He got his doctorate in Germany."

"And then Berkeley welcomed the Nazi swine with open arms."

"No, he was accused of being a Communist." Solberg delivered the line with a smile.

"Like me?" Weaver said with a rough grin. "Oh, I get it."

"Look, bullshitting aside, I see you as a hard-case man who's done good things for people in Missoula. That's the nut of it."

Weaver eyed Solberg. "Last time I was stroked that nicely, it cost me $1 a minute at the Mustang Ranch."

Solberg chuckled. Weaver's attacked his eggs like cholesterol was a vitamin. Matt sipped coffee, waiting.

"Alright," Weaver said, resting his fork in the goo. "That whole business about the Montana Tree Monkeys is total crap. I know for a fact that those eco-pansies are not in Montana anymore and most of them went straight. One's a realtor in Santa Fe, for Christ's sake. Another turned hard-right Republican down in Texas. So don't waste your time chasing those sellouts."

Solberg eyed the man. He was telling the truth, but not all of it. "Thanks. The FBI suspected the Tree Monkey angle was bogus from the start."

"So why the fuck did you have me look into it?" Weaver asked in an angry whisper.

"Because we didn't know for sure. Now we do."

Weaver stayed stirred up. "So who else do the FBI geniuses figure for this?"

"They've got no idea," Solberg said.

"Fucking Feds," Weaver growled.

There was a lot Weaver wasn't saying. Solberg studied his face—a pissed-off mask.

"Alright, but one last thing," Solberg said. He pulled a photo from his shirt pocket and slid it across the table. It showed a horribly burned Linda Merchant. Her face was red slaw. "This is the kid," Solberg said. "Just in case you think of anything else."

Weaver's eyes got wide. "That ain't fair, Matt."

"No, it ain't."

34

Bernie Katz shook his head cynically. "So Ed Merchant is back with Blanca Chacón. It's another Hollywood miracle."

"And it gets better. Merchant bought Mercedes for Blanca and two of her cousins."

Bernie leaned back in his chair and thought out loud. "Bribes of some kind. But why? Usually, they're paid in exchange for a favor or silence. My guess is silence. Maybe Chacón had something on Merchant he didn't want to get out. But that's a stretch in Hollywood. Infamy sells tickets just as well as honor. If it didn't, Mel Gibson would be out of business. Unless it was rape, and we've heard nothing on Merchant. So that leaves us with an old standby—insurance fraud. Maybe Merchant and Blanca burned the house down to get a fat check."

Solberg sat up straight. "You mean Blanca and Merchant staged the whole thing, including the breakup? But that would only signal that Blanca had a motive. And why would Merchant stay in the house with his daughter on the night the fires were set? It doesn't make any sense."

Bernie nodded. "If you assume competence and honor, you're right. If you set them aside, anything's possible."

"Meaning Chacón's cousins fucked up," Solberg said, tilting his head.

"If they're even the guys. Maybe the fire starters got the date wrong. Maybe Merchant wanted an alibi too close to the fires. 'I just stayed there with my kid,' he could say. Like he loved the place so much he'd never dream of destroying it."

Solberg scratched his head. "But Merchant is filthy rich. The insurance check would be chump change to him."

"Assuming he's actually rich. Secretly going broke is a show biz tradition. People in fancy houses eating bologna sandwiches."

"Guy makes $16 million per movie. Where did the money go?"

Bernie counted on his fingers. "Drugs, gambling, too many houses, travel, boats, planes, bad investments, IRS audits, and getting ripped off by the schmuck who manages your money. Fortunes never last. And Merchant's got a divorce down the line where his financial records would be exposed. Maybe he figured he'd cash out the Mann Gulch house by collecting the insurance money, then hide it before divorcing his wife."

"Blanca would have to be a sociopath to pull off a con like that. Linda Merchant loves her and those fires nearly killed the girl. How could a woman that evil fool a sweet kid?"

"Kids want to be loved," Bernie said. "So they can be as blind as the rest of us."

35

Bill Knight pulled his white Dodge Ram to the side of a gravel road. Clicks and pings as the engine cooled off. He walked into the tinder-dry woods, greeting the plants: heartleaf arnica, Oregon grape, kinnikinnick. Each was a familiar component of this habitat type, but the vegetation crunched like peanut brittle under his boots.

And it got worse. Decades of fire suppression had allowed ground, surface, and aerial fuels to accumulate to dangerous levels. Dead-fallen, crisscrossed trees formed perfect fuel ladders for transferring flames from the land into the canopy. The stage was set for a massive stand-destroying fire.

Knight saw it clearly. At some moment of perfect stochastic logic, a seemingly random event would deliver an ignition source—probably lightning, possibly human—to set this patch of the desecrated world ablaze. The fire *could* happen this year.

He walked deeper into the woods and reached a pinegrass glade. This was the place where Molly had once pulled him down, kissed his chest, and then lingered below, while late-leaving osprey winged toward Sonora and the sky turned deep lapis until darkness and home.

A new log house crowded the edge of the glade. Wastefully large and wretchedly close. "Come not within the measure of my wrath," Knight said theatrically.

He pressed his face against the bark of a large ponderosa pine. It smelled like vanilla. Purity and health. This tree might survive a burn—a low margin of elk sedge surrounded it and adjacent fuel loads were slight. This matriarch might live to sprinkle the ash with seeds and grow a kinder world.

Knight lay on his back, watching puny cumulus clouds drift over the crest of the Bitterroots. No hint of rain—the clouds were temptresses. To the east, the snowpack of the Sapphire Mountains was a memory. A rust-colored smear revealed where beetles had killed thousands of water-starved pines.

It wasn't a hot, dry year. It was a hot, dry world. If there was a God, the fire should happen *now*.

36

The young woman pulled over at the base of a remote draw she'd targeted using Google Maps. It was thick with dry timber and crowded with dying shrubs. Better yet, it formed a perfect shoot up to the Big Sky Resort, a gated compound of the rich and famous near Bozeman. "Drifters," she called them. Rootless people up to no good.

The woman got out of her old pickup and leaned against the fender listening for engine noise heading her way. There was no rush. She was patient and certain of her cause.

There was nothing about her that stood out. Not pretty or otherwise. Not heavy or thin. A regular Montana gal: ashy-haired and average, it seemed. Almost invisible, which was part of her pain.

After ten minutes, she decided the coast was clear. The woman retrieved six paper popcorn bowls from behind the seat. Straight from the Dollar Store and untraceable. Covered with cartoon characters designed to delight. Sent a message—"I'm really going to enjoy watching this."

Then she grabbed a large vodka bottle that was really filled with Everclear—95 percent alcohol and eager to burn. The label was a ruse: vodka is a liquor that cannot ignite. A cover story in case she was stopped by the cops. Another pause as she listened for trouble. The forest was as quiet as a sleeping moon.

Her planned escape route was an even rougher dirt road over the Madison Range and down to Ennis. She'd be drinking beers at the Long Branch Saloon by sundown. Watching a ballgame and waiting for the news droids to break the story. Her story.

She grabbed a plasma lighter and the rest of her tools and walked casually for fifty yards to the edge of a cursed forest. She laid the first popcorn bowl beneath a ninebark shrub and half filled it with Everclear. Then she placed the other five bowls about ten yards apart and slowly poured in the accelerant. Pride in precision.

The next part came easy. She'd run track back in 2013 as a senior at Hellgate High School in Missoula. The woman trotted back to the first popcorn bowl, flared the plasma lighter, and set fire to the paper rim. Then she ran to the next bowl, then the next, until all six were lit. Fire slowly crept down toward the fuel that would give it meaning.

The woman smiled and laid a small plastic action figure in plain sight on the dirt road. "That should stir up the bastards," she said, smiling.

Then she got back in her dented pickup and slowly drove away. In her rearview mirror the world glowed yellow, red, and goddamn right.

37

Rob Tabish struggled up the trail, sweating. In his smokejumper prime, this hike would have been a stroll. Now he needed breaks to catch his breath and calm his thudding heart. "Never get old," Tabish said, panting.

"Don't expect to," Fleming said, scratching his butt.

The men hiked through dry grasslands toward a giant hillside letter on the face of Mount Jumbo in Missoula. "The L." Stood for Loyola Sacred Heart High School.

"During Trump's visit to Missoula, we used bolts of plastic to turn the L into LIAR," Tabish said. "I was part of the big red I. Trump got the big red ass when he saw it."

"Politicians," Fleming huffed. "Fuck 'em all."

"And let *me* sort 'em out," Tabish said, grinning.

They reached a switchback and trudged to the edge of a coulee. Tabish sat on a fescue tussock, grabbed a water bottle from his pack, and drained it. He gazed down at the Missoula Valley, where a hundred thousand people were jammed into a basin. Lolo Peak rose above it like a burial mound. "Fine view of perdition from up here," he said.

"Just a groovy-ass city to me," Fleming said.

"Wasn't always," Tabish said. "Missoula used to be a real place." He lowered his head and retrieved a large metal flask from his pack. "Care for a dram?" he asked, holding the flask out.

"I like beer," Fleming said.

"Ah, a man of rudimentary tastes," Tabish said. "Me, I'm just rude." He took a pull of whiskey and wiped his mouth on his sleeve. "In the old days, Mount Jumbo never had many trees," he said. "Now, look north of here. Forests have invaded the prairies and crowded out the grass. Bad news for elk. Worse news for bighorns and badgers."

"And the trees are only there because we put out fires," Fleming said.

"Bingo," Tabish said. "Logi taught you well."

"Who the hell's Logi?" Fleming asked.

Tabish chuckled. "Logi is the Norse god of fire. He's the boss around here."

Fleming had a visible headache.

Tabish cured it. "Logi is the one and only Dr. Bill Knight. The guy you're working for."

"Working for?" Fleming said. "I never thought of it that way."

"No other way to see it," Tabish said. "That's why I sent you to his office."

"Because I didn't know shit?" Fleming said.

"And now you know an ounce of shit," Tabish said.

Fleming actually smiled. "Dr. Knight is amazing. He teaches me everything about the woods. Even tells me where to go."

Tabish nodded. "Years ago, Knight gave talks to us smokejumpers out at the Fire Depot. Tried to help us understand fire better—and it did some good. But he was cagey about it."

"I don't always understand him either," Fleming said.

"What I meant was Knight had double meanings for things. He'd say fire was good for the land, then show us how to fight it. He'd say how useless we were, then build us up. Knight used fire scars, dates, and theories to make it look scientific, but I got his message."

"That fire fixes everything?" Fleming asked.

"Partly," Tabish said. "Knight slowly convinced me that smoke-jumping was a waste of time. Said the problem was people living in the line of fire, so to speak. That's why I nicknamed him Logi."

"But you're proud of your smokejumper days," Fleming said.

"And I always will be."

"But why?" Fleming asked, confused.

Tabish smiled. "Being brave at stupid things is the history of men."

Fleming scratched his head.

Tabish grinned, then cinched his pack. "Let's head into the coulee. Got something to show you."

Fescue and bluebunch wheatgrass gave way to a thicket of haw-thorn, serviceberry, chokecherry, and wild rose. Deer droppings covered the shady ground. A rubber boa slithered. A yellow swallow-tail flew.

Tabish took the lead, bushwhacking upslope. He pulled branches and let them whip back. Fleming got slapped until he caught on.

Finally, Tabish stopped and sat down on a fallen gray tree trunk. "This is the Medicine Tree. Dead as a carp for seventy years now. Have a seat."

Fleming sat down, looking lost.

Tabish pulled out the flask and chugged. "We're sitting on the corpse of a massive ponderosa pine. I'm sad to see her gone."

"But trees are wrong up here," Fleming said.

"Except where they're right, like this coulee," Tabish said. "Salish Indians used to visit this tree seeking health and a good life. Wisdom too, which they called medicine. They believed the spirit of old trees held the world together."

"You really believe all that spirit stuff?" Fleming asked.

"Once upon a time."

"And now?"

"It's more of a guideline." Tabish grinned.

Fleming whiffed on the joke. "How did this tree die?"

"Bill Knight himself figured it out. He wrote that it was over three hundred years old when some assholes cut it down in 1949. That year ring a bell?"

Fleming strained and failed.

Tabish angrily finished the flask. "Well, 1949 was the same year those smokejumpers died in Mann Gulch. You get the connection?"

Fleming didn't.

Tabish spit on the ground. "After '49, the Montana landscape began to fail. The world heated up, the woods got sick from assholes like me putting out fires, and Californians built houses in the thickets."

"Damn," Fleming said. "No wonder Logi got mad."

"Lotta people got mad," Tabish said. "And that Mann Gulch mansion paid the price."

"But Dr. Knight is still angry," Fleming said.

"Logi will die angry. Just like all gods."

38

Solberg hiked up Spring Gulch in the Rattlesnake Recreation Area and cut back to the creek. Hank Weaver waited for him beside the remains of an old homestead cabin. "I can't get the picture of that little girl out of my mind," Weaver said.

"Good," Solberg said.

Weaver looked tormented. "Matt, I've got some hard information for you. Hard because it's personal. I'm not sure, but two guys I know might be involved in the Merchant fire."

"Okay," Solberg said. He held back, not wanting to push.

Weaver rubbed his face. "Alright. When men get drunk they brag, right?"

"Part of our lifestyle," Solberg said.

"And when they brag, it's usually bullshit."

"This is widely known," Solberg said.

"Okay, so don't jump to any conclusions about what I'm about to tell you."

"Not my nature," Solberg said.

Weaver studied Solberg's face, searching for an FBI sting. It wasn't there. "Last night, I was drinking way too much tequila with Rob Tabish and Jim Steele in my backyard. Just old fuckers shooting the shit."

"The smokejumpers," Solberg said.

"In the flesh," Weaver said. "Known 'em for years. Hale men well met. Them and a twist-tie kid named Fleming that follows them around like they're the second helping of Jesus. You saw him at the North Side party."

"Beard, tattoos, and nasty aroma?"

"That's Fleming. Anyway, after a while we're all pretty drunk and things heat up, as they do. Vietnam. Iraq. Obama's phony liberalism. Trump's genuine fascism. The usual shit. Right up until I mentioned the Mann Gulch fire. When I did, Tabish goes off on a rant about running the rich bastards off because Montana is going down the shitter."

"Hell, we've all said that with enough booze in us."

"You bet, but then things went sideways. Tabish starts saying, 'Merchant deserved all of it.' Meaning the girl too, I think."

Solberg face got hot. "He really said that?"

"He did. Then Tabish goes into my yard and piles up pine needles and lights 'em on fire with a cigarette. Steele gets some wood from my garage and pretty soon they've got a pretty good blaze going on my goddamn lawn. No fire ring, nothing. I'm not one to water much, so the dry grass catches fire and it spreads. Tabish thinks this is fucking hilarious. Starts chanting, *Logi, Logi, Logi.*"

"Norwegian fire god," Solberg said. "One of my ancestors, no doubt."

Weaver frowned. "But then these guys pull out their dicks, and piss on the flames. Fleming too."

Solberg cringed.

"I know," Weaver said. "Piss really stinks when you burn it."

"Every Cub Scout knows that," Solberg said.

Weaver leaned forward. "But then Tabish and Steele yell at Fleming to sing a smokejumper song with them. And off they go. Words like 'See the fire down below. Run for the rocks.' Stuff about 'thirteen crosses in Mann Gulch.' Gave me the chills. I mean those guys died horribly back in '49. But Tabish went from honoring them to calling the Merchant fire 'revenge,' even with that girl burned so badly. Called it 'good science,' like he was repeating something he was told."

"Was Tabish bullshitting or confessing?"

"Hell if I know," Weaver said. "Later, they all passed out on the ground. I laid blankets on 'em and the next morning they were gone. Haven't seen 'em since. Fleming included, which is a blessing. The weasel steals anything that's not tied down."

"So why are you coming to me with this? Tabish and Steele are your buddies."

"Because they've turned drunk and hateful. Really bums me out to watch those guys slide downhill."

Solberg shifted gears. "Tabish ever work as a potter?"

Weaver looked confused. "Why the fuck would you ask that?"

"Just something I'm checking out."

Weaver went along. "Not that I know of, but he could have had an artsy girlfriend back in the old days. Hell, who didn't?"

Solberg spoke softly. "Thanks, Hank, but why did you bring this to me? Was it the picture of Linda Merchant?"

Weaver nodded. "If Tabish and Steele hurt that little girl, 'buddies' becomes past tense." The stern look on the man's face convinced Solberg it was true.

"And this Fleming character?"

"Dumb as dirt, with tombstone eyes," Weaver said.

Solberg waited for more.

"Work the problem, Matt," Weaver said.

"I appreciate this," Solberg said.

"Gotta go."

"Can we talk again down the line?" Solberg asked.

Weaver frowned. "Down the line, this conversation never happened."

39

The next morning, Solberg gave Bernie Katz two names to check out about the Mann Gulch fire: Rob Tabish and Jim Steele. He'd confided this without sharing all he feared. It would be a travesty to sic the FBI on two firefighting legends if they were innocent.

At 10:00, Solberg pulled in to the Missoula Smokejumper Center beside the airport. It was already 90 degrees and the forecast called for 107, another record high. Climate change is a punch you can't duck.

The Missoula Smokejumper Base was a standard government-issue building, but legendary. The Loft was the hub of the place. It was pierced by a tower for rigging parachutes that had a blue twenty-foot smokejumper painted on its front. Eighty smokejumpers were based here—it used to be 180. Only 320 left in the country. Federal budget cuts were inflicting structural damage. The base was where crews stored gear and hung out waiting for the call. This year, it came early and often. Fires raged in the Payette National Forest in Idaho, the Deschutes in Oregon, and across a swath of Montana.

Smokejumpers are a first-strike weapon, dropped in to hit remote ignitions and gain the upper hand. Crews work the first forty-eight hours with no sleep. Paid just $17.50 an hour, with hazard pay added when on the line.

Solberg walked into the Smokejumper Loft. Sign read "STUPID HURTS." A line of ready room lockers held jumpsuits, packs, Pulaskis, hard hats, fire shelters, first-aid kits, chainsaw slings, and pre-rolled parachutes (including a reserve and drogue in case things went bad). A person's name was scrawled on masking tape above each "cubby."

White-and–blue-striped chutes lay on long tables being tended to by riggers. Square-shouldered men sat at beat-up sewing machines mending gear.

A modest wall display served as a Smokejumper Hall of Fame. Plaques for Tabish and Steele hung near the top.

Solberg always felt humbled here. These men and women risked their lives doing something epic, heroic, and a little nuts. They parachuted into burning forests from fifteen hundred feet and hit the ground ninety seconds later carrying sixty pounds of gear. It's called "Initial Attack."

All to save what? Timber? Bambi? Solberg was nearly as jaded as Bill Knight about fighting forest fires. The purpose wasn't ecological—forests needed regular burns to stay healthy. Too often, firefighting was about saving houses built in the woods because no one had the balls or brains to stop the construction.

But the bravery of smokejumpers—of all firefighters—was staggering, and their losses echoed like a bugle at Arlington. Solberg knew the litany by heart. The 1910 Big Burn in Montana and Idaho: whole towns lost and seventy-eight firefighters gone. Over in Washington, Ernani St. Luise and Douglas Ingram died like warrior priests in 1929. A blowup in California chaparral killed twenty-five in 1933. The doomed Mann Gulch crew flew out of this very depot. In 1994, a local legend named Don Mackey and thirteen other firefighters died in Colorado fighting the Storm King fire. An Arizona blaze killed nineteen hotshots in 2013. The list was tragic and grew longer every year.

Despite Solberg's doubts, the Smokejumper Loft felt like a cathedral.

He took stairs to the loadmaster's office. Rocky Hilger was on the phone. "My guys have worked twenty-one goddamn days in a row and they're due some time off!"

Hilger was a retired smokejumper—five foot eight and hard as a frozen anvil. "So they'll land in Missoula in forty-five minutes?"

Blather.

"Alright," Hilger said. He hung up and turned around.

"Hi, Rocky," Solberg said.

"The infamous Dr. Matthew Solberg," Hilger said. "Writing another big-ass book?"

Solberg smiled. "Tackle me if I get the urge."

"Happy to." Hilger motioned to a chair.

"NICC on your ass?" Solberg asked, sitting down.

"The mother ship, known to you civilians as the National Inter-agency Fire Center, likes to throw their weight around. To them, 'coordinating men and equipment' means telling me what the fuck to do. Ah, they're mostly good folks." Hilger eyed Solberg. "What's on your mind?"

"I know you're busy, so I'll get right to it," Solberg said. "I'm investigating the Mann Gulch fire for the FBI."

"Can't believe it happened again," Hilger said, shaking his head.

"That place is a coffin and a shrine."

Hilger blew air out his mouth in agreement. "How can I help?"

"We've got squat for leads about who set the fires. There's an out-of-state suspect, but I've got my doubts. About all I have locally is a notion that will royally piss you off."

"Why shift gears?" Hilger said, checking his watch.

Solberg gathered himself. "Do you personally know Rob Tabish and Jim Steele?"

"Course I know those guys. Nine feet tall and covered with hair, as the fable has it."

Solberg nodded. "Yes, but what are they *really* like?"

Hilger rubbed his nearly bald head. "I can't believe you're mentioning those guys in the same breath as that fucking Merchant fire. Especially with a kid burned up."

"Me either, Rocky," Solberg said.

"So what's got you so damned interested in Tabish and Steele? Fill the room with the faintest whiff of why these guys—retired mother-fucking smokejumpers, by the way—were involved with that shit storm in Mann Gulch."

Solberg felt like he was being hit by a strong wind. "A friend of these guys thinks they might have set the fires."

"Who said that load of crap?" Rocky asked, frowning.

"Can't say."

"Anonymous sources," Rocky said, scowling. "I'm convinced already."

The roar of a plane made Hilger turn around. An OV-10 "Bronco" landed and taxied past the window to a stop. It was a twin-engine, turboprop aircraft developed for war that was now used to observe fires. The plane had large cabin windows and FIRE written on its twin tails. Two men emerged carrying notebooks, binoculars, and laptops.

"I thought satellite images made scout planes obsolete," Solberg said.

"Not to me," Hilger said, turning back. "Fire has to be seen with human eyes to know what's on its mind. You've worked out there; you know I'm right."

Solberg considered that high praise. "All the more reason I was reluctant to mention Tabish and Steele in this mess."

"But you did," Hilger said, eyes boring in.

"I figured you'd know whether it's bullshit or not."

Hilger glanced at his watch. "My guys land in half an hour. You've got until then to convince me not to snap your Norwegian neck."

"Alright," Solberg began, swallowing hard. "Like I said, Mann Gulch is holy ground. Maybe Tabish and Steele took that literally."

"Like an Indian burial ground?" Hilger said. "Pretty woo-woo shit, Matt."

"Hear me out. Maybe those guys figured that Edward Merchant, Mr. Zillionaire Movie Star, built his mansion on a kind of smoke-jumper battlefield and desecrated the memory of the fallen."

Hilger leaned back, thinking.

"But I don't know Tabish and Steele like you do," Solberg said. "Would those guys be capable of something like this?"

"You think I keep track of every smokejumper that comes through this place?"

"Yeah, I kinda think you do."

Hilger sighed. "Alright, pains me to say it, but I hear they practically live at Red's Bar. Too many stale stories and fresh drinks. Steele is a follower; that's about all I know. But word is Tabish can be a fire-breathing asshole when he's lit."

"Words or actions?"

"Couldn't say," Hilger said. "But I hear Tabish says lots of angry crap about Montana changing too much. Course, that's a favorite pastime around here. Hardly makes him special."

"But he *is* special. Smokejumpers are wired up different than most people. Like you—born risk takers with a massive sense of honor. Fierce about the camaraderie, the..."

"Yeah, I know the drill, but I'm not sold. Drunk and surly isn't the same as evil. You're asking me to believe that Rob Tabish, a first-rate smokejumper, destroyed his honor over one fucking house? A little girl almost died, for Christ's sake."

"Her name's Linda."

"Damn," Rocky said. "How is she?"

"She'll live, but she'll never be the same."

Rocky's face softened. "You really think Merchant's house made Tabish *that* angry?"

Solberg lowered his voice. "Let me put it this way. Are you happy that a mansion was built overlooking Mann Gulch and the crosses of your dead buddies?"

"I never met those guys. Leave them out of this."

"Okay, but you knew Don Mackey, the smokejumper based out of here who was killed in Colorado back in '94."

"Yes, I knew Don very well. He was a really good man. All fourteen who died at Storm King were first-rate people."

"Alright," Solberg said quietly. "What if somebody built a mansion next to Don Mackey's memorial in Blodgett Canyon? How would you feel?"

Hilger stood and raised his binoculars, impatiently scanning the sky for an incoming plane. One bringing his crew safely home. Then Rocky Hilger turned around slowly and looked directly into Solberg's eyes. "If someone did that, I'd skull-fuck him."

40

By 3:00 the temperature read 108 degrees on the shaded thermometer in Solberg's backyard. Chickadees splashed happily in the birdbath. "A lovely choice, *mis amiguitos*," Solberg said.

He called Bernie Katz. "I just talked to Rocky Hilger, the smoke-jumper boss."

"What's his take on Tabish and such?"

"Hilger was defensive at first. Which I'd expect when his way of life was insulted."

"But then?"

"Then he confided that Tabish and Steele were mean drunks who spewed hate about newcomers building mansions. Especially Ed Merchant and especially Tabish—he's the alpha. Hilger implied it was possible their clichés turned into action."

"Implied?"

"Hilger said he'd do unmentionable things to anyone who defiled a smokejumper memorial like Mann Gulch. I connected the psychological dots to Tabish."

"Dots aren't a line," Bernie said. "I need proof."

"Then let's find it," Solberg said.

"Deal," Bernie said.

"There's one more thing," Solberg said. "It's probably nothing."

"Let me decide," Bernie said.

"There's a marginal creature named Fleming who's got kneepads on for Tabish and Steele. You know the type—long beard and more tattoos than teeth."

"Sounds like half of U of Montana students. Girls included. What about him?"

"Not sure. Just see if you have anything on a white male, about thirty, named Fleming. All he goes by. Fleming is a dodgy street character so the Missoula cops may know him."

"Alright. Will you be reachable?"

"Yes, unless I'm on a search in the mountains."

"We've still got mountains?" Bernie joked. "Hard to tell through all this *schmutz*. You seen Bill Knight lately?"

"No, but with all these fires, he's probably in the woods checking things out."

"Checking exactly what things out?" Bernie asked slowly. That cop-ish tone again.

"Don't tell me Knight is still a suspect."

"Until this is solved, Gandhi is still a suspect."

41

Solberg finally caught up with Bill Knight at his office.

A framed quote from conservationist Aldo Leopold now filled the spot where a photo of Bill's wife used to be: A THING IS RIGHT WHEN IT TENDS TO PRESERVE THE INTEGRITY, STABILITY, AND BEAUTY OF THE BIOTIC COMMUNITY. IT IS WRONG WHEN IT TENDS OTHERWISE.

Solberg pointed. "Dusting off Leopold's maxim, I see."

Knight glanced over his shoulder. "Never hurts to remember wisdom. Especially these days."

Solberg studied Bill as he moved papers around on his desk. The man looked downcast. "Say, do you remember a smokejumper named Rob Tabish?"

Knight nodded slightly. "Vigorous mammal, as I recall."

Solberg sat back, trying to read the Good Doctor's eyes. "You gave him training sessions in fire ecology years ago, right?"

"Like dozens of other smokejumpers," Knight said, a bit too quickly.

"So you don't remember anything specific about that legend?"

"Your wording is transparent, Matt. If you have something to ask, just ask it."

Solberg nodded and leaned in. "Alright, I have reasons to believe that Tabish might be setting fires."

"Reasons are not evidence," Knight said, hands folded.

Solberg smiled. "Alright, did you see anything in his behavior or character that would make a rationale person suspect him of arson?"

Knight sipped tea. He obviously relished controlling the moment when verbally jousting with Matt Solberg. "My job was to instruct jocks about science. Smokejumpers see ecology as a zero-sum game. If fire wins, they lose. That leaves no space for nuance."

"And your career is about nuance," Solberg said.

"I'm a scientist. My job is learning how things work."

Solberg drummed his fingers on the arm of the chair. "Alright, so Tabish would never give an inch to fire?"

"Not in natural times," Knight said.

"Are these natural times?" Solberg asked.

"That climate died thirty years ago," Knight said with certainty.

Solberg crossed his legs and waited for more.

Knight almost smiled. "This is about Mann Gulch."

"It is," Solberg said, leaning forward.

Knight stared at the ceiling. "And you're wondering if I broke my covenant with reason and instructed old smokejumpers to set fires. Is that about right?"

Solberg felt foolish. "Sorry, it sounds insane when you say it that way."

Knight's eyes drilled in. "No other way to say it."

"So Tabish doesn't stand out to you?"

Knight shook his head. "In size, yes. In intellect, hardly. But Tabish took lots of notes during my Fire Lab training sessions."

"And why would you remember that?"

"Because the pencil looked like a toothpick in his hand."

"Nothing else?"

"It just looked funny to me."

Solberg shook his head. "Nothing funny about arson, especially at Mann Gulch."

Dr. Bill Knight leaned back. "Smokejumpers are a weapon, and I aspire to remain a peaceful man."

Solberg felt the brush-off and sat back, recalculating. "What do you make of that fire set next to Big Sky?"

Knight almost smiled. "The popcorn bowl bandit."

"So you don't think that was serious?"

Knight shook his head. "Setting fires is always serious. The arsonist took out seven houses, but it could have been fifty. Luckily, the run-up was too long, so fire crews had time to get ahead of it."

"Therefore an amateur did it," Solberg said, nodding.

"Or a committed beginner, learning as they go. Makes them dangerous."

Solberg considered that. "Do you really think they'll start more fires?"

Knight tilted his head. "I need more data to figure out their game."

"Sounds pretty grim to me," Solberg said.

"No, it's *always* a game," Knight said, drumming his fingers on the desk.

42

After talking with Bill Knight, Solberg phoned in a report to Bernie.

"Do you believe Knight about Tabish and what's his name?" Bernie Katz asked.

"Not sure," Solberg said.

"Don't overwhelm me with details, Matt."

"Knight played verbal cat and mouse, but that's typical. About all he said that mattered is that Tabish took lots of notes during fire ecology training sessions."

"Aren't students supposed to take notes?" Bernie asked.

"Most smokejumpers are kinesthetic learners; they remember through experience."

"So Knight gave you no other reasons to suspect Tabish?"

"He said reasons are not evidence," Solberg said.

"He'd make a lousy cop," Bernie said.

"And you'd make a lousy ecologist."

"I hate bugs. Tabish may or may not be a legit suspect. If being drunk and stupid was a crime, Las Vegas would be a dungeon. But what does your gut tell you about Knight?"

"I hate even thinking about it."

"So you suspect something but are too loyal to say so," Bernie said, eyebrows raised.

Solberg sighed. "A master of facts can't become a master of fiction."

Bernie rolled his eyes. "Let me know when your head clears."

Solberg was finally off duty. He headed to the basement to unwind in cooler air. A "CRO-MAN CAVE" sign hung on the wall. He opened a Negra Modelo and sat on an old brown couch that dated back to his marriage.

A text came in from Becky. Matt felt a flash of fear—was his daughter okay?

"I miss Mom," is all she said. No emoji for effect. Just sadness.

Matt exhaled. Finally, an opening to talk. "Me too, sweetie," he replied.

Two minutes went by. Was that it?

Then another text. "I'm having a hard time. Portland is tough."

"It's a big city compared to Missoula."

"Not what I meant. Things are difficult. Brace too."

"Are you alright?" Matt texted. "I can come out there right now."

A minute went by. "Internet is full of scary Montana fire stories. You get mentioned a lot."

"Just trying to help."

"Don't die."

"I'll do my best."

Matt waited half an hour. No more texts came in.

Solberg went to bed exhausted, but his mind would not let him rest.

43

Bill Knight finished his last sample and sat back. In March, he'd drilled cores and cut wedges from forty large ponderosa pines below Lolo Peak. The arduous analysis of rings and fire scars was finally done. "Trees remember," Knight said with satisfaction.

His moment of calm vanished. Molly was really gone. Not out of town—dead.

For years, finishing a data set was an occasion to celebrate with his wife. They'd go to the Victor Steak House and sit in the back. Molly would have salmon and he'd have a rib eye. They'd share a slice of huckleberry pie for dessert. Then head home for a nightcap under the glow of the Milky Way.

Bill Knight pulled out a bottle of Laphroaig, poured a shot, and held it up. "Here's to you, Molly," He slugged the whisky.

Knight dove back into his data for comfort. Facts are patient and immortal. He scrolled through screen after screen, feeling reassured. Science was Knight's meditation. A practice to salve his grief—not just for Molly but for the forests and a dangerously stupid world. Facts were a sacrament, and dendrochronology was his scripture. It required intense focus and a mindful selection of trees. Some grow in moist, rich sites little affected by want; they're called "complacent." Those homogeneous rings reveal nothing. "Sensitive" trees root in dry places and their rings faithfully record variations of rain and snow.

Knight was called to learn the master chronology—the deep history of the forests. It was a highly quantitative process charmed by polynomials, exponential functions, multiple regressions, and eigenvectors. These mathematical indices were vital. They proved that explanations existed for things. Knight's work felt like forensics, like a crime was being solved.

He smelled someone standing in the doorway.

"Hey, Dr. Knight."

Knight looked over. "Mr. Fleming. You're just in time."

Fleming sat down in the student's chair opposite Knight. "You said something really cool last time I was here."

"Exactly what was that?" Knight asked, arms folded.

"You said fire heals the world."

"Perhaps I did. Do you think that's true?"

"Hell, yeah, we need to burn the place down!" Fleming said, rising to his feet. "So I..."

"Remember, it's never that simple."

Fleming sat back down.

Knight studied the boy. Fleming was angry and confused—a way of life. His shaggy beard had grown shaggier since his last visit. His eyes were more urgent and his stink had evolved. Aged sweat and urine were now infused with pine pitch and charcoal. "You've been in the forest," Knight said.

"Oh, yeah, I've been out there. Moved around to different places like you told me. Blue Mountain burned up just like you said it would."

Knight carefully closed a notebook. "And where else did I send you?"

"The Rattlesnake National Recreation Area."

"And what did you see?"

"Fat hikers and fancy bikers."

"Other than that."

"Lots of trees were cut down to open things up for the others."

"And who are the others?" Knight asked patiently.

"Birds, I guess. Deer and elk too. It looks kinda weird, though."

"Why?"

"The woods didn't burn for real. Forest Service just piled stuff up and lit it."

Knight almost smiled. This inky barbarian had stumbled upon an eternal truth. Thinning does not replicate burning. Fertility is not dispersed. Fire mosaics are not created. Cutting trees is a mechanical parody of Nature's grace.

"Alright," Knight said. "Let me show you something." He opened a file on his computer and turned the large screen toward Fleming. "What do you see?"

1713
1739
1751
1764
1790
1807
1825
1886

"They're years, right?" Fleming said.

"Of course," Knight said. "What story do those years tell?"

Fleming stared again. "Who the fuck knows? I wasn't alive back then."

"But the trees were alive," Knight said. "Some of them still are."

Fleming nodded in half awareness.

Knight sipped cold oolong tea. He was about to share sensitive information with a damaged soul. Knight had "taught" Fleming several times when his grief needed to ignite someone with darkness. The outcome of that sick counsel was suspected, but still unknown. "Alright," Knight said. "Do you know the Bitterroots very well?"

"Not really," Fleming said, "except for Blue Mountain."

Knight took a deep breath. This man-child was trouble. A cruel temptation. "Okay," Knight said. "I just finished analyzing forty pines near Lolo and the Taylor Creek Valley. They averaged 313 years old."

"Wow," Fleming said. "Real geezers."

"Show some respect," Knight said. He spread out a map of the area. "For most of their lives, lightning-caused or Indian-set wildfires moved through as often as every four years, clearing away brush and small trees. The big pines barely noticed. They shed a layer of bark and went on with their lives, nourished by released nutrients."

Knight picked up a wedge cut from a pine and showed it to Fleming. "But every thirty years or so, a hotter fire burned these curving, dark-brown scars across each 'catface'—a damaged part of the trunk. They're called fire scars. Those events had to be hot enough to cause damage, but not hot enough to kill the tree."

"So the fires didn't change anything," Fleming said.

"Not true. As you wisely said, they opened things up for others."

Fleming smiled with dense pleasure.

Knight studied his eyes. "My work shows that fire scars stopped in 1886. In just over a century, fire suppression created an ecological nightmare. A sunny, open savanna of big, well-spaced pines was transformed into a crowded, dim mongrel of a place." Knight hesitated a beat, then laid his fly on the water. "And then what happened?"

Fleming bit. "All those fucking houses got built."

"Crudely worded, but precise," Knight said.

"Mongrel," Fleming said, shaking his head.

"It's a metaphor," Knight said.

Fleming stroked his scraggly beard. "I know exactly what to do with a mad dog."

44

Since her Big Sky fire, the ashy-haired girl had been busy. She torched an abandoned house in Drummond, then watched flames spread into the hills. Set another burn near Seeley Lake that took out some old hunters' cabins. Then a small ignition at Helmville that blended into a lightning-caused blaze.

No popcorn bowls or action figures were left as clues. Those fires were noise, not signal. Experience Points in a fantasy game she favored. A way to add to the summer's chaos as cover for her true crime to come. The Big Sky fire did some damage, but not nearly enough to gain respect.

And so far, her game had no other players.

Paladin was the action figure she left behind at Big Sky—a protector with many faces through the ages. Warrior knights. Lately, Paladins were major players in Dungeons and Dragons, her chosen myth.

The symmetry with Dr. Bill *Knight* was irresistible.

The media never reported any of that, which was a sour disappointment. Either they didn't know or investigators—FBI types and

Bill Knight himself—were withholding the information. She'd never met Knight, nor wanted to. But from the sound of things, he had an extraordinary ability to decode fires and determine the story. Logic, mathematics, imagination.

She saw Dr. Knight as the Dungeon Master. A big shot with too much control. And now, she was ready for her campaign to challenge him. Or at least mess with his elder mind.

The woman drove past working cherry orchards on the east shore of Flathead Lake. She had no quarrel with fruit growers. Her hatred was reserved for rich fools who replaced old sturdies with palatial homes. They'd fucked up the lakeshore beyond redemption. Built immense wooden houses with cedar shake roofs. Basically asking for it.

She passed Blue Bay, with the wide beauty of Flathead Lake stretching west. Trophy houses everywhere. The owners named them things like Loch View, Gull Shores, Idyll Times. The yearly property taxes were three months' pay to a working Montanan.

No moral alignment in that fantasy world she favored. Depravity.

She drove up a small dirt lane and headed into the lower slopes of the Mission Range. It was midweek, so the dry woods were empty. This time her work was simpler. Lay a single paper popcorn bowl beside the road and half fill it with Everclear. The woman had timed it just right. It was 8:30 on a summer night and the air was cooling up in the high country. Soon it would sink, then gain force, pushing whatever lay in its path downhill.

In this case, it would be fire. An unusual path since flames usually race uphill, drawn into their own heat. But in this precious spot, her fire would be blown downslope toward fifty monuments to a single class. Drifters.

She set the popcorn bowl in the brush and sang a Lorde song—*And we'll never be royals.* A giggle. But how to sing it to the FBI? Might be dangerous fun. She carefully poured Everclear until the popcorn bowl was half full. Then the plasma lighter was applied. The lid of the paper bowl flickered, then slowly burned. The mountain breeze was fresh and strong. Nature saving Nature.

No need to linger. She laid a plastic Paladin figure in plain sight. It was different than the first ones, but close enough for someone clever to catch on and start playing. She got in her old truck and rolled downhill, clutch pressed in, key turned, until she jump-started the rig.

She didn't look back, certain she was a Fighter.

45

The *Missoulian*'s front page the next day offered a terrifying list.

RECORD HEAT AND DROUGHT
SNOWPACK GONE
NATIONAL FORESTS CLOSED
SIXTY-ONE FIRES BURNING
SUSPICIOUS FIRE AT FLATHEAD LAKE DESTROYS 31 HOMES SO FAR
DRY LIGHTNING STORMS COMING
BRACE YOURSELVES, MONTANA!

Solberg glanced at his watch—6:14 p.m.—then walked inside the Missoula Airport. As always, he said, "I'm sorry, old one" to a stuffed grizzly bear. Native Americans had named him Charlo after a great chief, a man who'd resisted newcomers taking over the land.

Solberg waited at the bottom of a flight of stairs outside the security checkpoint.

The first person to emerge was Edward Merchant, carrying a leather bag. "Hi, Matt. Thanks for coming on short notice."

A woman approached, holding a slip of paper and a pen. "Sorry to bother you, Mr. Merchant, but can I have your autograph? It's for my husband."

Merchant looked cheesed off. "What's his name?"

"Jeff," the woman said nervously. "He's a big fan of *Revenge Force* and all the sequels."

Merchant signed quickly then thrust the paper and pen at her.

"Thank you, sir," she said.

Merchant fake-smiled and walked toward the door.

"You have baggage?" Solberg asked.

"My things are waiting for me the DoubleTree Hotel."

They got in Matt's truck and headed to town. "How's Linda doing?" Solberg asked.

"She's through a bunch of skin grafts. We take things day by day."

"I wish her all the best. So why the urgency in coming to Montana?"

"Heard you decided who to blame for torching my house."

Blame, there was that word again. "We've got a theory."

"A fucking theory. FBI guy said it was more than that. Idiot."

"Bernie Katz is hardly an idiot."

"He said you were close to nailing some people. Retired smoke-jumpers, right?"

Solberg was shocked. It wasn't like Katz to blab about cases. Meant he was up to something. Solberg made the light at Higgins Avenue, but got stopped at the next. "Red skies over Montana," he said.

"What?" Merchant asked, staring at Matt.

"See the old post office on your left? That stood in for the Forest Service headquarters in the old movie *Red Skies over Montana.* Richard Widmark walked right up those stairs."

"Didn't take you for the starstruck type."

"I'm not. That movie was loosely, and I do mean loosely, based on the 1949 Mann Gulch fire and the smokejumper deaths." The light changed and Solberg accelerated.

Merchant shook his head. "I got lots of crap about where I built my house. Not sure I need to watch that particular film."

"Or maybe you do." Solberg pulled into the DoubleTree's parking lot. Merchant checked in and they took an elevator to the third floor. He key-carded a door open.

A woman with long black hair sat on a shaded balcony overlooking the Clark Fork River. She came inside, smiling. "Eduardo, I'm so glad to see you." She kissed Merchant on the cheek, then gestured at Solberg. "Is this the man who found Linda?"

"Yes. Blanca Chacón, meet Matt Solberg."

She rushed forward, arms open. Solberg extended his hand, but she hugged him and held on. "Thank you," she whispered. "*Muchisimas gracias* for saving my daughter."

My daughter. Did she mean it?

Blanca released her grip and stepped back. "Sorry, I just met you. Please forgive my lack of manners."

"No problem," Solberg said, nodding. The woman was beautiful, but toughness lived behind her eyes.

"Linda said you talk to her sometimes," Blanca said.

"Yes. We spoke the other day and she seemed upbeat."

"Thanks to you," Blanca said, squeezing Solberg's arm. "See, there I go again."

"Don't worry. We Norwegians are touchy too. But that just means we're crabby."

Blanca laughed and flipped her hair. Solberg studied her. She was too cheery—behavior he didn't trust.

"Say, let's have a drink," Ed Merchant said.

"You bet," Solberg said. "There's a bar here with seating on the river."

"I can't. Public places are a minefield for me."

"Oh, right," Solberg said.

Merchant shrugged. "Blanca, where's that tequila I asked you to bring?"

"Got it," she said, raising a bottle.

Merchant grabbed glasses and they all sat on the balcony. He eased the cork out of the bottle and poured carefully. "It would be alcohol abuse to waste a drop of this. It's Casa Dragones Blanco Joven, one of the finest sipping tequilas in the world."

"I'm Blanca and this is Blanco," she said smiling. "*Salud.*"

Everyone raised their cups. The woman wasn't acting natural—she was performing.

"*Skål,*" Solberg added.

"*Chai-yo,*" Merchant managed. "The only Thai I learned in Bangkok."

Everyone took slow sips of tequila. Merchant eyed Solberg for a response. "Wow," Matt said. "Very smooth with a clean peppery finish. Extremely good."

Merchant smiled and seemed to mean it.

Blanca watched people float down the river in rafts and inner tubes. "Is it always this hot here?" Blanca asked, wiping her forehead. She was five foot two, slim, with shiny black hair hanging down her back.

"No, it rarely gets this bad," Solberg said. "You probably never experienced this kind of weather over at the old house."

Blanca looked anxious at the mere mention of the burned-down place.

"Sorry," Solberg said.

Merchant and Blanca exchanged looks. Cryptic. Empathy or deceit?

"Do you know who burned the house down?" Blanca asked. She sat back, sizing up Solberg.

"No," he said. "Too many unanswered questions."

"What kinds of questions?" Merchant asked, refilling his glass.

"Motive and opportunity, same as always."

Merchant huffed. "Remember when I offered to pay you real money to find the arsonist? Maybe you should have taken it."

Solberg sipped his tequila. Was Merchant's offer part of his cover story as the aggrieved father? If so, it was convincing. But then again, Ed Merchant was an Academy Award–winning actor.

Blanca suddenly looked tired, maybe burned out by her act or all the questions.

"Matt and I need to talk," Merchant said. "Will you be alright if we leave you here alone?"

Blanca did a dramatic eye roll. "Sometimes I'm better off alone." There was a hard edge to her words.

Merchant embraced her. The affection appeared real, but the hug lingered a bit long, like a gesture to make amends or project an image. Blanca patted Merchant on the arm and backed off the hug. A mystery lived inside her dazzling smile.

Once outside, Solberg and Merchant walked along the Clark Fork on the Riverfront Trail. Missoula has a large system of parks, trails, and open space lands. A city embraced by beauty.

"Man, it's scorching out here," Merchant said, adjusting his Dodgers baseball cap. "No wonder everyone's in the river."

"Only sensible," Solberg said.

Merchant turned serious. "Matt, I flew up here because I'm tired of waiting for answers. I need to know who you're going to lay this on."

"You've got the right."

"Damn straight. My girl is going through hell and I want to know who should join her."

Solberg's fatherly instincts agreed, but his gut wasn't sure about this guy. "Alright," he said. "Since Bernie Katz talked to you, I guess I can too. As you said earlier, we think two retired smokejumpers might be the arsonists."

"But I thought smokejumpers were steel-shank heroes around here."

"They are. But these two make dangerous noises about how the fires made things right for the men who died in Mann Gulch."

Merchant stopped walking. "Holy shit."

"It could just be drunken bullshit."

"No, it makes sense," Merchant said, walking again. "Very theatrical."

"But here's the problem. Smokejumpers would no more set fires than crap on the flag. Arson is inherently evil to them. It kills their kin. But there's something off about these two guys, one of them in particular. A man named Rob Tabish. He has a malfunction of some variety."

"And what's that?" Merchant asked.

"Beyond my pay grade."

"Okay, but your theory sounds right. Are they going to be arrested?"

"No, for now it's just a theory."

Merchant exhaled loudly. "Hell, I should have built my house in Santa Fe."

Solberg held his tongue.

They reached a wooden deck overlooking a rapid called Brennan's Wave. It was named for a respected Missoula man who died kayaking in Chile. Surfers took turns riding the standing wave, doing spins and tricks until they fell backward into the water. About thirty people stood watching, but Merchant went unnoticed in the crowd.

"Here's a bench," Solberg said.

They sat in precious shade watching the surfers. Young women on bicycles with baby trailers pedaled by. Some of the trailers held dogs.

"How close are you to solving this?" Merchant asked. For the first time, he looked nervous.

"The FBI is in charge, not me."

"But I can hire guys who..."

"Bad idea," Solberg said. "Your guys would turn this into a clusterfuck with no reach-around."

Merchant smiled slightly. "A great line from *Full Metal Jacket*."

At that moment, Solberg felt a watt of friendship for Edward Merchant.

The movie star glanced around the park. Still undetected. "Alright, does the FBI have any other suspects?"

"Just two," Solberg said. "And today I met them."

"Me and Blanca? You've got to be shitting me?"

"Come on, Ed. The FBI questioned you, then Blanca, because she had a motive—the breakup."

"And the psychopathic rage to hurt Linda, someone she sees as her own flesh and blood? That's crazy. Besides, me and Blanca are back together now. You think I'd live with a woman capable of such a thing? Jesus." Merchant walked to the river's edge and stood by himself. Two surfers shared Brennan's Wave, sliding back and forth along the break.

Solberg eased over. "I was just being straight with you."

Merchant tilted his head. "Tell me this, why would I burn down my own fucking house?"

Solberg took a leap. "FBI suspects insurance fraud, with a divorce coming."

"Like I need the fucking money," Merchant said, flipping off the sky like he owned it.

"*Do you* need the money?" Solberg asked.

"Fuck you, asshole," Merchant said, eyes boring in.

Solberg was not intimidated. "And they're also checking out your estranged wife."

Merchant cooled off. "I married her for tits, not brains. You follow?"

"Any of that tequila left?" Solberg asked, blowing by the slur. Maybe Merchant would let his guard down and implicate himself.

"Sure, and two bottles in reserve."

They walked back to the hotel. "So you and Blanca reconciled?" Solberg asked.

"Yeah, and the media loves saying what a philandering asshole I am. They make Linda's mother sound like some kind of jilted saint, and trust me, the Hell Bitch is not a saint."

"*Lonesome Dove*," Solberg said.

"Best western ever written," Merchant said.

They walked on for a while before Solberg whispered, "With such a tragic ending."

46

Fleming awoke in a hawthorn thicket upslope of I-90 in Missoula. There were hiking trails nearby, but no one had found his camp. He got out of his sleeping bag naked and vigorously scratched his balls with both hands. His arms were covered with colorful tattoos, paid for by a string of burglaries in Bozeman. He retrieved a failing toothbrush from a pack and brushed his teeth without paste. A well-worn copy of *Into the Wild* rested on a stolen lawn chair nearby.

Fleming weaved out of the thicket and pissed in a ravine. Then he squatted and shat. Balsamroot leaves were his wipe and dirt was his powder. He'd let his leavings dry in the sun, then mix them with grass to make cooking fuel. If he stayed here until fall, that was.

Back in camp, Fleming ate fistfuls of nuts and raisins, then chugged water from a two-liter Coke bottle he'd filled down at Westside Park. With breakfast over, he put on blue jeans and a fishing shirt. His brown leather boots had thick red laces. Fleming shoved on a black baseball cap, inspected the contents of his pack, and strapped it on.

Time to get back to work. His partner was waiting down at a Circle-K, if they hadn't lost their nerve.

47

Not quite three years ago.

On a sunny October day, Bill Knight led a hike up St. Mary's Peak. His pack held a cremation box with Molly's ashes. Bill had hand-crafted it from Douglas fir and stained it the color of burgundy blood.

Molly had always loved his woodwork. Homemade tables, chairs, and hutches that warmed their home. When Michael Slaton killed his wife in a senseless car crash, Knight gave those treasures away. Molly had touched their grain. He replaced everything in the house except an old blue vase she filled with white daisies every summer.

A small procession followed him up the trail that day: four neighbors, three cousins, and Matt Solberg. No one spoke during the 3.8-mile hike to the summit. Larch needles were at their golden peak. The sky was a bluebird's wing.

As they gained elevation, Bill paused now and then to gaze down at the valley. Everyone stood back and gave him time.

The mourners moved through whitebark pines and switch-backed into alpine rocks. The sun felt warm to Solberg, but his friend's grief chilled his core. Molly Knight had always been so kind: a patient, luminous light. Solberg forced back tears, thinking of Judy. Three years before, his own wife had dropped dead right down there, just below Totem Mountain.

Death arrives on silent feet. Or it kicks you in the gut.

The procession stepped up the last pitch to the top. No one was in the lookout tower; fire season was over until next summer.

Bill Knight stood on the summit and turned to the congregation. His boots were scuffed and dusty. His eyes were hollow. To the west was a cliff with a thousand feet of open air below him. A height that tempts you to surrender. The gray granite summits of the Heavenly Twins stared back, unconcerned. "Eternal friends," Bill said, pointing behind him. "Mountains are the only ones."

He held the cremation box in his hands and stared at the cinders. A gust of chilly air blew by and Bill Knight released his love forever.

Molly's ashes looked like rising smoke.

Bill Knight snapped back to the present. He sat outside his house, drinking a Rainier, thinking about that awful day and Molly's killer—Michael Slaton. The third anniversary of that crime would soon be here. He'd been dwelling on it lately and spending dangerous amounts of time alone. Sitting, brooding, plotting. He'd even spent time with Fleming—a dense, oily cur.

A downdraft rushed out of Big Creek Canyon, a glacial valley aimed east like the barrel of a gun. Knight had bought his 320-acre ranch back during the 1980s real estate crash and it stood in the crosshairs of intense down-canyon winds. The cottonwoods were ragged and the birds were strong.

A boom of thunder rolled in from the south. The highest peaks, the range's only ten thousand footers, pierced towering black thunderheads. Trapper and El Capitan were the first summits to feel the bolts. Then lightning cambered across Castle Crag, Sky Pilot, and St. Mary's Peak.

St. Molly's Peak, Knight used to call it, just to hear her laugh.

He did a mental countdown. On cue, the sky was slashed by jagged strikes landing from Darby to Lolo across a fifty-mile front. The onslaught built in intensity as bolts ripped the sky and died on shoals of blackening air. Rolling thunder forever. Red, green, orange, and blue pyrotechnics rose from the valley. People broke the fireworks ban and lit up the storm.

But still no rain. The slanting signs were there, high above the peaks, but the world was drenched only in arid wind and laser light. If you wanted to burn down a planet, everything was in perfect motion.

Knight allowed himself an empty laugh.

That day's *Missoulian* ran extensive coverage of the Bitterroot fires. Buried amid banal quotes from firefighters, politicians, and the Forest Service was a central relevant fact—417 more houses were destroyed. Knight read the passage over and over. Another fire took out 58 homes and counting beside Flathead Lake—a place he never expected to burn. It was clearly arson, maybe set by the same person who tried to burn down the Big Sky resort.

The rules, as Dr. Bill Knight knew them, no longer applied.

He went indoors and rinsed his face. Stared at himself in the mirror, then flicked off the light.

Knight retrieved an old briefcase from his bedroom closet. He slowly looked through photos of Molly taken back when Montana was a hidden kingdom. Pictures of hikes together in the Bitterroots, Pintlers, and Missions; of fall rafting trips surrounded by blazing cottonwood leaves and cobalt skies; of cross-country skiing at Lolo Pass and snowbank picnics with clever ravens. He'd scanned the collection into his computer, but recently deleted the file. Prints are more intimate. Some even had Molly's handwriting on the back.

Thanksgiving hike up Bear Creek, 1977
Turquoise Lake backpacking trip, 1993
St. Mary's Peak, July 2012

Hundreds of photos like that. Scenes from a life spent outdoors with your one true companion. Solace in a landscape that was now being destroyed, house by house. Each picture filled Bill Knight with aching love and sickening loss—grief's rancid chemistry. He tucked his favorite picture of Molly in his shirt pocket and buttoned it. One where she smiled lovingly at the camera after they had made love in a blue camas meadow. Such a gentle face: unguarded, unaware of her fate.

Then Knight dumped the rest of the photos in a trash bag and carried it outside. The rocky edge of the fire pit was overgrown with bluegrass. His last fire had been with Molly three years before. They'd gathered here often over forty years of marriage, enjoying the warmth of crackling logs, sipping red wine, sitting in chairs side by side, fingers entwined, as sparks danced toward Venus.

That all ended in a fiery collision just one mile away.

Bill Knight sighed and pulled the bag of photos to his chest. A cow bawled in a far pasture. Five minutes went by. Then he tipped the bag over, its contents falling onto old ashes. He tossed the bag to one side, retrieved a gas can from the shed, and doused his life with fuel. Knight pulled a cigar lighter from his shirt pocket and kneeled beside the pit. "I have to let you go, sweetheart."

Knight flicked the lighter and touched a picture of his smiling wife. A *whoomp* of flame quickly spread across the pile. He watched Molly's face burn away, again and again. Bill Knight sat on the ground and wept. Deep wracking sobs.

"No!" he yelled, rising to his feet. "No more of that." He went inside, heated a can of beef stew, and ate supper at the kitchen table while doing a crossword puzzle. The gulf south of Yemen—*Aden*. Central points—*foci*. He finished and poured a cup of black coffee. The last picture of Molly was placed within the pages of a book of Rumi poems she loved.

Dr. Bill Knight sat in his recliner and calmly opened a notebook. He'd kept a dangerous secret locked inside himself until this moment. With Molly even more gone, he could finally calculate what she would never abide. Knight carefully wrote the formula down in clear printed letters.

The future of the Bitterroot Valley depended on: Dr (cos H tan L sin F) = X, where Dr = exponential rate of population growth × sum of: (cos of Houses × tangent of Land × sin of Fire) and where X = non-random, directed trajectories: dimensionless numbers conceived of as options.

$$Dr \ (\cos H \tan L \sin F) = X$$

Knight studied the model. It was more a sketch than an algorithm—qualitative, biased, and irreproducible. Nonetheless, Bagnold's work on sand transport and Schumm's debris load calculations from rivers were evident in its spirit. But this was a far different kind of entrainment. One that Knight felt pulling him downwind, downstream to a place that wasn't possible when Molly was alive.

Knight needed more data. He pulled the Ravalli County Comprehensive Plan from the shelf. There, amid childish goals and sinister objectives, was the story of a housing boom gone vicious. It was born in the 1970s, stalled in the '80s, and had roared back to life since.

Knight worked methodically, using a calculator. Ravalli County was 2,386 square miles—24 percent, or 573 square miles, was privately owned. The remainder was in Forest Service, Bureau of Land Management, and State of Montana hands. Of the private land, when he subtracted the floodplains, wetlands, big game winter range habitats, prime soils, historic sites, and scenic river corridors—when the honorable portions of the landscape were set aside—it left only 250 square miles even vaguely suited to development.

The 1970 population of Ravalli County was fifteen thousand. It was now forty-five thousand, many of these newcomers. Ravalli County now had the lowest percentage of native-born Montanans in the state. It once had the highest.

Knight felt an ideal population density was one family per forty acres: about 64 people per square mile. It should actually be fewer, frontier style, but 64 seemed reasonable when towns were included. With a population of forty-five thousand and a maximum developable area of 250 square miles, the actual population density of Ravalli County was now 180 people per square mile. Simple mathematics revealed the truth: there were twenty-nine thousand too many people living in the Bitterroot Valley.

Which ones should leave first?

Knight thought of the Molly's killer, Michael Slaton. He was a Californian—one of thousands of Californians in the Bitterroot. Knight stared at the equation, retracing his logic. *Could it really be that simple?*

He picked up the *Missoulian*. The letters to the editor contained the usual ferocious ignorance. He picked up the Montana section. Stories about a new distillery and an old gold mine. Finally, he found a "human-interest" piece about a family whose house had recently burned down in one of the Bitterroot fires. Their name was Owen: he was a commodities trader, she a book designer, three kids, a massive dream house. They were from Orange County, California.

Knight poured his attention into the print. "We came here trying to make a new life," said Donald Owen, "trying to get away from crime, earthquakes, and fires. Looks like we didn't get away after all."

Owen was asked what he would do now. "Probably rebuild, but my wife just wants to go home. I'll say one thing, we'll definitely tell all our friends in L.A. that Montana's no paradise."

Knight was riveted. There at the end, almost as throwaway lines, were two vital facts: twenty-three of the thirty-seven recently burned houses were built by Californians in the last five years. And ninety-five hundred people, or 21 percent of Ravalli County's population, were California transplants.

Knight nodded. His equation could now be completed. He picked up his notebook and added two letters to the page. It now read: Dr (cos H tan L sin F) = HC, where HC = Houses of Californians.

Knight chuckled. HC was the code for "HAZARDOUS CARGO" on highway signs.

When the number of Californians was subtracted from the county total, the population pulled back to about thirty-five thousand. The Bitterroot Valley would revert by fifteen years Far from ideal, but Knight considered it an acceptable preliminary result. One where a firestorm would run Michael Slaton off and those like him. And it might do more.

Although the ignition sites remained to be located and the likelihood of all this was still unknown, Knight knew his theoretical equation was no longer undirected. It was now "a supervised classification." A targeted result.

48

"We caught the putz," Bernie Katz said at the screen door.

Solberg's head snapped around. "Dammit, Bernie. I lost a year off my heart."

Bernie let himself in and sat at the kitchen table with Solberg.

"Which putz?" Solberg asked, wiping hangover from his eyes.

"The little shit that tried to burn Lucy Beauchamp's house down. A neighbor caught 'em trying to lay out another garbage bag bomb. This time on the perp's own family ranch, if you can believe it—the place right next to Lucy's."

"What's his name?"

"*Her* name is Shelly Pinsonnault. Twenty. A local from Cyr."

"Really? A woman?"

"Didn't take you for a sexist, Matt. Women commit crimes too."

Solberg nodded. "Any motive?"

"Pinsonnault isn't saying much, but the fire seems to have been aimed at new houses built on land her parents sold. Motive could be a family grievance, vandalism, or thrill-seeking. *Meshugeneh* is my working theory right now. She's getting a public defender assigned, so I'm letting her stew in a cell for a while. You got coffee?"

Solberg poured him a cup. Kitchen clock read 9:23 a.m.

Bernie sipped coffee and brooded. "We got the girl, but how would she know how to use a garbage bag bomb? Had to be someone else involved."

"I agree," Solberg said. "Any ideas?"

"A rogue chemist or a Unabomber crank," Bernie said.

"Or a firebug."

"Or a firefighter," Bernie said, frowning.

Solberg nodded. "This is Montana. Take a number."

Bernie took a sip. "Say, Lucy took a shine to you during that search operation. Suppose you could go out there and talk to her?"

"About what?" Solberg said, cradling a steaming mug.

"About why this girl with no record suddenly commits a felony."

"You sure Lucy knows her?"

"Lucy's a Beauchamp. She knows the shoe size of everybody in a fifty-mile radius."

"Why can't you or one of your people do it?"

"Sheriff Cousy says Lucy hates the Feds, particularly ones of my exotic persuasion. She learned it from her daddy, old Baptiste himself. You're the fair-haired boy on this one."

"And every other one in this godforsaken summer."

"You turning martyr on me?"

"Just beat up."

"Self-inflicted, judging from the stink of tequila on your breath. Can you get out there today?"

Solberg rubbed his temples. "Alright, I need to know why you threw me under the bus with Ed Merchant."

Bernie smiled. "Sorry, I needed to stir the pot. You learn anything useful?"

"That Casa Dragones tequila punches back."

Bernie snickered. "And leaves a bruise. What else?"

Solberg smiled. "I learned Ed Merchant is a complicated guy. One minute you sort of like him, the next you loathe the arrogant son of a bitch."

"Actor."

"Merchant flew in Blanca Chacón, making a big deal about how much he loves her."

"She came to Missoula three days ago. Strange he didn't travel with her."

"Media's hounding him pretty good," Solberg said. "He's laying low."

"Fair enough. Were they close or faking it?"

"Blanca was happy to see him, but her reaction was way over the top. Fake. And she's still plenty angry about something. Maybe the reconciliation isn't what it looks like."

Bernie got right to it. "Do you buy Chacón as the arsonist?"

Solberg refilled his coffee cup. "I'm not sure. East Los is tough and it injures people. Her anger at Merchant might have touched an old nerve and set her off. Hell, maybe she's just pissed at having my Norwegian face in her business."

Bernie nodded. "And Merchant?"

"Like you said, he's an actor. The man's clever and could be covering up a scandal."

Bernie's bushy eyebrows jumped. "Cheating on his wife? Hollywood would give him a lifetime achievement award."

Solberg paused for a moment. "But Merchant turned into a real pig when he talked about his wife. I know you ruled her out, but it would be hard to blame her for kicking this guy in the balls."

"True, but we've got enough to move past her."

Solberg nodded. "But if Blanca had someone set the fires, Merchant would look batshit for taking her back. His daughter almost died. That stink would definitely cost him work."

Bernie scowled. "Except in some *fakafta* reality show."

"You bet. He'd be a tabloid punch line the rest of life."

"And then there's the money," Bernie said. "If Chacón is behind this, the homeowner's insurance company would pay in full. If she and Merchant worked together somehow, then it's fraud. A lover's conspiracy gone bad, that kind of thing."

"I went right at him with that."

"Bold of you," Bernie said, smirking.

"Just following your lead. Merchant got rip-shit about being accused, mostly about the idea he needs money. Bad choices or bad luck aside, he still makes $16 million a movie."

"For the dreck he's in lately?" Bernie said.

"Dreck is gold internationally," Solberg said. "Violence and bad dialogue."

"Sounds like a Trump rally."

Solberg stayed on point. "The big-ticket item for him would be a divorce based on a scandal, and there's no telling how that would turn out."

"True," Bernie said. "In a regular divorce he'd lose half his fortune—*rumored* to be $60 million—unless there was a pre-nup, which we don't know. We're digging into his finances to the degree we can. But if he's dirty with this fire, he would take a much bigger hit. He might even lose custody of Linda for being an unfit parent."

"What a fucked-up mess." Solberg rubbed his eyes wearily. "And now we've got these fires at Big Sky and Flathead Lake."

Bernie sat back. "My investigators are still trying to tie them together. The idiot left clues at both sites, messing with us. Popcorn bowls and toys."

Solberg sighed. "Unless they're not an idiot. Maybe they're someone clever trying to distract us from bigger cases."

"No, arsonists always think they're smarter than we are. Part of the profile and why they often get caught. I'll let you know what we figure out."

"Like I need more to deal with," Solberg said.

"Welcome to life at the Agency," Bernie said. He sniffed at Solberg like a Customs dog. "Catch a shower and go see Lucy Beauchamp. I've got something to check out."

"What's that?" Solberg asked.

"Mapping analysis of the Bitterroot fires."

"Bo?"

"Didn't she tell you?".

Solberg looked surprised.

"No," Bernie said. "I guess she didn't."

49

Solberg followed a dirt road to Lucy Beauchamp's house. Maile Felder sat beside him.

"You sure Lucy will talk to us?" Maile asked. "She's a tough cookie."

"She will because you found her," Solberg said. "I'll just follow your lead."

They pulled up to the Beauchamp place. Five brown horses grazed in a pasture being irrigated by a rolling wheel. An old white horse loafed in the front yard. The door was open, but Solberg knocked loudly on the frame.

"Yeah, yeah," came a woman's voice. "Don't get your panties in a twist." Lucy Beauchamp appeared at the door, wiping her hands on a dishrag. "What do you peckerwoods want?" she asked, squinting.

"Hi Lucy, it's me, Maile Felder. From that day of the fire."

Her eyes cleared. "Alright, I know you now. That Federal called and said someone might be out this way. How ya doing, Millie?"

"It's Maile—like smiley."

"Whatever you say, girl. Come on in. The both of ya."

Maile and Solberg walked inside. The house smelled like a grease trap.

Lucy stood, hands on hips. "If you're feelin' peckish, I've got eggs and mysteries burnin'."

Maile scrunched her face. "What are mysteries?"

"Why, they're sausages, girl."

"Sure, that sounds great," Maile said, unconvinced.

Lucy went to work and soon fried eggs and blackened mysteries appeared on three mismatched plates. They sat down at a wooden table to eat.

Maile lifted her fork and caught a scowl from Lucy.

"You raised by sheep, Millie? We say grace in this house." Lucy reached out her hands and the three of them joined up.

Lucy did the honors. "Lord, thank you for the bounty of this food and for a mighty short visit by these guests at my table. I'll pass over the usuals since you know 'em by heart. But there's one thing I want these folks to hear. That just like Jesus, a good horse knows where he's going even when you don't. Amen."

"Amen," Maile and Solberg said, smiling.

Lucy dove into the food. Her guests waded.

"Well," Maile said, swallowing hard. "I hear you know Michelle Pinsonnault. Any reason she set that fire?"

"Shelly Pinsonnault is sewed together funny," Lucy said, waving her fork. "Born that way."

"So she had no real reason?" Maile asked.

Lucy washed a bite down with coffee. "Didn't say that. Sure, she had a reason. At least for tryin' to run *me* off. You see, there's always been dust-ups between the Beauchamps and Pinsonnaults. Goes back to when my daddy, old Baptiste, rest his rascal soul, stiffed that girl's granddaddy out of a section of prime hay ground down by the crick. Would have been back in the '50s, I suppose."

"What did Baptiste do?" Maile asked, covering her uneaten mysteries with a napkin.

"Let's just say my father wasn't always ace-high. Paid for the land, mind you, just not what the family or anyone else saw as a fair price. Rumor was he four-flushed 'em somehow."

"And they're still holding a grudge after more than sixty years?" Maile asked.

"Time don't matter with grudges. You'll know that firsthand when you get older, girl. You see, that deal put the Pinsonnaults in a hole they're still in. Without enough hay for the winter, they could never build up enough herd to get ahead. Even with the high beef prices lately. So they turned to subdividing their ranch to stay afloat. Five houses built so far, with twenty more comin'."

"A feud," Solberg said. "Is that what this fire was about?"

"Enjoy your nap?" Lucy asked, shaking her head.

Solberg grinned. "You got any idea why this girl would set fire to her own place?"

"You're the geographist. But it might have something to do with exactly *where* Shelly was tryin' to set it. Comes down to the seven deadly sins. If the fire was aimed at her daddy's house, that's wrath. If it was aimed at the betterments on the lots they sold, that's greed. If it was aimed at me again, she's plumb loco. Not one of the seven, but you catch my drift."

Solberg nodded. "What else do you know about this Pinsonnault girl? She have friends around here?"

"Not really. Ones she had moved away to find work, but not her. She's as useless as a cut dog. *Sloth*—that's one of the seven! Knew they'd come in handy. Anyway, this girl gets by on paintin' fingernails, food stamps, and griftin' at bars. Anything to get beer and pot money. She figured the family ranch was her retirement plan. Her parents thought otherwise."

"When's the last time you saw her?" Solberg asked.

Lucy took a sip of coffee. "Hard to forget that day. I was ridin' Smokey, the distinguished gentlemen dining in the front yard. We were over on Fish Crick like usual, having a poke-around. And I swear I saw Shelly Pinsonnault skinny-dipping with some lickspittle character."

"What did he look like?" Solberg asked.

"My eyes ain't so good anymore. Had a long beard, I suppose. Hell, turn men upside down and they all look the same to me."

Solberg immediately thought of Fleming. He glanced at Maile—*time to go.*

"Lucy, thank you so much for the meal," Maile said, rising.

"Thanks for comin', Millie. And oh, you weren't no trouble the day of that fire."

The women shook hands. Solberg got a one-bounce shake.

He and Maile walked out the open door. Smokey leaned against the porch, half asleep in the shade.

Lucy came outside. "Damn horse always looks half roostered."

"I bet he doesn't touch a drop," Solberg said, smiling.

Lucy smiled back. "Don't step in the used hay on your way out."

50

Fleming rested in his hawthorn thicket, eating shoplifted salami and hand-out cheese. He slept hard at first, then napped restlessly.

Two weeks before, Fleming had met Shelly Pinsonnault at a bar in Alberton and they'd hit it off. She had liquor and a car. Checked both boxes of his job interview. Fleming quickly got Shelly stirred up enough to help him place a garbage bag bomb on Lucy Beauchamp's ranch. She was torrentially pissed off at Lucy. Blind as a baby bat. Child's play.

The ranch was featured in Dr. Knight's research and Fleming hoped his teacher would be pleased. *Their* fire had torched thousands of acres and two new houses, but it was only a partial success in Fleming's view. The Blue Mountain Complex showed him what was possible when fires got big.

Fleming itched to go back to Cyr and finish things off. Shelly Pinsonnault was child's play again. Beer and blaming rage. This time they'd burn down her parents' place and run off anyone who dared to build on *her ranch*. She'd get even once and for all. She had no plan after that.

Fleming had let her solo this time to get her hands dirty. That way she wouldn't squeal if they got caught. Fleming's mentor had taught him well.

"Lay the bag down in dry grass, arrange the mirrors, and walk away easy," Fleming had said. But Shelly took too long to summon the courage. The cover of darkness was lifting as she set the bomb beside a county road. She got caught right away by a neighbor driving by who put a gun on her until the cops arrived.

Fleming had watched the plan go south from the bushes. Stranded, he hiked thirty miles back to Missoula, cursing Shelly Pinsonnault the whole way. "Stupid bitch! Evil twat!"

Fleming stuck to the woods when he could and the dark when he couldn't. Drank from side creeks and cattle troughs. At the Crossroads Exxon, he stole candy bars from a Chevy and bananas from a Jeep.

And only now, after resting in his thicket for a few days, did he feel ready to get back to work. Who knew when that Pinsonnault girl might give him up to the cops? Time to keep moving, but Fleming's mentor was done for a while. Said he'd "study the situation." That seemed old and weak to the man-child. He'd wet his beak and wanted more before blowing town.

It was nearly dark when Fleming stuffed all his meager possessions into a pack and walked into Missoula on Orange Street. Once in the North Side neighborhood, he strolled casually. Rushing attracts attention. The cops knew him by sight, like they knew most of the homeless in this spruced-up college town. But since he never got popped, they assumed he was harmless.

Fleming turned the corner at Shakespeare and ambled down an alley. He stepped over a low fence into Rob Tabish's yard. The man's truck was gone and the house was dark. Fleming tried the back door—locked. Ditto the front door. "Where's the love, brother?" Fleming said under his breath.

He dropped his pack, sat in a lawn chair, and lit a Camel. Fleming felt free from prep school prison and medication hell. Soon he'd gain the respect of Rob Tabish and, he hoped, Dr. Bill Knight. The bulls of the woods.

During past visits with Tabish, Fleming had noticed that a guy two houses down owned a blue mountain bike. It was always stashed in a shed, unlocked, leaning against snow tires. Fleming eased down the alley and sure enough, the bike was there. He inched the shed door open and slowly pedaled away.

Fleming glided through Missoula, blending with partiers moving from drink to drink. Griz Bar, Stockman's, Missoula Club, Rhino.

He paused on the Beartracks Bridge to watch the Clark Fork River flow west. Light from a quarter moon danced on the falling water.

It was 1 in the morning when Fleming pedaled to the top of Whittaker Drive and stopped for a rest. Missoula twinkled hundreds of feet below in the smoke. Endless rows of yellow streetlights carved up the valley. Fleming pissed in the knapweed and shook his dick at the city.

To the south, fires glowed in the Bitterroot and Sapphire Mountains. Despite the summer's epic drought, the blazes were not fully in command. "Help's coming," Fleming said.

He rolled southwest on Rimel Road through the Line Ranch, then entered a sprawl of suburban houses called the South Hills. Fleming accelerated across Miller Creek Road. It wouldn't do to be spotted so close to his target. Twenty minutes later, he braked to a stop overlooking a swath of new houses in the Taylor Creek Valley. Starter castles lined up like targets.

He dismounted and walked the bike downhill. From checking Google Maps at the public library, Fleming knew that an irrigation ditch ran the length of the valley paralleled by a dirt levee. He hid the bike in some bushes and walked quietly uphill.

Grand homes were surrounded by pines and dry bunchgrass. Each had a fancy entrance gate with a name written in steel: Casa de Starrs, Mockingjay Way, McIntosh Farm. Fleming passed several promising sites, then stopped at the biggest house he'd seen. It was thirty yards upslope, surrounded by tall grass and small trees. Recently completed, but unoccupied.

He lowered his pack and shoved aside jerky and candy bars until he retrieved a metal bottle of gasoline. He paused for a moment and listened. No one around. He poured gas on pine cones and dry grass. A six-inch area, no more. Then he pulled out a coil of hemp fuse and measured a length. After a quick cut with his Buck knife, he laid the fuse on the ground, starting on the dirt road and ending in the gas-soaked circle. Fleming flicked his lighter, lit the fuse, and lowered it to the ground. It sputtered, then came to life, burning slow and steady.

His tests back in the thicket indicated it would take half an hour to reach home. Plenty of time. He gathered his tools and sifted back down the road. Three minutes later, he stopped below a huge log home and repeated the process. Pour gas, cut fuse, light, move. This was repeated two more times, each site evenly spaced to maximize damage. Fleming recovered his bike and looked up the valley. None of his spots were on fire yet. Things were going as planned.

Fleming pedaled across the Taylor Creek Valley to the Bitterroot River. There were no bridges in this remote reach. He retrieved sandals from his pack, changed footwear, tied his bootlaces together, and slung the Keens over his neck. With his pack cinched tight, he lifted the bike and rested it across his shoulders. Fleming stumbled to the bank and waded across the Bitterroot River in the weak moonlight, feeling water move over rocks. The lights of Lolo were a beacon.

More work waited on the far shore.

51

ARSONIST STRIKES!

Sitting in his den, Bill Knight scoured the online *Missoulian*. Overnight, four fires had been set along Taylor Creek and three more across the river above Lolo. Three houses destroyed and more in danger. "I'll be damned," Knight said.

He checked the Situation Report of the National Interagency Fire Center. There were now eighty-two "Incidents" in the state described by name, type, general location, lat/long, and acres involved. Each with comments on the fire's status and the resources deployed to fight it. Maps showed the boundaries of each burn.

Knight quickly found the new fires. Each was located in the "Wildland-Urban Interface," where homes are built in fire-dependent forests. Knight rubbed his chin, evaluating the geography. "You chose poorly."

He thought of Fleming right away, but couldn't be sure.

The next morning, Knight drove to Missoula through a tunnel of smoke. He stopped to glass the slopes above Lolo. Hotshot crews hit the blazes hard around clusters of houses, slurry bombers dropped veils of orange retardant, and helicopters doused them with water. A major push was underway. Knight admired the choreography, but not the mission.

He parked at the Fire Ecology Research Center and trudged up to the third floor. Matt Solberg waited for him at his office door. "Good morning," Knight said walking up. "Katz sent you about these new fires?"

"We have an understanding."

"Bernie Katz couldn't track an elk through snow."

"That's why I'm here," Solberg said, ignoring the slam.

Knight opened his office, sat down, and exhaled tiredly.

"You alright?" Solberg asked, taking a seat.

"Perfect in every way," Knight said. "Have to take a leak is all."

Solberg studied the Good Doctor's awards nailed to the wall. Regents Professor plaque. MacArthur "Genius" fellowship. National Academy of Sciences membership. Knight played in the majors.

Knight returned from the restroom. "I piss with the frequency of an elf these days." He sat down, wincing in pain.

Solberg smiled, but felt concern. "You see a doctor about it?"

"I had a poke and prod last week."

"And?"

"Just being an old coot, I suspect."

Solberg didn't push.

Knight gathered his energy. "I checked the fire websites and satellite images at home. Even had a look driving through Lolo this morning. Very sloppy work."

"Yah, only three houses lost so far, but people had to bug out in the middle of the night. Kids must have been terrified."

Knight took out a pad of paper. "What's the time sequence? Online sites weren't clear."

"Not sure," Solberg said. "Ignitions were stretched out over two hours. Forest Service and the FBI are interviewing homeowners to nail it down. I was hoping we could go out there once the firefighters get more containment."

Knight blew by the suggestion. "Any moron with a lighter and some Coleman fuel could have done it. Besides, the fires were set in a scatter of houses. Bad locations."

"Yeah, but not the worst I've seen," Solberg said.

"You're right; they're mediocre," Knight said.

A provocative choice of words. Typical of the Good Doctor.

"Hell of a fire season," Solberg said. "Reminds me of 2000."

"Drier," Knight said, looking up. "A more conducive regime."

Solberg studied the man's tired face. "You've been working very hard lately. That must be tough with the anniversary of Molly's death coming up."

"Molly." Knight spoke the word without emotion.

"And like I said, I can join you at Taylor Creek and Lolo to have a look."

"No, I'll work alone. The arsonist made stupid choices I need to figure out."

"Stupid in what way?" Solberg asked.

Knight's eyes flitted around the room. "The satellite image shows short run-ups, few houses in the swaths, and ignitions spaced too evenly. Besides, the Bitterroot River forms a firebreak between Taylor Creek and Lolo. No way for the burns to link up."

"Which implies what?" Solberg asked.

"A novice," Knight said. "Someone with enough knowledge to cause trouble, but not enough to wreak havoc."

"If that was their goal."

"The goal is *always* havoc," Knight said, forehead wrinkled.

"Unless a single place is targeted," Solberg said.

"Incorrect. When a single house burns down, the psychological damage is worse. The person knows they were attacked. That haunts the mind."

"Of people like Edward Merchant," Solberg said.

"Assuming he and/or Blanca didn't set the Mann Gulch fires," Knight said.

"How did you come up with that?" Solberg asked, surprised.

"Logic. What does Bernie have so far?"

Solberg hesitated. Should he share information with Bill Knight? The man the FBI suspected of eco-terrorism? Sitting in this reassuring office, a place of scotch and friendship, his paranoia felt ridiculous. "Merchant's not as rich as we thought, but he's still loaded. But money is weird for people like him. There's never enough even when there's plenty. So Bernie is focused on insurance fraud. But we really don't know."

Knight almost smiled. "In any case, Merchant will never rebuild that place. Neither will Richard Walker up Powder Gulch. *That's* havoc."

"What about these new burns at Lolo?" Solberg asked. "Will people rebuild?"

Knight waved his hand. "Yes, because the targeting was poor and the outcome was weak. Again, that's the signature of a beginner."

Solberg nodded. "Or two beginners, since burns happened on both sides of the river."

Knight cracked his knuckles. "Or one person who waded the channel. They'd have to be young and agile to pull it off, even with this weak water. But there are tons of athletic people around here, which doesn't help you very much."

Solberg felt relieved by his reasoning. "There's something you're skipping over, though."

"What's that?" Knight asked.

"That *houses* were the only target."

Knight stared at Solberg in disbelief. "What other targets are there?"

Solberg was taken aback. "Critical infrastructure like power lines and bridges, commercial property, government facilities, high-value..."

"*I wrote the list,*" Knight said angrily. "I meant what other targets exist where *these* fires were set? Dammit, Matt, focus. Do rich or famous people live there, like at Mann Gulch, Big Sky, and Flathead Lake?"

"Don't know. Are you looking that far north for suspects?"

"The Flathead is close enough to consider. That arsonist might be someone you already suspect, like Rob Tabish, working with an accomplice."

"Good point." Solberg thought of Fleming once again.

"Or it could be someone out of the blue," Knight said.

"That doesn't narrow it down," Solberg said.

Knight nodded. "Chaos is the law of nature and order is the dream of men."

"Nietzsche?"

"Henry Adams."

"A fine historian and novelist," Solberg said.

"What's the difference?" Knight said.

52

The ashy-haired girl drove slowly down a dirt road with her headlights off. There was a strong moon, but the air had a yellow cast from all the smoke. She'd explored this back road several times before, scouting her objective with no evidence in the truck. Even brought a fishing rod in case she encountered suspicion. Lincoln Creek was renowned for native cutthroats.

During those probes, she'd seen a realtor's sign next to a long driveway. It led to a vacant house in exactly the right location: hidden from view, surrounded by stressed trees, and directly downslope from the true target of her campaign.

It was a large wooden house where *he* still lived after his mega-rich parents moved away. Back in high school, the girl desperately wanted to be accepted by them and their wealthy neighbors. She'd lived in a dry rot house on the bad side of Missoula with a chambermaid mother and a work-comp dad. Grim monotony. Nothing evil, just no love. So, when *he* showed the slightest interest in her, the girl innocently saw a different life opening up before her bright-blue eyes. An escape from nothing to something.

But one afternoon in that house, it happened—down in the playroom when she was fourteen and *he* was seventeen. The boy didn't force himself on her; he pretended to love her. But when it was over and she was bleeding, *he* laughed at her before driving her home. At school, the guy told his buddies and they laughed at her too. They called her Bloody Mary. A cruel nickname that plagued her for years. Even some of the girls used it because she was so plain and unconnected. A brainy nerd who barely spoke.

But on this yellow moon night, Mary Callahan would finally scream.

The Dungeon Master was still unaware of her despite those oh-so-obvious clues. She wondered if Dr. Bill Knight was distracted or if he wasn't all he seemed to be. So Mary decided to leap ahead and resolve this on her own terms. Those previous fires had earned her enough Experience Points to finally go ahead and destroy the Demon.

She knew that Dungeons and Dragons was just a fantasy, a game to keep her entertained and confuse the old coots. But tonight it felt intensely real, different, personal. No one had been injured in her fires, just as she'd hoped. Houses were the enemy, not people.

Until now.

Mary sat in a wicker chair on the back porch staring uphill. Through a weave of branches she saw window lights. *He* was home.

The old pickup held her usual supplies. She carefully aimed eight paper popcorn bowls, filled them half full of Everclear, and stood back. She laid a blue Paladin action figure on the irrigated lawn, certain it would be found. Her D&D character was now her brand.

A pause before igniting the fuel—last chance to stop. Other people lived up this narrow canyon, people who'd never hurt her. A dog barked in the distance. A warm breeze sifted by. The lighter felt like a gun in her hand. "This is officially weird," she whispered.

Five minutes went by, then five more. "Conscience is an angel on your shoulder," Father Kelly always said. "God's way of protecting us from doing harm."

"Protecting us," she whispered.

She looked uphill through the waiting trees. Lamps burned cheerfully in *that fucking house*. Mary Callahan bent over and cried.

53

Solberg ate a Caesar's salad at the Good Food Store and downed a liter of water. The temperature outside was already past 100. He'd spent the morning at the Missoula County Clerk and Recorder's Office going through plat books. None of the people affected by the Taylor Creek and Lolo fires were famous or obvious targets for a vengeful smokejumper or anyone else. Bernie Katz had found nothing either, but said he'd keep digging.

After thirty minutes, Solberg reluctantly left the air-conditioned store and cringed as heat roared from the asphalt. He drove north on Orange Street. Up ahead, the Rattlesnake Mountains were smothered in smoke. Radio said a suspicious fire had broken out up Lincoln Creek. Thirty expensive houses were already torched, with more in danger. "Who the hell set *that* fire?" Solberg said.

Ten minutes later he pulled up to Rob Tabish's shack on Shakespeare.

Solberg exhaled nervously as he knocked on the front door. No answer. He walked to the back door and knocked again.

The sound of slogging footsteps. Rob Tabish appeared, looking half asleep and a quarter drunk. "Not in the market," he growled, and began to shut the door.

"Wait, Hank Weaver is a friend of mine," Solberg blurted.

Tabish sized up this stranger, then dim recognition appeared in his eyes. "You were at the North Side party on the Fourth."

"You gave a fine reading of the Declaration."

Tabish scratched his haunch with one hand. "You talked with Hank Weaver for a while. What do you want from me?"

"Can we talk about the fires?" Solberg asked.

"You a reporter? No comment."

"No, my name is Matt Solberg, I'm..."

"You're the egghead who wrote that fucking search book, aren't you?"

Solberg let the shot go by.

Tabish had made his point. "Shit, it's baking out there, come on in."

The house was a wreck—dishes in the sink, beer cans scattered, thrift store furniture. An American flag hung upside down on a wall. A shelf of colorful ceramic mugs, maybe keepsakes from a past relationship.

Solberg scanned the shelves for pyrometric cones. The kind left at the Mann Gulch fire. None visible. Could be stashed.

"Let's go down to the basement," Tabish said. "It's cooler below ground."

They walked downstairs and sat on beat-up recliners facing each other. A stereo with a turntable squatted on a crate. A collection of vinyl records, stretching ten feet long, was anchored by cinder blocks. Posters of Lenin and Lennon were tacked to the walls.

"Beer?" Tabish offered, taking three from a fridge.

"Why not?" Solberg said, catching a tossed Bud.

Tabish drained half a beer and ran the can across his forehead. "So, you writing another dumbass book?"

"No," Solberg said. "I'm here, off the record, to talk to you about the Taylor Creek and Lolo fires."

"No one is *ever* off the record." Tabish finished his beer and opened the next.

"You're right," Solberg said. "Let me lay it out then. I'm trying to figure out who set those fires and the ones at Mann Gulch. I was brought in when the Linda Merchant went missing and I've kept at it ever since."

"Brought in by who?" Tabish asked, averting his eyes.

"Search and Rescue at first. Then the FBI, once they knew Mann Gulch was arson."

Tabish shook his head. "The Fucking Bureau of Intimidation. I'll say one thing, you've got a big pair of hairy balls to come here. Like I said upstairs—no comment."

"Not even about Taylor Creek and Lolo?"

"I know nothing about those burns," Tabish said.

Those burns. Solberg noted his wording.

"We through here?" Tabish shouted, throwing his empties into a corner barrel.

Solberg felt physical danger. Tabish was in his sixties, but still a beast. "Linda Merchant's in bad shape," Solberg said, trying to calm him down. "I thought you could help."

"That's a real drag about the girl," Tabish said, showing a flash of humanity.

"You're a smokejumper," Solberg said. "I figured you've heard something. It was Mann Gulch, after all."

"Mann Gulch." Anger flashed on Tabish's face.

"There's no politics here," Solberg said. "I'm just trying to help a kid out."

Tabish laughed cynically. "No politics? Well Opie, unless you've got FBI creds and a warrant, get the hell out of my house."

Solberg set his beer on a table and stood up. "Sorry for breaking up your busy day."

Tabish scowled and followed Solberg upstairs. At the door, Solberg turned and took a gamble. "Who's this Fleming guy you hang around with?"

Tabish bowled Solberg over, sending him through the open door and sprawling on the ground. "None of your fucking business, you right-wing sack of shit!" Tabish picked up a broom and charged.

Solberg jumped up, dodging the first swing of the broom, but he took the second hard in the chops. He juked his way to the street with Tabish in pursuit, until he felt a slap across his backside.

"Fuck off!" Tabish screamed.

Solberg jumped in the Ford and patched out, Rob Tabish roaring in his wake.

54

Bernie Katz sat at his desk, failing to suppress a grin. "Need another tissue there, Matt?"

Solberg pulled a bloody Kleenex from his nose and dropped in it the trash. "Glad I provide you with entertainment."

"I warned you not to go to Tabish's house by yourself. And oh, with no training, badge, gun, warrant, or backup."

"You finished?" Solberg said, feeling his cheek. The welt was rising.

"Yeah, that's about it," Bernie said. He pulled a bottle of Maker's Mark from his desk and poured two shots. He pushed a brimming glass forward. Solberg emptied it in one gulp.

Bernie took a sip and set his glass down. "Tabish is someone you shouldn't mess with, Matt. We've checked him out and the man is chancy. Not Jersey chancy, but he'll do around here. Tabish is pissed off and, at least in his rhetoric, radicalized."

"What's he angry about?"

"In the immortal words of James Dean—what have you got? Montana changing, no pension from the Forest Service for risking his neck, 'fascist greedheads' running the country. I know this one is personal for you and it was your idea that this smokejumper might be behind the Merchant fire. But you can *never* do that again. Clear?"

Solberg nodded. "I took a shot. Sorry."

"Quite a shot, from the look of that shiner you're growing." Bernie said.

They smiled.

Solberg rubbed his face. "It may be nothing, but Tabish's place has a shelf of ceramic pots. Maybe he had access to pyrometric cones like the ones found at Mann Gulch."

"You see any?"

"No."

Bernie shrugged. "This is Missoula. If you can't throw a pot, you don't get a driver's license."

"Maybe Tabish lured one of those potters into his scheme," Solberg said. "A former sweetheart with a political grudge."

"Missoula is thick with legitimately pissed-off women," Bernie said. "That doesn't exactly single anyone out."

Solberg nodded. "Okay, but what do you make of Tabish going nuts?"

Bernie poured Matt another Maker's. "If it was back home, I'd say he was a tough drunk defending his rep."

"And in Montana?"

"Could be that or you squeezed Tabish and fear shot out his ass."

"He didn't look scared to me."

"No, I suspect you freaked this guy out pretty good, especially with that question about Fleming. It's why he bloodied you. Could be the two of them worked together setting burns."

Solberg let the idea sink in. "Which ones?"

"I've got suspicions—Flathead, Big Sky, Mann Gulch—but no proof," Bernie said.

"What about Fleming?" Matt asked. "You have anything on him?"

"Some. Malcolm Fleming came from wealth—a Main Line suburb outside Philly."

"Malcolm?"

"No wonder he ditched it. Hardly a shock, but this is one troubled guy. Kicked out of several prep schools for fighting, theft, and vandalism. Has a mental health history, but it's sealed. A few petty busts back East, nothing here. No known addresses in the last two years. Missoula cops say he's a street person they keep an eye on."

"A hungry ghost," Solberg said.

"A what?"

"In the Buddhist wheel of life, a hungry ghost is a spirit trapped by desires."

"Fancy name for a shitheel," Bernie said.

"Maybe. But I think Fleming aches and can't find a remedy. Nothing satisfies his hunger."

"For what?"

"Sex, power, beer."

"Sounds like Congress," Bernie said. "What makes him special?"

"Maybe he isn't, and that's his problem," Solberg said.

Bernie Katz leaned forward. "I'll play along. What's the remedy for a hungry ghost like Fleming?"

"A jar of nectar."

"Great, I'll buy him some Smuckers."

Solberg smiled. "Nectar in his case is respect. I saw the need on his face at the Fourth of July party. Fleming is desperate for someone like Tabish or another big man to give him his due."

"A big man like Dr. Bill Knight?" Bernie asked.

Solberg huffed. "So you're back to that nonsense."

"Is it nonsense?" Bernie asked, bushy eyebrows dancing.

Solberg held his ground. "Look, suspicious fires have been set in a dozen counties. One on Mount Helena. Another in the Rimrocks above Billings. A burn near Seeley Lake that torched some old hunters' cabins. Two high-priced fires at Big Sky and Flathead Lake. And now this burn up Lincoln Creek. Jesus, man."

"Not my savior," Bernie said, deadpan. "Investigators say the arsonist in the last three used popcorn bowls and some kind of accelerant. That is one mean son of a bitch."

"Why mean?" Solberg asked.

"The popcorn bowls send a message that this is entertainment to them. Hard to catch somebody if that's all they're up to. But I think they *want* to get caught."

"Why?" Solberg asked.

"Remember when I said we found dolls at some ignition sites?"

"Yup."

Bernie nodded. "They found another one at Lincoln Creek. The dolls are weird-looking things we still can't figure out. Each one is kind of different." Bernie found images on his phone and showed them to Solberg.

"Paladin," Solberg said right away.

"Like in the old TV western?" Bernie asked, sitting up.

"*Have Gun—Will Travel,*" Solberg said. "No, these Paladins are right out of Dungeons and Dragons. Three versions of the same character."

"How the hell do you know that?" Bernie asked, incredulous.

"University students are still kids," Solberg said.

Bernie leaned forward. "Does that mean the arsonist is a kid?"

"Maybe, but it's definitely someone getting their jollies fucking with us. The original Paladins were knights protecting Europe from invaders."

"Really?" Bernie said. "So we're back to Bill *Knight* protecting Montana?"

Solberg stiffened. "Probably a semantic misdirection or coincidence. I was with Knight during the hours the Flathead fire was set. Besides, why would he leave such a ham-fisted clue guaranteed to get him caught?"

Bernie spoke softly. "You can't always predict what people will do. Even ones you swear you know."

"No, it's gotta be someone playing a game," Solberg said, waving the idea away.

"What kind of game?" Bernie asked, leaning in.

"Dungeons and Dragons, of course," Solberg said, smiling.

Bernie stayed serious. "Okay, exactly how does that game work?"

Solberg shrugged. "Not sure. It's about adventures and campaigns, adopting the identity of a character."

"Like Paladin," Bernie said, making a note.

"Yup, fantasy stuff."

"Except this shit is getting real. So we're looking for a gamer dweeb with a grudge against rich people. Missoula bars are hip-deep in them, so keep your eyes open."

"Damn, you're making me paranoid, Bernie."

The agent slouched in his chair. "It never hurts to be paranoid, even about Bill Knight."

Solberg sighed. "Will you finally give it a rest? Again, the mix of arson fires rules out Bill. There's no pattern or motive that makes any sense. Especially when he's done nothing except *help you*."

"Maybe," Bernie said.

"Maybe you just hate us fucking academics," Solberg said, smiling.

Bernie scowled. "Cost me a hundred grand to send my kid to college. The genius majored in Theater."

"Have I seen him in anything?" Solberg asked.

"A Wendy's drive-thru," Bernie said, half joking.

The men drank whiskey and mulled.

"Alright," Bernie said, "I'll pass this Paladin theory on to my people and see what they come up with." He exhaled tiredly. "Let's focus on Fleming for the moment. You know this state, so assuming the evil little shit is setting fires, what's his next move?"

"Why don't you just pick Fleming up and interrogate him?" Solberg asked.

"He'd lie and then run off to set fires somewhere else. No, we need to trap the rat bastard *here*. And I need your local brain to help us do that."

Solberg was being drawn even farther across the line into an FBI investigation. He was now sure it was more than Bernie covering his ass. The agent had busted major players back East. Mafiosi and real estate pimps. He'd have no fear going after a movie star like Edward Merchant or an egghead like Dr. Bill Knight. But with this outbreak of fires, Bernie Katz needed help in a place he still didn't understand. He needed a *yeshuvnik* he could trust.

Solberg relaxed. "Whoever Fleming is trying to impress, he needs to do something epic. Much larger than Mann Gulch or the Flathead—more houses and more fear."

Bernie nodded. "Lots of houses have been totaled up Lincoln Creek and the fire is still uncontained. Even took out the schmancy estate of a hedge fund billionaire named Archer Stone. His twenty-something son barely made it out alive. Believes the fire was aimed right at him, and he could be right. Isn't that enough fear?"

Solberg scratched his neck. "Flood the zone with shit."

"An old tactic," Bernie said. "Distract us with the sheer volume of crap."

"So we can't make sense of things," Solberg said.

Bernie shook his head. "There's nothing I can do with that. And beyond all the other suspects, I'm still grappling with Blanca Chacón. She makes sense and then she doesn't. Chacón had a motive, but from there we're just speculating on how she pulled it off. Not saying she didn't, but the idea of working with Merchant still makes more sense."

"So what do you want to do?" Solberg asked.

Bernie sighed. "For now, let's give priority to Fleming and Tabish.

Yet that still leaves me with a problem. Why would that kid suck up a broken-down smokejumper? A guy with no record of violence or radical actions, as far as we know. Mostly Tabish spins yarns and shits on the moon."

"Until now," Solberg said. "Maybe." He sighed as he rubbed his eyes, then sat back. "What if this Fleming kid is Paladin? He's the right age for a gamer."

Bernie shrugged. "For all I know, Paladin is Jimmy Hoffa." He returned the whiskey bottle to a desk drawer, then leaned forward on his elbows. "Before you go, humor me. Where does Tabish fall in Buddha's wheel of fortune home game?"

"He's easy," Solberg said. "Rob Tabish is a titan at war with the gods. Remember, he was a fire*fighter* who jumped into battle hundreds of times."

Bernie rolled his eyes. "You're going kind of Berkeley on me."

Solberg smiled. "If it's untrue, reject it."

"As the Buddha would advise," Bernie said, smiling back.

"Yes grasshopper," Solberg said.

Bernie folded his hands. "What exactly is smokejumper Rob Tabish's remedy?"

"Buddha arrives carrying a flaming spear."

55

Dr. Bill Knight desperately needed the reassurance of familiar tasks. He slowly cranked the steel borer into the cinnamon-colored trunk of a ponderosa pine. Sawdust sprinkled his boots. He paused to catch his breath as the tool neared heartwood. A blue grouse watched from ten feet away. Montanans call them fool hens. He could have picked up a rock and killed it with one throw, but he felt empathy for the simple bird.

He unzipped and peed a trickle, feeling a pain in his core. That morning the cause of his discomfort was finally diagnosed. Knight had prostate cancer.

"Your Gleason score is 9 and your PSA is 20," the doctor had said. "Our tests indicate it is Stage T3, meaning the tumor may have escaped the gland. If you'd had regular checkups, we would have caught this much sooner. However, while you have an aggressive form of cancer, we have a tremendous range of treatment options. It's possible you will die *with* this disease, not *of* it, if we get started right away."

While the doctor explained the relative risks and benefits of surgery, radioactive seeds, chemo, and targeted radiation, Knight tried to remain calm. But he'd heard enough to know what the blather meant. He would die of cancer. Not right away—maybe years from now if he got treated, but his miserable course was charted and there was nothing this bright young physician could do to stop it. "I'll think it over," he'd said to the doctor.

Knight felt a powerful urge to carry out the project that until today had been just an intellectual exercise. His fire equation had started as a fantasy to channel his rage, a way to corner the bastard and science it into submission. HCs = Houses of Californians. A dark joke.

But now Knight was free to do as his data insisted. If he had the evil heart to comply. He'd seen fires take innocent lives and spare guilty ones. Knew that burns release millions of tons of carbon dioxide, speeding up climate change. If he did this irrational thing, he would be defeating himself and damaging the world he'd sworn to protect. The whole thing felt alien and cruel—not at all like him.

Or at least who he had been.

Knight torsioned the increment borer out of the pine. He turned a knob at the end of the shaft and withdrew a perfect core cradled by a thin metal band. He blew the sawdust off. The sample was the diameter of a straw, with stripes of varying thickness—the tree's annual growth rings made by light, hidden by darkness until this moment. Knight carefully transferred the fragile core into a groove he'd cut in a board. He wrote the site number, tree species, and "heart" and "bark" at the appropriate ends in black marker. Knight reversed the borer out of the tree and rested.

The forest was reassuring, the peaks unchanged. At that moment, his cancer diagnosis felt ridiculous. Cancer killed other people, not him.

A white-tailed doe stared at him from the bushes. "Sorry, honey, I have to make a racket now."

Knight put on protective goggles and Peltor earmuffs. He checked the fuel level in his chainsaw, hoisted the tool into place, and fired it up. He made a level cut across the bottom of the tree's "catface"—a gouge where repeated fires have damaged the trunk. He withdrew the saw and made an angular cut down to where the other ended. Soon a semicircular wedge wiggled. Knight made a final push, withdrew the saw, and shut it off.

Towhees sung with joy. Bill Knight smiled at the birds. "It's your valley again."

He tugged the wedge free. There, recorded in the wood, was the message he needed—fire scar data to boost his spirits on his second-worst day. He smeared the wound with salve. Pine pitch would do the rest. Two more sites remained, and the sun had already arced west over the Bitterroot Mountains.

On the drive to his next plot, Knight counted changes in the land. His vision was acute like never before. So was the pain in his body and heart.

> *Eleven new houses near Stevensville—hay ground gone*
> *Forty-seven trailers on the Burnt Fork—Molly's picnic site gone*
> *Eight pairs of osprey nesting in the Metcalf Wildlife*
> *Refuge—proper*
> *Eighty-three houses along Ambrose Creek—spoiled*
> *Hundreds of houses in Hidden Valley—monstrous*

He steered the pickup down a dirt road, hands shaking on the wheel. The reality of cancer flooded his brain and sweat poured down his face.

Bill Knight pulled over and ran into the trees. "Molly!"

56

Two days later, Solberg's face still ached from Tabish's beatdown. He walked in the back door of the Griz Bar, hoping to be inconspicuous. The place was crowded with locals—men and women with generic faces you forget.

Barkey Boyd busted him right away. "Nice shiner, Matt. My wife get cross with you?"

The guys along the Flight Deck grinned. Solberg grinned back, cringing from the pain. Barkey got a glass from the bartender and poured Matt a beer from a plastic pitcher.

Solberg took a long pull. "Thanks, Barkey."

"You bet. No, really, what happened? You look like shit."

"Had a dust-up."

"And the other guy?"

"Untouched by human hands."

"Who was it?" one of the men asked.

"Can't say," Solberg said.

"Must be FBI shit," Barkey said.

Solberg drank beer.

"About the fires," Barkey went on.

More beer and silence.

"Means it is," Barkey said.

"You're not as dumb as you look," Solberg said.

Barkey smiled.

A young woman sat on a nearby stool sipping a pint. A regular gal with ashy-blond hair who blended into the background. Mary Callahan.

Solberg barely noticed her, but lowered his voice anyway. "What do you hear about the fires?" No harm in checking in. He trusted these guys.

Barkey shrugged. "I hear the usual nonsense. Conspiracies are as common as cow shit around here. How about you, Matt?"

"Well, the burns at Taylor Creek and Lolo were likely set by an amateur. And if their goal was taking out houses, but they picked some lousy sites."

The ashy-haired girl was handed another pint by the bartender. The place was getting crowded, so Mary casually moved her stool a bit closer. Being polite, but quietly listening.

"Maybe the Lolo fires were personal," Barkey said.

"You guys know anybody who lives on Taylor Creek?" Solberg asked.

A tall guy chimed in. "Bunch of rich out-of-staters with big houses and tiny balls."

"You do a personal inspection?" Barkey asked, smirking.

Some laughs.

"That's about all we have," Solberg said.

"Bullshit," the tall guy said. "Tabish's drinking buddies over at Red's say he's being checked out by the FBI. That true?"

Solberg wished he'd kept quiet. "The Bureau would know, not me."

"Don't kid a kidder," Barkey said. "I heard it too. Tabish is a paranoid son of a bitch, but that doesn't mean the Feds aren't out to get him."

"But why would they be?" Solberg asked, fishing.

"Mann Gulch," the tall guy said. "When he's lit up, Tabish speaks well of those fires."

Solberg lowered his voice. "So do lots of people. Maybe Tabish is just trying to claim somebody else's work."

"Why the hell would he do that?" the tall guy asked.

"To seem bigger than he is," Solberg said.

Barkey grinned. "Tabish was big enough to give you that shiner."

"How the hell did you know?" Solberg asked.

"Garbage man friend of mine saw the whole thing," Barkey said. He reached over and searched through Matt's hair.

"What're you doing, Barkey?"

"Checking for broom straw."

The Flight Deck burst out laughing.

"You guys knew the whole time?" Solberg asked, embarrassed.

They kept laughing. Barkey got another pitcher of beer and poured the men a glass.

Solberg sighed. "Let me ask you guys a question. Do you think Rob Tabish really set the Mann Gulch fires? Is he capable of hurting a kid?"

"Burning, yes, the kid, no," one guy said. "But he's as mean as a snake when he's drunk."

"Barkey?" Solberg asked.

The man rubbed his scruffy chin. "Tabish has the anger and the know-how, but he's too beat up to cover Mann Gulch all by himself. He'd need a young set of legs to help."

Solberg thought of Fleming: a rich kid from Philly, maybe with a fancy art background. That would explain the pyrometric cones the guys didn't know about.

"How about these new burns down by Lolo?" Matt asked. "And the one up on Flathead Lake?"

Barkey shook his head. "Lolo is bone dry, so no wonder it went up, but the Flathead surprised me. Thought it was too wet up there."

Solberg resisted talking about climate change. The guys were smart and getting there on their own.

Barkey slugged some beer and put his glass down. "But why the hell would Tabish do it? There's no smokejumper history in either place."

Solberg brooded.

"Truth is," Barkey said, "things are pretty crazy right now. Not just at Mann and Lolo, but everywhere. We even got a new fire up Lincoln Creek that's out of control. Perfect cover for anybody with a grievance and a Bic."

Solberg held back what he knew. "We've got nothing on that burn."

Mary Callahan remained invisible. She dove into a burger, watching a baseball game on the set. A sip of beer and a secret smile.

Solberg was oblivious. "That's the problem with these fires. Too many angles."

Barkey nodded. "Yup. Arsonists can be dumb as dirt or smart as the devil."

"Not sure all these fires are dumb," Solberg said.

"I agree, so don't overlook the second half of that."

"Meaning?"

Barkey set down his beer. "Someone smart could get away with massive shit right now. There are so many fires that no one can make sense of them. Perfect time to settle an old score. Hide in the chaos and ambush somebody. Like this new fire up Lincoln Creek. No way to catch a bastard if they keep it simple. Hell, there was a guy in Culbertson who waited thirty years for payback over a girl in high school. Then he torched fifty grand's worth of a rancher's hay."

"So these fires might be about something old," Solberg said.

"Or something new," Barkey said.

"And they may not be linked."

"Or they are."

Solberg shook his head.

Barkey lifted his glass. "Say, Matt. What do a Rubik's cube and a dick have in common?"

Solberg grinned. "No idea."

"They both get harder the more you play with them."

The guys all laughed.

Mary Callahan stood up and paid her tab. Her arms swayed defiantly as she walked out the door. No one gave Paladin a second look.

57

A dry lightning storm tattooed the face of the Bitterroot Mountains. Bolts slashed through the darkness, illuminating everything from Lolo to Darby. Thunder rattled windows for forty miles and caused a cattle stampede in Victor. There were so many lightning strikes that the National Interagency Fire Center website couldn't keep up.

Bill Knight watched the storm from his yard, sipping scotch. He'd tried to trance away his cancer diagnosis with fieldwork. Read websites about treatment regimens and survival rates. One night, he even sought Molly's wisdom at her favorite reach of the river. For a second, she was a trout flashing in a riffle. A wild, silent ghost.

But that morning he got more horrible news. "Our latest test shows your cancer has spread outside the prostate gland," the doctor had said professionally. "It has metastasized and you need to get treated immediately."

Knight told the doctor he'd take a day to consider that. But it seemed even more pointless, a foregone conclusion. His body and soul ached with cancer and loneliness—he felt nauseous and halfway out of the world. Knight's only respite came in blaming Michael Slaton for his misery. He knew this was only party true, but he needed an enemy, a target, a final release. Shrinks call it closure.

Through binoculars, Knight studied a dozen new fires pock-marking the high-elevation forests of the Bitterroot Mountains. A few lightning strikes even hit the base of the range on private land where new houses squatted in the trees.

The timing was perfect. It was a summer Saturday night, so lots of people might be blamed for starting a fire. Careless kids, drunk barbecuers, random arsonists, Paladin—a mysterious figure being reported in the news.

Knight had prepared for weeks, but ran through his bullet list anyway:

- Regular boots—tracks meant he was examining plots
- Jeans and cowboy shirt—generic Bitterrooter
- Soiled John Deere hat—shield his face
- Mud-covered license plates on the old GMC—typical ranch rig

If Knight was seen near a burn, he had the perfect excuse: a famous ecologist in the line of duty. Besides, in the chaos he believed no one would solve his pattern. "Too much scatter," he said out loud.

Knight got in the Jimmy and fired it up. He pulled out of the driveway, turned right on Bell Crossing Road, and crossed the river. A small wooden cross marked the site of Molly's death at the intersection with Highway 93. Knight didn't stop to lay a pebble at the shrine as he still did sometimes. He accelerated west toward the Bitterroot Mountains.

Unlike Fleming, the fool he suspected had set the Taylor and Lolo fires, his sites were strategically chosen: hundreds of houses, denser fuel, a seemingly erratic spacing of ignitions, and easy escape routes downwind. No one would get hurt and Michael Slaton wouldn't be targeted. Knight would terrify the killer and run him off. That might be enough.

Site #1—St. Joseph Road

A lightning-struck snag rose above a forest over-grown with houses. Knight parked out of sight and followed a contrail of smoke. After ten minutes of bushwhacking, the burning tree led him into its light. Fire crackled in the crotch of a double-trunked ponderosa, but there was no sign of spread.

Knight tasted the wind with his tongue—a gusty southwest current. More than sufficient. He picked up a dry branch and allowed the wand to touch fire. The wood was eager and crackled in relief. Knight licked the air and estimated the optimum direction of spread. More than a thousand houses lay downwind. From his research, he knew that half were HCs, Houses of Californians.

Knight knelt at the base of the pine. He slowly brought his torch in contact with dry grasses and pine needles. Ten seconds later he withdrew the branch and watched the fire blink awake. It stretched outward in a swath. Knight moved fifty yards and added a second burn to hedge his bet.

Site #2–Rattler Creek

No fire-struck trees visible. Knight's equation played over and over in his head—this was a dense collection of Californian houses built in a beetle-killed forest. A prime site, yet lightning hadn't found it.

Knight walked into the trees and listened to the electric storm. He pulled the powerful cigar lighter out of his pocket. Extend tongue to wind, walk, think like lightning. Knight moved on to a patch of dying pines beside a gravel lane. Stray bottle rockets, cigarette butts, or firebrands might be blamed.

He got down on one knee and flicked the lighter. A powerful blue flame. Knight moved it in contact with a pile of resin-filled pine cones. They burned cheerily, spawning meanders of fire toward the mansions of stock cheats, real estate lawyers, and trust fund naturopaths.

Site #3–Magpie Estates

This subdivision contained 305 custom homes built by a La Jolla developer. Mostly HCs. A tall pine in the middle of a pasture had been hit by lightning, but the fire went out on its own. Knight made a quick foray into seedlings, deployed his lighter, and was soon back on the road, moving south toward Pinesdale. Knight had no quarrel with the singular people of this polygamous Mormon town. They had enough trouble of their own making.

Site #4–Manor Vista Road

Despite the fancy name, this development was a dense mixture of HCs and modest houses. So far his fortunes had been good; just a couple of cars had passed, but only when he was rolling with his head bent forward. Knight banked the truck through a smerge of house types. Targeting was impossible here. The site was compact and certain to kill.

"No way," Knight said to himself. He holstered his lighter and moved on.

Eldorado: the valley's densest concentration of Californians. More than two thousand homes in all. Knight was in luck. A fire had started from a strike just below the Selway-Bitterroot Wilderness boundary. Thick smoke provided excellent cover. With an updraft forming, any ignition down here would be sucked west at splendid speed. Fire would leap the iron gate and forage for eight-thousand square-foot HCs like a ravenous force of canon law.

Knight parked in a dirt track invisible from the county road. He strolled into the trees, knelt, ignited twigs, and returned. Three minutes later he was safely back on Highway 93 as a reddish glow raced toward the mountains.

It was fully dawn when Knight got home. He glassed the slopes with a spotting scope. His St. Joseph fire was progressing nicely, sending a column of brown smoke high above the valley. The Rattler and Magpie Estates burns were also thriving.

Knight turned his attention to the prize—Three Badger—the gated community infected with Californians. As he'd predicted, *his* project was being drawn upslope and joining forces with the wilderness blaze. Dr. Bill Knight had created fire weather, a vortex of pressure that might mature into a second Big Burn. Something so potent that only fall rains could stop it.

Knight pulled back from the scope. All this felt thrilling and bizarre, larger and more brutal than the equation. It was no longer a mathematical fantasy or desperate joke. He had crossed a violent threshold was crossed and its force shocked him to the ground. Heartbeats thundering in his ears.

58

"The fire situation is now out of control." The dazed young woman gave a live TV update from the Aerial Fire Depot in Missoula. She had to yell over the sound of slurry bombers straining to take off.

> Sources tell us that some 120 fires are now being reported state-wide. Fourteen people died in the Colter fire near Yellowstone National Park, and there are more than forty people missing across

Montana. All available manpower and equipment are engaged to fight these terrible blazes. As of now, all activities on public lands are prohibited. The woods are officially closed and voluntary evacuations are widespread.

Up the Bitterroot, there are more than twenty fires caused by last night's lightning storm. While many of these are high up in the mountains, houses are already reported lost along St. Joseph Road and in a string of fires extending southward toward Hamilton. The Three Badger development is engulfed, and many houses are already lost. Currently there are no reports of casualties.

The National Interagency Coordination Center in Boise sent additional smokejumpers, hotshot crews, and slurry bombers to the Bitterroot. But the center was depleted by more pressing needs at the Colter fire by Yellowstone. People had died there—famous ones. PAC people. So there few resources left to send to less well-connected burns.

Across Montana, what was left of federal, state, and local forces were assembled and the National Guard was deployed. The governor called a press conference to say he was considering a declaration of martial law.

President Trump tweeted: "There is no reason for these massive and costly forest fires in Montana except that forest management is so sad. Billions of dollars are given each year and still they fail. No Raking, No money!" Montanans were unified by their disbelief. When Trump was excoriated for a lack of empathy, he pretended to praise the bravery of firefighters. Montanans were unified by their disgust, although some kept it hidden.

Bo and Matt watched the news for hours, dazed by the sheer scale of what was happening. At 4:00, they went up to Solberg's rooftop deck. Through binoculars the Bitterroot Mountains looked like newsreel footage of Dresden. Smoke columns swallowed nine-thousand-foot peaks and foraged for more. Firebrands rode the whirlwind. The Bitterroot Range was a cauldron giving birth to afterlife.

"Damn," Matt said in a whisper. "Have a look."

Bo peered south and said nothing for two minutes. Her hands shook. Matt touched her on the shoulder.

"We have to do something, Matt." She set the binoculars down.

"I'm working with Bernie and I'm sure to get search and rescue jobs."

"The National Guard's up the Bitterroot, so maybe you won't."

Matt hoped she was right. "What do you want to do, Bo?"

"I need to map what's going on."

"The Feds are all over it."

"I don't care. *I* need to do something, alright?"

"Okay," Matt said, touching her shoulder again. "I'll come with..." His cell rang and he checked the ID. Unknown number. "Matt Solberg."

"Matt, this is Rocky Hilger from the Fire Depot."

"Hey, Rocky, how are..."

"I need your help." A desperate voice.

"Name it," Solberg said.

"I need you to go up in a scout plane to check out these Bitterroot fires."

Solberg swallowed hard. "Don't you have personnel for that? I'm not..."

"They're all deployed at the Colter fire and elsewhere. Boise sent me a scout plane, but I've got nobody left to put their eyes on these blowups. Neither does the Fire Lab. You're experienced and I need to know what's going on."

"Try Bill Knight, maybe he's..."

"There's no time for that! You coming or not?"

"Fifteen minutes," Solberg said.

"Make it twelve." Click.

Solberg put the phone in his pocket. "Say, I've gotta go do this thing for the Fire Depot."

"Don't tell me you're actually going to fly into this horror?"

"You heard?"

"Guy was shouting. Of course I heard."

Matt reached out but she stepped back. "No," she said. "I can't stop you, but don't expect me to agree with it."

Solberg checked his watch. She waved him away with the back of her hand.

59

Eleven minutes later, Solberg screeched into the parking lot of the Aerial Fire Depot. Rocky Hilger met him at the door. "Here's your map, note pad, and laptop," Hilger said. "You know Apple?"

"You bet," Solberg said, taking the materials.

"File is WildCAD Satellite. Has a red flame icon."

Rocky led him through the Smokejumper Loft onto the tarmac, where a twin-engine Bronco idled, its passenger door ajar. Solberg lowered his head and stepped inside.

"I'm Major Milliorn," the pilot said, offering his hand.

"Matt Solberg."

The men shook.

"Here's your T-10," Milliorn said, handing Matt a parachute.

Solberg strapped on the chute and buckled up. Milliorn revved the engines and taxied into position. The pilot squawked his identification, N875MC, roared down the runway, and lifted off. Solberg felt vibrations as the gear came up and the aircraft banked south.

Major Milliorn handed Matt a pale green Clark headset that allowed the men to talk above the racket of the engines. Solberg checked his map: a 1:62,500 orthophoto of the Bitterroot Valley. Roughly one inch to a mile scale, with contours lines and topographic features overlaid on a color photo. He fired up the laptop, clicked the WildCAD icon, and a satellite image appeared.

Solberg felt an updraft as Major Milliorn flew them over McCauley Butte. "Didn't know the Forest Service used military pilots," Solberg said.

"I'm not military, just Texan. Major is a first name down there."

"There you go," Solberg said. "What's our flight plan?"

"Commercial traffic is rerouted and civilian aviation is grounded. The sky is ours. Oh, except for slurry bombers and helicopters." Milliorn laughed, at home in the bedlam.

Solberg looked outside, then down at his map and laptop. "Let's have a look at Taylor Creek first."

Milliorn banked the plane east and descended. Altimeter read 1,750 feet. Down below were four evenly spaced Vs of blackened land. No flames visible, and crews were mopping up. "It's over with down there," Milliorn said.

Solberg made notes. "Now Lolo."

Milliorn turned west and Solberg felt a thrill in his stomach. He stared down at the slopes. "Not much spread here either," Solberg said. "Three spot fires, some damage, but no linkage with the big burns."

"Minor leagues. Let's go to the show," Milliorn said, a gleam in his eyes.

Solberg was not amused. To the south was a wall of smoke, cinders, and flames. As they flew, visibility dropped to a thousand feet, then to nothing.

Milliorn was all business, flying by instruments, keeping the thing level the best he could. Updrafts from blazes slammed violently into the aircraft. They careened across the sky, G-forces building. Solberg slammed his right knee hard on the door handle, twisting the joint and opening a gash. He cringed from the pain, but kept his mouth shut.

"Must be the St. Joseph fire!" Milliorn yelled. "Big son of a bitch!"

The world below them was a siege of red and orange flames boiling up toward the plane before dying as swirls of black exhaust. Solberg caught glimpses of the devastation. Too many burned houses to count.

Two minutes later the air evened out. Solberg exhaled. He'd torn his map from holding on too tight. "Damn," he said, wiping his bloody knee with a rag. "Bumpy up here today."

"A tad," Milliorn said, grinning.

Solberg looked out the window. He recognized Harley Creek's narrow slot with the wider One Horse Canyon beyond it. "Not everywhere is involved," he said, making a note. "So far, the St. Joseph fire hasn't moved south."

Bang! The plane shuddered from an impact. Milliorn hung onto the yoke for dear life.

"What the hell was that?!" Solberg yelled.

Milliorn tested the ailerons and shook his head. "A firebrand just nailed my six. No damage, I think. But I'm getting us out of this mess." He banked east and gained altitude to twenty-six hundred feet above the valley floor. Still far below the fire-mauled summits. "You still got the need?" Milliorn asked. "It's gettin' dicey."

"It's your airplane."

Milliorn wiped his mouth. "Alright, where's our next site?"

"Rattler Creek. Take a southwest bearing."

Milliorn checked an aeronautical chart. "Sounds right."

Eight minutes later they flew low over the Rattler and Magpie fires. "These fires have stayed local so far," Solberg said. "Can't tell where they're heading though."

"Uphill would be a good guess," Milliorn said.

"Unless the wind moves them sideways. Bitterroot canyons crank out gales." Solberg entered data on his map and laptop. They headed south, burning debris flashing by the windshield. The plane rose and fell hundreds of feet in seconds.

"It's gettin' interesting," Milliorn said. "We almost at Three Badger?"

Solberg looked down at a massive fire front. "We're there." Flames twisted into funnels rising hundreds of feet into the air. "Wow," Solberg said. "Biggest fire whirls I've ever seen."

"In Texas, we call 'em pillars of fire. It's a Baptist thing."

Solberg half smiled. "This fire's as big as St. Joseph. Might cover eight square miles, but with this schmutz, it could be double that. Spreading fast to the west, south, and north." Solberg recorded notes and labeled spots on the map. It was too turbulent to use the computer anymore.

"Schumtz, huh?" Milliorn said.

"It's not a Baptist thing," Solberg said.

"Care for a closer look?" Milliorn asked. "I see a gap."

"Lovely," Solberg said.

Milliorn grinned. He retarded the throttle as he pushed down on the yoke and the plane descended rapidly. It was like flying into an erupting volcano.

Solberg was transfixed. He'd never been this close to the heart of a fire. There was a desperate beauty to it, a primeval truth.

"More than five hundred homes lost," Solberg said. "No sign of containment."

A voice came in over the radio. "Bronco N875, be advised slurry bomber operating in your area at two thousand feet."

Milliorn responded. "Roger, have him in sight."

A deafening roar filled the cockpit as the slurry bomber flew by way too close.

"Jesus!" Solberg shouted.

Milliorn was unfazed. "Yes, my son."

The immense plane descended, banked south, and dropped orange slurry onto a slope at the edge of the fire. Hundreds of homes were in danger. Three helicopters dropped buckets of water on the flames.

They flew over the immense Manor Vista development. A clot of Californians. "Don't see anything going on down there," Solberg said. "Strange that it was spared in this madness."

"Strange or suspicious?" Milliorn asked.

"Both," Solberg said.

"Enough fun for one day," Milliorn said. He turned the yoke northeast and they passed through a shroud of smoke. Waves of sparks and debris bounced off the windshield. Milliorn studied his instruments, as calm as a lama.

Bo, Solberg prayed. *Becky.*

The sky finally opened as they flew over Taylor Creek. The yellow shirts of the firefighters looked like Christmas tree lights.

60

Major Milliorn made a smooth landing back at the Fire Depot and taxied to a stop. Solberg closed his eyes and exhaled.

"You done real good up there," Million said, shutting down the engine. "Most Yankees sweat like a whore at church when it gets dodgy like that."

The two men took off their headsets.

"Thanks," Solberg said. "But I'm from Montana—how can I be a Yankee?"

"You live north of Fort Worth," Milliorn said, smiling. He reached behind him and opened a strapped-in cooler. "What kind of Coke you want?"

"Coke, I guess."

Milliorn chuckled and handed him a can. Solberg drained the contents.

The passenger door opened. "You two done with your tea break?!" Rocky Hilger shouted.

Solberg turned to Milliorn and shook his hand. "I hope I never fly with you again."

Milliorn smiled big. "Feeling's mutual."

Solberg limped into the Fire Depot and gave his observations to Rocky Hilger, improving the accuracy of his map scrawlings and expanding on details from his notes. Hilger transcribed the information into a mass email as Solberg spoke.

When Solberg was done, Hilger sent his message and sat back, overwhelmed. "Two serious motherfuckers with multiple ignitions in between. Jibes with what we see on the satellite images. This could get evil real quick."

"Already is," Solberg said. "If the Three Badger and St. Joseph fires join up, we'll see another 1910 firestorm. It's time to evacuate everyone in the forests between Hamilton and Lolo."

"The whole west side of the Bitterroot?" Hilger asked. "No way that's happening. Too much politics."

"More politics when people start dying. But don't take my word for it—check with Bill Knight."

"Been trying. He still hasn't called back."

Solberg shook his head. "That's weird. He should be front and center at a time like this. Maybe he's doing fieldwork."

"Fieldwork!?" Hilger grabbed a landline. He paused before dialing. "Thanks, Matt. You earned your keep today."

Solberg stood up and winced when he put weight on his right leg.

"Get that looked at," Hilger said.

"It's nothing," Solberg said. He knew better. A gash and strained ligaments.

Solberg limped through the Smokejumper Loft. Every cubby was empty. Just as Rocky Hilger said, all hands on deck. No one left in reserve.

Jumped out.

61

Matt called Bo on his way back to town.

She picked up after one ring. "Matt! Are you alright?"

"I'm fine. Just a little bumpy up there."

Silence on the end of the line.

"Didn't mean to scare you," Matt said.

"Just promise me you won't fly again in this mess."

"Trust me, I have no interest. But I can't promise that."

A long pause.

"Bo, you still there?" Matt asked.

"Yes. I'm here. Come to the Geography Lab. There's something you need to see."

"I'll grab a sandwich at Wordens and be right there. You want anything?"

"Jellybeans and a diet Sprite."

"You really are a Gemini," Matt said, laughing.

Bo didn't laugh. "Just get here."

Twenty minutes later, Solberg entered Parsons Hall and hobbled down a corridor to the Geospatial Research Laboratory. It contained thirty computer workstations with a dozen colorful maps pinned to the walls. Bo Xiong sat in front of three large screens.

"Got your jellys," Matt said.

Bo raced over and hugged him. "You're such an asshole," she whispered.

"Sorry about that," Matt said.

"No, you're not." Bo pulled back. "What happened to your leg?"

"We hit an updraft."

"Do you need a doctor?"

"It's just a boo-boo. What do you need to show me? Sounded serious on the phone."

"It is," Bo said. She ate a handful of jellybeans and clacked away at her keyboard. Bo was a nationally respected expert in geographic information systems, or GIS. Layering maps and imagery to determine patterns on the land.

Matt pulled up a rolling chair and gingerly sat down, looking at the screens. "Alright, it's the Bitterroot Valley," he said. "Fire ignitions and spread from the look of it."

"I classified the fires by type," Bo said, "but I used different criteria than the Feds. On the left are the arson fires along Taylor Creek and above Lolo. Whoever set them didn't even try to make them look accidental. The spacing of burns is weirdly even. Means the locations were chosen for ease of access."

"On foot." Matt leaned in for a better look. "The ignition sites are close to houses but there's a river between the two areas. Which could mean a kid or..."

"...someone on a bicycle, or a fast runner..."

"...with a pair of river shoes, like Bill Knight predicted. But that leaves us nowhere."

"Precisely," Bo said. "Now let's shift to the Bitterroot Valley. This screen shows all known lightning-caused fires. They are mostly in the mountains, but not always, like this ignition beside St. Joseph Road."

"Strange for a low strike to take off like that," Matt said. "You sure it was lightning?"

"It's complicated," Bo said. "There are two points of ignition fifty yards apart when you zoom in on this new image. Either there were two strikes close together, or an arsonist used one strike to set the second fire."

"That'd take a very cool customer," Matt said.

"This was not a thrill seeker; it was someone intelligent."

Bo clicked on the keyboard. The Rattler, Magpie Estates, and Three Badger fires came up as red splatters on the center screen.

"These other fires are even more suspicious," Bo said. "There are no reports of lightning at Rattler, but it might have been ignited by burning debris floating over from St. Joseph."

"Easily. Just a mile away."

Bo nodded. "And a tree was struck at Magpie Estates, but the satellite image shows it's a single pine tree surrounded by irrigated alfalfa. Hardly the place a burn could start."

"Unless sparks spread the fire when the wind came up."

"Possible, not probable," Bo said.

"Thought you said the arsonist was intelligent?"

"Smart doesn't mean wise. Or sane." Bo said, looking at Matt.

"Where are you going with this?" he asked.

Bo pointed at an image of the Three Badger fire. "This one started next to a fancy gated community. Over twelve thousand acres involved and the thing's growing exponentially."

"I saw it face–to-face. Fearsome. Any lightning strikes nearby?"

"Not sure."

"Firebrands from the wilderness burn could have ignited it."

Bo shook her head. "No, the wind is blowing *west*—away from the development at thirty miles an hour. Unlikely a firebrand can defy physics."

Matt felt queasy.

Bo worked her keyboard until a field of black stars appeared against the red background of burns. "Each star is a house destroyed by fire in the past ten hours."

"My God," Matt said. "I had no idea it was this bad. What's the total?"

"Over eight hundred homes lost so far and we're just getting started."

Matt lowered his head. "Casualties?"

"Thankfully no one's been killed, but lots of smoke inhalation and psychological trauma. An emergency shelter is set up at Hamilton High School and the Forest Service has ordered mandatory evacuations in multiple areas."

"*Namaste*," Matt said.

"*Namaste*," Bo answered.

"There's more," she said. "Of the eight hundred houses lost, at least half were built in the past ten years. Which likely means..."

"Californians," Matt said. "No surprise there."

"I cross-checked those sites with Bill Knight's fire scar sites featured in his article in the *Journal of Forestry*. A 62 percent match."

Matt's face flushed. "You're accusing Bill Knight? Of obvious dumb-shit cases of arson!"

"I'm sorry, Matt, but these new fires are not in the dumb-shit category like Taylor Valley. They're analytical and precise. When you told me how angry Bill is about the Bitterroot being overdeveloped, I began to wonder. And when you add his hatred of Michael Slaton..."

"Is Slaton's house at risk?" Matt snapped.

"No."

"Then don't jump to irrational conclusions!"

"I wasn't being irrational, just trying to..."

"And what about the Manor Vista development? It's choked with

Californians and has no fire at all. I saw it from above and the place was left alone. How does that fit your seamless model?"

Bo was pissed, but kept her cool. "It doesn't. The *Missoulian* is fixated on someone called Paladin. Regardless, to pull off these Bitterroot fires the arsonist would have to possess real knowledge. That's why I thought of Bill Knight."

Matt shook his head. "The Taylor Creek and Lolo burns took out houses. Why don't you..."

"Four houses. These fires will destroy thousands."

62

A white glow appears in the darkness and young Matt races toward it. Wally Groff lies curled up on the ground. "Wally!" Matt yells. "You okay?" He kneels down and touches Wally's face. Ice. He holds Wally's hand. Fingers snap off and fall to the ground.

Wally opens his dead eyes. *"Why didn't you save me?"*

"Naww!" Solberg screamed, sitting up in bed, hands clawing the air.

"Matt," Bo said. "Wake up."

His eyes raced around the bedroom.

"You're safe," Bo said.

Matt was awake now, but shaking.

Bo stroked his shoulder.

He managed a nod.

"I'll get some water," Bo said, getting out of bed. She returned and Matt drank the whole glass without stopping. Bo wiped his sweat away with a towel. "Was it about your wife?"

"No, Wally Groff."

"Same dream?" Bo asked.

"Kind of."

"You couldn't find him?"

"No, I found him frozen to death."

"Matt, you were thirteen years old. It wasn't your fault. How many times do..."

"It *was* my fault," Matt whispered.

Bo touched his arm. "From what you've said, *he* was the one who ran ahead, not you."

"But I knew Mill Creek Canyon better than he did. I should have stopped Wally."

"How, by tackling him?"

"Maybe, or by keeping up with him. Wally was in better shape than me."

Bo gently massaged Matt's neck. His need to be super fit was well known. "You've never said why he ran off."

Matt sighed. "We'd hiked to a high lake that day, much higher than we'd planned. It got late and very cold. Our flashlights conked out. That's when Wally got scared and tore off ahead of me." Matt rubbed his face with both hands.

"What was he scared of?" Bo asked in a whisper. "I'm sure you had jackets and..."

"Wally was afraid of the dark. More than anyone I've ever known. Bears and mountain lions didn't worry him, but darkness—" Matt fought back tears.

"Do you know why?"

"No," Matt said. "But he was and like a fool I didn't bring a spare flashlight or batteries."

"He didn't either."

"Light was *my* job. Not his."

Bo resisted asking why.

The next morning, the air outside was a sludge of smoke. Although it was 9:00, the streetlights were still on.

Matt's phone rang.

"Don't answer it," Bo said. "Enough."

Matt checked the screen. "Hey, Bernie, what's up with the Bureau this crappy morning?"

"Fleming is missing," Bernie said. "Your search team been called yet?"

"How do you know he hasn't moved on?" Solberg asked.

"Come down to my office and I'll show you."

Matt looked at Bo, seeking permission. None came. "Alright, but I can only stay a few minutes," he said. He ended the call and said to Bo, "FBI has something for me to look at. Shouldn't be too long."

Bo wouldn't speak.

"I'll be back in an hour," Matt said. "If not, I'll call you."

"Will you tell Bernie Katz my theory about Bill Knight?"

"I'll try."

Bo frowned. "I'm sorry you had a shitty night, but I'm pissed at you. You yelled at me in the lab last night, which really hurt. Then you dismissed me as irrational, which women *just love* to hear. And after I showed how Bill Knight might be setting fires, you say *you'll try* to tell Bernie. Hell, the guy already suspects Knight. What the fuck, Matt!"

"He's my friend and I need more time to…"

"We're running out of time!"

63

Solberg stood at Bernie Katz's door. "Alright, what's so goddamned important?"

"Good morning to you too," Bernie said. He tossed his pen on the desk.

"Sorry, my day started rough. Will end rougher."

"You need coffee?"

"A bucket. What do you have on Fleming?"

Bernie poured Matt a mug of coffee, then scowled at the debris filling his office. "Let's go to the conference room."

They went down a narrow hallway, dodging busy young agents. The "conference room" was barely bigger than Katz's office, but the table was clear.

Bernie sat and opened the file. He slid a piece of paper to Solberg. "This is a print from the security camera at a commuter lot up the Bitterroot. Picture was taken the night of the Taylor Creek and Lolo fires. The guy look familiar?"

It was a grainy black-and-white image of someone riding a bicycle past a row of parked cars. The figure was illuminated by streetlights. Solberg examined it and shrugged. "Could be Fleming. Could be Sinatra."

Bernie handed him a magnifying glass. "How about now?"

Solberg leaned over for a closer look. "The cap mostly covers his face. I see a beard, but no obvious—" Solberg stopped. "Except for his arms. They're covered with tattoos. Jagged shapes mostly, except for one."

"Yup," Katz said. "I noticed it too. Look again."

Solberg moved the magnifier up and down. "It's a Chinese character," he said. "Fleming had one of those on his left arm."

"You know what it means?" Bernie asked.

"No idea. There are thousands of Chinese characters, and tattoo parlors often get them wrong."

"Ah, the Rembrandts of ink," Bernie said. "I've sent a photo to a linguist in the San Francisco office, but no word yet."

Solberg inspected the image again.

"It's him, isn't it?" Bernie asked.

"Possibly."

Bernie grinned. "My gut says this picture shows Fleming, the evil little putz, riding happy as a clam away from the scene of the crime."

"It's been two days; the guy could be in Idaho Falls by now."

"Doing what, converting to Mormonism? No, he doesn't show up on the next security camera three miles south, or on the one set up on the East Side Highway."

"Did he head north through Lolo?" Solberg asked.

"No photo evidence there either. I figure he's hiding up in the mountains, waiting for things to blow over."

"Problem is..."

"Problem is, the mountains are a death zone," Bernie said. "Unless he found a high lake Malcolm Fleming is either in serious shit or crispy. Can you and your crew go find him once it's safe?"

"Safe? We're two months from safe. Why is Fleming so important to you?"

"Missoula cops found his camp," Bernie said. "It was above town in some bushes."

"You sure it's his?"

"Cops questioned hikers who frequent the open space system and they reported seeing Fleming's furry little face. Nebbish even left some hemp fuse behind for good measure."

"Is that enough to link him to Taylor Creek and Lolo?"

"Forensics says yes. I also have Shelly Pinsonnault's confession.

When I pressured her, she sang like a mockingbird about how she and Fleming set the garbage bag fire on Lucy Beauchamp's ranch. Said it was revenge for Baptiste screwing the Pinsonnaults on a land deal years ago."

"Baptiste Beauchamp was a lying scoundrel," Solberg said.

"Surprised he wasn't president. Anyway, then this Fleming kid conned this Shelly character into placing a second garbage bag bomb on ground her family sold for development. Preyed on her 'I hate Mommy and Daddy' *mishigas*. Turns out Fleming is one hungry ghost, as you called him. Angry as hell about whatever you got."

"Wants power and has none."

"That's the profile of most arsonists. So maybe he's behind these bigger fires."

"Could be. He might be trying to earn the respect of old silverbacks like Tabish."

Bernie nodded. "What about Mann Gulch? You still think Tabish is the guy?"

"Possibly," Solberg said, sitting back. "But that little shit Fleming sure adds to the mix. So does Blanca Chacón."

"I suppose," Bernie said. "We're checking her out and coming up empty. Maybe we were overthinking things."

"Could be. Being ripshit at Merchant doesn't mean you're violent."

"And she's probably afraid of cops, based on her life in East Los Angeles. Explains why she acted weird when we questioned her. Then a *pinche* Anglo like you shows up." Bernie's eyes twinkled.

Solberg smiled. "Which leaves us where we started. A volatile couple, but not arsonists."

"Maybe it's that simple," Bernie said. "But I hate simple."

"Why? Parsimony cuts through the clutter."

Bernie huffed. "Care to translate?"

"All things being equal, choose the explanation with the fewest moving parts."

"That doesn't match my cynical view of humanity. I've seen too many actual conspiracies."

"Fair enough," Solberg said.

Bernie tilted his head. "Alright, Inspector Poirot, who else you got?"

Solberg limped over and shut the door. He sat back down, resting his hands on the table.

"What's with the gimp?" Bernie asked.

"Aviation is inherently dangerous."

Bernie shrugged.

Solberg spoke softly. "Bo ran her GIS magic on these latest fires and I think she's onto something."

Bernie tapped the face of his watch with an index finger.

Solberg took the hint. "Alright, Fleming is too small a fish to have pulled off St. Joseph and these other huge fires. He doesn't have a car, the right motivation, or the brains. But maybe he's in on Mann Gulch, drawn in by Tabish's noise about the evils of Ed Merchant's house. Fleming might have been involved there to suck up to the guy, but not these Bitterroot jobs. Smokejumpers are being dropped in and Fleming would never risk their lives. If someone dies, there goes Rob Tabish's respect. Worse, Tabish would kill the little prick."

Bernie mulled this over. "Unless Fleming had no idea how big these fires would get."

Solberg exhaled. "I guess, but someone else might be setting them."

"Which, as always, leads us back to Bill Knight," Bernie said.

Solberg spoke in a whisper. "Bo's analysis suggests that these new fires are located too effectively to be the work of an amateur. There was clear logic in where they were set. There's only two gaps—the Manor Vista development and Michael Slaton's neighborhood. It would take someone with both experience and nerve to use a lightning storm to cover his tracks like that."

"But why would Knight do it?" Bernie asked. "These fires haven't hurt Slaton."

Solberg sighed. "All I know is that Bill's a wreck. He's exhausted and the anniversary of his wife's death may have pushed him over the edge."

"She died three years ago. Why is he cracking now?"

"Not sure, but…" Solberg hesitated. He was implicating his dear friend.

Bernie waited.

Solberg gathered himself. "Bill Knight studies how fire keeps forests open and healthy. He made a national name for himself by proving that forests are crowded and sick because we put fires out."

"So Smokey Bear is full of shit?"

"Mostly, yes. But now with climate change and fire suppression we've created forests that are unnatural. So when the flames come they wipe out everything in their path."

Katz looked confused. "But what about the people? Is Knight a psychopath?"

"No. He might see too many houses as a problem he needs to solve."

"The land being destroyed by development?" Bernie scratched his head.

"And his wife getting killed by a guy *from* a development."

Bernie Katz nodded. "Makes twisted sense, except..."

"...Bo's maps show that Michael Slaton hasn't been targeted."

"Sure makes Dr. Knight look innocent, doesn't it?" Bernie said.

"It does," Solberg said. "Or it makes him look sinister. Like an owl hooting until a rabbit freaks out and runs."

"Enough with the Wild Kingdom *shtick*," Bernie said, closing his notebook.

Solberg stood up to leave. "Hell, maybe it's really this Paladin dirtbag. They seem bent on making a name for themselves."

"So how can we make sense of someone randomly burning down houses?" Bernie asked.

"We can't," Solberg said.

"Then what do we do?" Bernie asked.

"Figure out how it isn't random."

64

Fire consumed the planet. The sky was a crematorium, like Mount St. Helens had exploded again. That night, firebrands blew in from fires in the Bitterroot Mountains. Burning constellations fell to earth across Missoula. Solberg stood on his widow's walk, hosing down his roof. Whenever a fiery shard landed, he doused it. All over the Lower Rattlesnake, all over the city, his neighbors did the same. Water pressure and hope were dropping.

A text from Becky pinged on Matt's phone. "I read you went up in a plane over the fires. Are you okay?"

He answered right away. "I'm fine. Just hosing down the sky." He added a smiling elephant emoji.

"I wish things were different," Becky wrote.

"This summer is the worst," Matt replied without thinking.

"I don't mean the weather."

"I can be there in nine hours," Matt wrote, feeling his heart jump. A long delay. "When the fires are out, we'll talk."

Solberg was relieved that Becky wanted to finally open up. Assuming that's what she meant. But the tone of her texts worried him. What was she going through over there? Had that douchebag Brace hurt her? He resisted the impulse to get in the truck and just drive to Portland. But Becky was in her twenties and he'd honor that by staying put.

Solberg watched the spectacle rain down on the city. He'd seen burning embers for decades out in the woods, but never in town. Embers took out Wallace, Idaho in 1910. Paradise, California in 2018. Their glowing beauty belied their deadliness. Orange and red fireflies swarming, spinning, dancing, falling everywhere. People launched drones to film the spectacle. Others shot them down.

Missoula was a siege of fire and water. When embers landed in gutters choked with pine needles, unguarded houses burned to the ground. Fire engines wailed everywhere. Embers were a blitz now, miles from the fire front, so beautiful they bewitched people into pause, giving just enough delay for fire to achieve its primal need.

Combustion—fuel, oxygen, flame. No ethics or meaning beyond physics.

Solberg slept on his roof, letting a sprinkler stand guard. When he woke up, the fireflies were gone, but ash turned daylight to dusk and exhaustion to paranoia. There was an irrational fear that these fires might never end. Missoula itself might burn down. Conspiracy theories went viral about who set the fires. Putin, Soros, Hillary, the government.

Fires raged across Montana, and arson was suspected in half of them. People fled to stay with relatives in the farmlands of Eastern

Montana. Others chose the Pacific coast or the rock-bound safety of Utah.

The fires were national news. NBC's Arlene Newcolm reported:

> All we can tell you for now is this—something is happening in Montana that is symptomatic of a general turmoil in the West. It would appear that a war has broken out. Its weapon? Arson. Its target? The houses of rich newcomers in the Bitterroot Valley and other parts of the state. Its outcome? That is what remains unclear.
>
> But authorities have released some information about fires at Big Sky, Flathead Lake, and Lincoln Creek in hopes of getting tips from the public. The arsonist left small action figures at the sites of their burns. According to our sources, the FBI now calls this person Paladin—a reference to a knight protecting a homeland. The name also refers to a 1950s TV western with a gun-slinging hero. Fiction now appears to be fact.
>
> Here's the bottom line, fear is now rising in Montana. And its name is Paladin.

65

Up the Bitterroot Valley, Bill Knight shut off his television. Suspicious fires had destroyed homes all over the state. At first Knight was angry. Maverick fires were contaminating his work. Then he realized that something elegant was happening.

Confusion was in its full glory, forming a perfect disguise. The Colter fire near Red Lodge had killed people, but it was caused by lightning strikes in lodgepole pine forests—ecosystems that are born to burn. The lesson of the gigantic 1988 Yellowstone Park fire went unlearned, and ignorant people paid a karmic price.

Up Lincoln Creek, the *Missoulian* said, Paladin's fire had destroyed sixty-two luxury homes, including the mansion of a hedge fund sleaze. Knight figured the Paladin nickname was ironic and cagey. An homage he didn't want, but one he might use.

In the Bitterroot Valley, things were more complex. Diverse forest types, a patchwork of land development, and both arson and lightning fires. Knight felt confident the underlying pattern of his burns would never be detected. All except the unburned Manor Vista development. It stuck out like a sore thumb. A necessary miss.

Knight thought about the Californians he hated, rechecking what he knew. It was clear they lacked courage or they would have stayed to fix the mess they'd made of their own state. They ran away to Montana, but not to the real place—they ran to the *idea* of Montana. They wanted it easy, and Montana is never easy. Californians sought peace and brought violence. And now they were experiencing what they had fled—a pure burning rage.

Then there was Michael Slaton. Knight had driven by Slaton's house earlier that day to see if the fires had run him off. They hadn't, but Slaton had sent his family away, from the look of things. A sprinkler on the roof leaked a pathetic trickle. Slaton was trimming tree branches using an electric chainsaw suitable for a fifteen-year-old. "You clueless bastard." Knight drove away. Slaton was playing the brave husband defending home and hearth, but so far, all he'd suffered was dread.

When the time was right, Knight might transform dread to agony. The moment spun closer, pulling on him like vile justice.

66

"Paladin, Paladin, where do you roam?" Mary Callahan sang as she drove. The media had finally recognized her skill and damage path. Paladin was exactly the name she'd hoped for. Reporters regressed to a 1950s western, but she'd take it. A quick Internet search revealed what they meant: a tall dark gunfighter with a silver chess piece knight on his holster. She'd even watched an episode of *Have Gun—Will Travel* on YouTube. A black-and-white saga of gunfire justice. "Ah, the '50s," Mary said.

The Lincoln Creek fire had finally put her on the map. The *Missoulian* even showed a Paladin action figure on the front page, which pleased her no end. Below it was an interview with *him;* the prick even got choked up about losing his mansion. His rich daddy would replace it with a much bigger one. "Poor baby," she said, then spit out the window.

Mary Callahan drove in the dark, feeling more powerful than

she'd ever imagined possible. She was now a person to be reckoned with, not what those fools saw when ordering coffee. A nobody. Baristas see it all—rudeness, stress, judgment. More kindness than she'd expected. It was the best job she could get in the Missoula, a whiplash-expensive city where a decent town used to be.

The media coverage was just what she'd hoped for, and she loved feeling famous. It was the best kind of fame: where you don't get recognized on the street. Or at the Griz Bar, listening to Matt Solberg, the head fire wonk for the FBI. A man certain to talk to Dr. Bill Knight, the Dungeon Master. They had no idea who she was and what she'd done. Or what was coming.

Whoever set those fires up the Bitterroot had done extremely well—far better than she'd dared—but they left one prize unclaimed. Mary was back to grab it. Manor Vista. "More like *Hasta la vista*," she said, giggling.

The most beautiful part was this: her next fire would unleash massive doubt and bigger fear. Make it much harder for the Dungeon Master to stay in charge.

"What a splendid turn," she said, pulling off a dirt road. As was her custom, she waited, listening for engines and voices. After a while, she retrieved her tackle from the truck: popcorn boxes, Everclear, plasma lighter, and a quite different Paladin. An Old West version of Richard Boone—the mustachioed heartthrob of that distant horse opera. Found it at a thrift store. Her Wikipedia search of Richard Boone only added to her pleasure. He starred in a 1952 movie—*Red Skies over Montana*. A pretend version of the Mann Gulch fire in which everything turned out hunky-dory. "Have fun—will travel," she sang, then laughed.

As she waited, a teenage girl appeared, riding a ten-speed in the dark. "Howdy, ma'am," the girl said, then she was gone.

A surge of doubt. Real people lived here, souls she didn't know. Ones who may have never done any harm like *he* did. Mary Callahan paused longer this time, choosing her future. "Fuck 'em all."

She moved quickly in case the girl pedaled back and saw her clearly enough to be able to identify her. Popcorn bowls, Everclear, plasma lighter—onward.

67

Fleming was on the run, lost in a nightmare of smoke and glowing ash. After setting his burns at Taylor Creek and Lolo, he'd camped up in the Bitterroot Mountains to lie low before leaving Montana.

A raging wall of fire changed all that. Fleming tried to move downhill to safety, but the flames cornered him. He followed a creek, but got shoved back. Heat seared his skin and baked his eyes. He coughed from the acrid smoke; his nose was choked with soot. Heading downhill was impossible now. No way to reach the protection of the Bitterroot River. Fleming backtracked to a trickling creek, dipped his cap in the water, and doused his head. A moment's relief.

He scanned in all directions. Pulsing red fingers grasped at him from three sides. He looked uphill. There might be protection in the granite cliffs above him. *Rocks don't burn. I'll survive and walk out a fucking hero. All the way to Missoula, cold beer, and goddamn praise. The old man will finally respect me.*

Fleming scrambled uphill, stepping over deadfall, face slashed by branches, legs heavy. He made five hundred feet of vertical advance without stopping. Lungs heaving, vomit rising. *Keep going.* A freight train raced toward him. Bright red light and furnace of heat.

Rocks don't burn.

68

Rob Tabish hiked toward Fleming's camp in the North Hills above Missoula. Huffing, sweating, spitting. "Where the fuck are you?" he cursed.

After twenty minutes, Tabish reached the brushy site. Trash, filthy socks, and flies dining on shit. A beat-up lawn chair lay on its side. Fleming was gone. "Ungrateful prick," Tabish whispered.

The man stared south toward immense smoke plumes rising from the Bitterroot Mountains. A local version of hell. One Tabish knew well from years of parachuting into misery. "Not a place you should be, boy."

The smoke surged higher, powered by unimaginable heat. Thick brown graves made of soot and ash. "Way bigger than a garbage bag bomb, isn't it?" Tabish waved his hand at the fires. "Ah, you're probably just sleeping off a drunk somewhere. Right?" He pissed on the ground and zipped up. "I'll have some burgers waitin' for ya at the house tonight."

Then Rob Tabish hiked back down to his truck, knowing none of that was true.

69

The stink of a burned human body is nauseating, but strangely sweet. Muscles and fat smell like burnt pork. Blood gives off a coppery scent. The brain and spinal fluids emit a rotten musk.

A smokejumper crew descended a ridgeline in the Bitterroot Mountains and caught wind of the stench. The crew chief radioed it in. "Got a victim on the border of the Manor Vista and St. Joseph fires."

"Alive or dead?" the dispatcher asked.

"Past dead."

"Damn. Can you bring the body down?"

"It won't hold together. The legs are burned off and the head has separated. The rest is mostly peeling skin and charcoal."

"What do you mean, mostly?"

"One arm is strangely intact. Must have been tucked under him."

"Any distinguishing traits?"

"Tattoos. A green thunderbolt and an Asian symbol of some kind."

"Get a GPS location, take pictures of the body, and get the hell out of there. There's only one safe route back to the valley. Head northeast, but the wind is rising, so get moving."

"Roger. We're gone."

70

Bernie Katz called sounding breathless. "Matt, we got him."

"Which one?" Solberg asked, fearing it was Knight.

"Fleming."

"Really, you caught the guy?"

"Fire did. Smokejumpers found his body this morning. Get in here."

Ten minutes later, the two men stared at pictures of human remains on Katz's computer. The lower body was a pile of ashes, with two bony trails leading to the remnants of boots. Charred ribs poked out of the chest, the exposed organs roasted and pecked over by birds. One arm was bent, protecting where the head should be. The skull lay two feet away, seared down to blackened bone and empty eye sockets; the mouth was wide open, teeth in a death grimace. Solberg exhaled to keep from puking.

"See those tattoos on the remaining arm," Bernie said, pointing. "There's even a piece of the Chinese one we talked about. It matches the security camera shot."

Solberg studied the image. "Sure looks like it."

"We'll recover the remains once it's safe," Bernie said. "Check the dental records and tie him to these big fires. But for now, there's no rush. The schmuck is as dead as Julius Caesar. Someone even found a Paladin action figure where the Manor Vista fire started—the one he died in. We got him."

Solberg shrugged. "I believe the body is Fleming and maybe he even set this one. But Bo still thinks Knight started most of the large Bitterroot fires. But we've still got two problems—no proof and no harm done to Knight's logical target, Michael Slaton."

"Oh, is that all," Bernie said, smirking.

"I know it sounds unlikely," Solberg said. "But Bill's behavior worries me. He goes back and forth between the man I know and one I don't. He looks pale and exhausted. And I'm really worried about tomorrow."

"What happens tomorrow?" Bernie asked.

"It's the third anniversary of his Molly's death."

"Probably a coincidence. He's had two anniversaries to go off his nut."

"You think I'm wrong?"

Bernie rapped a knuckle on his desk. "As long as Slaton isn't targeted, Bill Knight is clean. And beyond that old memo linking Knight with the Montana Tree Monkeys, which seems like horseshit now, there's nothing to base a charge on."

"Can't you just talk to Bill?"

"And do what, ask him if he's guilty?" Bernie said, smirking again.

"I've worked with the man long enough to know he'd tap-dance around my questions."

"But couldn't you get a sense of his state of mind?"

"Grief isn't the same as guilt," Bernie said.

Solberg sighed in frustration.

"Look," Bernie said, "you know Knight far better than me. Why don't *you* call him?"

"I did and he doesn't answer."

Bernie suddenly looked stern. "Keep trying."

Solberg tapped the arm of his chair. "Did the San Francisco office get back to you about what the Chinese symbol on Fleming's body means?" he asked.

Bernie fanned through a folder and handed Solberg a printed email. "See if you can make sense of this."

Solberg read the report. "The symbol isn't clear, given the damage to the body, but it could mean a number of things: harmony, balance, or sex. One meaning of the tattoo is 'to ease Nature.'"

Bernie started at a picture of Fleming's remains. "He doesn't look too easy now, does he?"

Solberg flinched. "I'd go with it—to ease Nature."

"Why?" Bernie asked.

"Because it explains a lot."

71

Solberg called Bill Knight for the fourth time. Still no answer, so he sent another text. Knight had been out of touch for several days and it was worrisome.

A moment later, Bo texted Matt to meet her in the Geography Lab at 7:30 sharp the next morning. She had something *very* important to show him. Her curt instructions meant she was still plenty pissed about their fight.

Matt slept poorly and arrived early. Bo sat working at a computer. "Hey there," he said.

Bo turned around, but didn't smile.

Matt sat down beside her. He could feel the anger radiating from her body. "I'm sorry I didn't listen to you at first. What you said about Bill Knight was brutal."

"Okay, but when you told Bernie, did he take it seriously?"

"He listened at first. But now that Fleming's body has been found, he's laying the blame on that fool."

Bo slapped the table in frustration. There was an awkward silence. Then Bo said, glaring at Matt, "Look, we had a fight the other day because I felt ignored and dismissed. Women feel that a lot. Do you understand?"

"I do," Matt said, folding his hands.

"Women still struggle to be taken seriously, even in the sciences where data are queen. Bernie is one thing, but I expected a lot better from you."

"I'm really sorry, Bo. I was a bonehead."

"Damn right," Bo said.

Matt reached out, but she rejected his hand.

Bo leaned forward. "You can *never* treat me that way again. Do you understand precisely what I'm saying?"

"You've got my word," Matt said, nodding.

Bo stayed tense. "Okay, but there's a lot more going on, isn't there?"

"There is," Matt said.

She softened. "Matt, we need to *talk* about things. About your wife's death, your need to save people, my parents' struggles as immigrants, my fears. I have big dreams too and some of them are about us."

Matt's eyes got wide.

"I know you're scared of committing," Bo said. "Me too."

"I tried it once and failed, you know."

"I'm not sure that's the right word," Bo said.

"What is?"

"There's a list," Bo said. "For each of us."

They sat in silence until Bo finally spoke. "I know someone who can help us talk. Are you willing to do that?"

"Completely," Matt said.

"What a perfect answer," Bo said. "And it might help you get closer to Becky. You agree?"

Matt nodded and held Bo's hand. They sat, flesh touching flesh, until their breathing calmed.

"Alright," Bo said, exhaling. "The FBI blames Fleming for everything, but I don't. You ready to do some geography?"

"Please," Matt said.

She turned to her computer and clacked away. "Here's my latest analysis of the Bitterroot fires." One by one, five bright red dots appeared on a satellite image.

Matt studied the pattern. "The points form a wonky square. Are these St. Joseph and the other big burns?"

"Yes, their points of ignition," Bo said. "Notice anything they have in common?"

"Ponderosa pine forests. Places I'd expect to torch in a year like this."

"Me too," Bo said. "But there's more." Another layer of points flashed on the screen in vivid orange. "These are the locations of current *lightning-caused* fires. Eleven of them."

"The dots don't match up," Matt said.

"No, they don't," Bo said. "It's highly unlikely that any of the burns I showed were caused by lightning."

Matt shrugged. "They could have been started by stray fireworks, untended campfires, chainsaw sparks. Any number of things."

"Except for the Manor Vista fire," Bo said. "Paladin, whoever they are, left an action figure there, but nowhere else. This time the TV gunslinger version. The kind an older person would use."

Solberg sighed his agreement. "Someone like Bill Knight. Could be a clue; could be a ruse by Fleming or someone else. Strange that the only fire with fatalities has Paladin's signature on it."

"Three young kids died," Bo whispered. She hesitated then dove back in. "But look at this next layer." She called up more information, this time displayed as light purple boxes. All the red dots—the suspicious fires—were located inside one.

"The points of ignition are all inside major subdivisions. Matches what we know." Matt scratched his arm. "Could it be Rob Tabish? He's got a real axe against mansions."

Bo shook her head "Improbable. Trailers and homemade houses were lost in the Manor Vista fire. Besides, there's no smokejumper connection, right?"

"Maybe he lost his focus."

Bo shrugged. "Let this next layer speak for itself." She worked the keyboard until a black frame emerged on the screen.

Matt stared. "That line puts a boundary around the fires. Maybe travel time by car."

"Good eye," Bo said. "I ran a gravity model using that variable."

"The northern one doesn't help," Matt said. "Half of Missoula could be involved."

The eastern line split the crest of the Sapphire Mountains. Matt pointed at it. "No one lives up there. What about the western boundary up Lolo Creek?"

Bo shrugged. "I massaged the data to create a point that wasn't in the middle of a huckleberry patch. Sleeman Gulch comes the closest."

"But you've got little confidence in it," Matt said.

"Low confidence, for sure," Bo said. "Sleeman is its own world. A peaceful, dead-end valley full of folks who lack a motive."

"You don't burn down what you can't see," Matt said.

"A reasonable assumption. Which leaves..."

"The entire Bitterroot Valley," Matt said, sighing.

"Not all of it." Bo sat back and let him think.

All five big arson fires were anchored on the south by a black line at Bell Crossing Road. Their points of ignition were a twenty-minute drive away. The Bitterroot Valley was widely known for crime, including arson, but its salty mixture of gypo loggers, hippie carpenters, stockbroker billionaires, and conspiracy trolls made it hard to figure out who was responsible.

Bo's new analysis changed all that. Her model showed a powerful correlation between targeted subdivisions and travel time from Bell Crossing Road. Bo zoomed in on the image, highlighting Bill Knight's house. She spoke softly. "When you said how strange Bill's been acting lately, I dug in deeper. I'm not saying he..."

"It's alright," Matt said. "I have my doubts. But this is just one set of fires."

"More data would improve the model," Bo said. "But..." Her voice trailed off.

Matt sat rigidly, considering the paranoid geography in front of him.

"Just remember," Bo whispered. "Correlation is not causality."

Matt shook his head. "Except when it is."

Bo looked solemn. "One more thing." She clicked the keyboard and three large Xs appeared on the image.

"What are those?" Matt asked, dreading the answer.

"Given the pattern of burned and unburned ground, these are the three most likely places the next fire will be set."

"They're predictions."

"Yes," Bo said.

"And if you're right, the real target is here," Matt said, pointing. Michael Slaton's house.

72

"So you and Bo are convinced I'm full of shit about Fleming," Bernie said, slouching at his desk.

"Not completely full of shit, just mostly," Solberg said, deadpan.

"Oh, so kind of you," Bernie said, smirking. "And you still don't know where Knight is?"

"I haven't a clue," Solberg said. "I've called, texted, emailed, checked his office, even driven by his house. Bill Knight has fallen off the face of the Earth."

"Damn," Bernie said. "Maybe he heard about Fleming's death and made a run for it?"

"Meaning he worked with that creep? No, he's probably doing fieldwork."

"In this chaos?"

"Work calms him down. Especially when the world goes crazy."

"And you're sure *he* hasn't gone crazy?" Bernie asked.

"Issue a phony press release to shake things up. See if he, Tabish, or Paladin responds."

"Saying what?" Bernie asked.

"I took the liberty," Solberg said, handing Katz a sheet of paper.

The body of an unidentified person was discovered by smokejumpers in the Bitterroot Mountains this morning. The victim died in the area torched by the Manor Vista and St. Joseph fires. The body was severely burned, but physical evidence, including very distinctive arm tattoos, provides a lead on who might have perished. The FBI is investigating a possible link between the deceased and a series of recent arson-caused forest fires in the Bitterroot Valley. The Agency will recover the body soon and report back once dental records determine the identity of the corpse. We look forward to closing this case in the near future.

Bernie finished reading and nodded his approval.

"The release does three things," Solberg said. "First is public safety. It sends a strong message that conditions are still extremely dangerous. The second effect is strategic—it tells the real arsonist that someone was killed in their fire. The third is far riskier. It sends the false impression that the FBI is pinning all the Bitterroot fires on a dead guy."

"Maybe a false impression," Bernie said, waving a finger. He stared at the memo. "Your reference to tattoos means Fleming is toast. If he and Tabish collaborated on Mann Gulch and elsewhere, that fact might back him off or bring him forward. You never know. If it's Paladin, we're back to nothing." Bernie paused, then leaned forward. "And if Bill Knight is setting fires, the news that he killed someone might shock him into stopping or confessing. But the suggestion that the FBI is homing in on another suspect to blame for *all* the fires might lure him into going after Michael Slaton."

"Damn, I hope not," Solberg said.

Bernie Katz shrugged. "Look, all this depends on Bo's prediction about where Knight will strike next, and on your ability to stop him."

"Me?" Solberg said, stunned. "With no agents in support? You reamed me out for *talking* to Tabish by myself. What's changed?"

"People are dying. Look, you know the Bitterroot far better than anyone I've got. My agents would stand out like a sore thumb."

"There's something else, isn't there, Bernie?" Matt asked with a wry smile.

Katz smiled back. "Like I always say, if the crap flies, I won't get smelly."

73

The next morning, Solberg answered his phone without checking caller ID. "Look, asshole..."

"Whoa," said Bernie Katz.

"Sorry, Bernie, didn't expect to hear from you so soon."

"Who can get under your skin like that?"

"I thought it was Ed Merchant. He sent me tons of emails last night. Guy wants someone to take the blame for Mann Gulch. And he keeps hassling me to find out who."

"And Mann Gulch is where I need to send you."

Matt looked at Bo in shock. She wrapped her arm over his shoulder, listening in.

"Hello," Bernie said. "You still there?"

"Yeah, I'm here. Who's missing?"

"Rob Tabish."

Solberg flinched. "No shit?"

"Zero shit. I guess your bogus press release stirred the pot pretty good."

"What do you mean?"

"Tabish left a weird note in his buddy Jim Steele's mailbox. He turned it over to us right away. It's a rambling thing you need to read before your team goes out."

"Why can't the Lewis and Clark County searchers handle this one?"

"Two reasons. One, you have a vested interest."

"Linda Merchant."

"Correct. And two, you know the ground inside out."

Solberg conceded the point.

"Come to my office, check out the note, then head over. I know you're tired, but I need this done."

Solberg hung up.

"I'm going with you," Bo said, rising to her feet. "And I won't be talked out of it."

Solberg was wise enough not to argue.

He sent a group text to Jake Pengelly, Maile Felder, and Ruga Snead telling them to meet up at his house in the Lower Rattlesnake in one hour. He'd summarize the job, and they'd all caravan over to Mann Gulch.

Ten minutes later, Solberg entered the FBI office. Just as Katz had warned, Tabish's note was long and incoherent. Solberg read it aloud with Bernie listening:

I have lived like a fearsome angel. Dropped into hellholes no man would dare. Brought others with me. Brothers of the silk. Sons of Rufus Robinson and Earl Cooley. The first smokejumpers to float into flames. Defenders, protectors. It was hard to breathe from the heat and goddamn smoke. But we breathed and hacked away at the red-assed beast. And usually we won.

Fleming wanted to be that. He couldn't, the stupid dead bastard. I led him on—used him, really. Had him set that garbage bag bomb fire. Fleming needed me and I needed someone to take the fall. Symbiosis. You ignorant cops reading this can look that one up—evil cocksuckers.

But this fire at Mann Gulch sticks to me and there's no scraping it off my boots. And here comes the whole deal. I never meant to hurt that Merchant girl. I swear I had no earthly idea that anyone was home. Pagan gospel truth, for what it's worth now. We went over there and Fleming just did what I told him to.

He set the Willow Creek fire; I torched the angel's side.

Those thirteen guys in Mann Gulch deserve far better than my sorry ass. I betrayed them. So I'm on the margin now, about to make my last drop. Not worthy of the center stage in that shrine of a draw. I'll have to take my chances on the nosebleed seats just over the edge. Maybe peek down at the markers for a second before I go.

That's all the apology a man can give.

Let no motherfucker say that Rob Tabish ended small!!

"I'll be damned," Solberg said.

Bernie took back the letter. "No, he will be."

A while later, Bo was at the wheel of Matt's pickup as they blasted up Highway 200 toward Mann Gulch. Jake followed in his truck with Maile and Ruga close behind in her Subaru. Matt studied a copy of Tabish's note. "He clearly takes the fall for the Mann Gulch fire. And he takes the blame off Fleming, not that it matters now."

"Do you believe him?" Bo asked.

"Yes. It's painfully honest and full of remorse. The guy was coming clean."

"I agree," Bo said. "It's a suicide note. People don't lie when they're checking out."

Matt read the message again. "What do you make of this part? 'I'm on the margin now, about to make my last drop.'"

"Again, suicide," Bo said. "Feeling marginalized, but the words aren't specific."

Matt studied the note. "Drop means a jump to these guys. Parachuting into a fire."

"Are there any active burns where we're heading?" Bo asked.

"I don't think he was talking about stepping out of a plane."

Bo exhaled heavily.

Matt plowed ahead. "Tabish said he wasn't worthy of 'that shrine of a draw,' meaning Mann Gulch. Outside the markers means the smokejumper crosses, and I'd say 'just over the edge' to him was literal. I suspect we'll find him somewhere on the rimrock."

"A lot of country qualifies," Bo said.

"I know, but what else have we got?"

74

Matt, Jake, Maile, and Ruga gathered around Solberg's pickup at the Departure Point access site on Holter Lake. Bo hung back, not wanting to intrude. She was respected, but not part of the crew.

Lieutenant Goebel of the Lewis and Clark County Sheriff's Office walked up. "The FBI has been throwing its weight around, Matt. We should have been searching for hours."

"I'm sorry," Solberg said. "That's not my call. Just alert the Life Flight helicopter they might have a job."

Goebel spit on the ground. "Tabish's car is parked at the ruins of the Merchant house, but there's no telling where he is." He got on his radio.

Solberg laid a map across the hood of his truck and gave his briefing. "Maile, you search Willow Creek because of your long legs."

"And youth," Maile said. "Don't forget my youth."

Everyone smiled.

"Jake and Ruga, you go up the Missouri River in the sheriff's boat, then sweep uphill through Mann Gulch, checking the ridgelines as you go. I'll cover the rimrock in between and coordinate things, with Bo's support."

There were no grumbles about her involvement. Solberg gathered the team in a circle. "Remember, his name is Rob Tabish."

The crew fanned out.

Matt and Bo drove up Beartooth Road and soon came in sight of the wreckage that used to be Edward Merchant's sprawling log home. They parked next to a beat-up Chevy pickup. First number on the tag was 4—the Missoula County designation. Rob Tabish's rig.

Matt felt the hood of the Chevy. Cold. "Tabish has been here a while," he said. "But the guy isn't in great shape anymore, so he still might be close. Take it slow on the rocks."

"Don't we have to hurry?" Bo asked.

"Slow is smooth, and smooth is fast."

Matt grabbed his search pack and checked Bo's. She carried what he'd asked for: plenty of water, a back-up GPS unit, and a large first-aid kit. They started out, Bo following close behind Matt, periodically checking a topo map. Hiking along the limestone ridge, they found a fresh set of boot prints. Maybe Matt would find Tabish—but probably not alive. He radioed in. "Got a fresh trail along the ridge. Any sign in your areas?"

Jake Pengelly was the first to respond. "Shitloads of sign in the gulch. Probably tourists and movie star stalkers. Hard to know if any of them is Tabish."

"Alright," Solberg said. "Double time it up the drainage. I'm southeast of the house and moving steady. Maile, you got any sign?"

Squawk and static. She was out of range down in Willow Creek canyon.

"If you hear me, Maile, head south toward the main ridge."

Mann Gulch opened up below them. The grasslands were scorched, struggling sprouts poking through the ash. Black skeleton trees were scattered here and there. Living Douglas firs still grew on the Willow Creek side, saved by a fuel break of rock. Each was more than seventy feet tall, with thick side branches.

Matt and Bo grabbed chokecherry bushes to circle outcrops. The prints they followed showed evidence of slipping and sliding. Tabish had had a tough time of it.

Solberg stopped to check the cave where he'd found Linda Merchant. Tabish might choose to die in the same spot. There was a deranged logic to it. Matt stepped over the low rock wall into Linda's fort. Just a lingering burned smell. He looked deep inside the cave. Empty.

The ridge gained elevation and they struggled along jagged rocks. Matt and Bo had to backtrack several times to relocate the boot marks.

The radio blasted static, then a voice pierced through. "Matt, this is Jake. You see what I see?"

Solberg toggled a switch. "What have you got?"

"There's a blue and white shape up a tree. Thing's getting blown around in the wind."

"Does it look like a parachute?"

"Could be, but even with my binoculars, I can't be sure. You're probably only a few hundred yards west of it."

"Thanks, Jake. Stay on your search. Out."

They picked up the pace, scrambling along limestone crags, ignoring the dangerous exposures falling away on both sides. A swath of blue and white fabric appeared up ahead, high in a tall branching fir. A smokejumper's parachute.

Matt and Bo raced to the chute, which was dangling from a stout branch with no one attached. They slid down the slope to where the lines reached the ground. The ends were freshly cut and bloody. A knife lay in the dirt, red from recent use. There were signs of a terrible impact, and a blood-smeared gash ran steeply downhill. Matt and Bo slid downslope on their butts to slow the descent, hands grasping at roots, heels digging in.

Rob Tabish's body was jammed sideways against the base of a huge fir. An arm was broken at a grotesque angle; a leg was in the same condition. Tabish's head was covered with blood and dirt. His throat was branded with blue-black choke marks.

Matt felt the man's neck. No pulse. He tried at the wrist, checking for any sign of life. Weak, erratic taps against his finger. Solberg grabbed his radio. "Jake, Maile—I have Tabish. He's alive, but in bad shape."

Bursts of squawking racket, then Maile's voice. "Can you call in a Life Flight chopper?"

"Negative. I'm below the ridge. Jake probably can't hear me on the other side. And there's no cell service down here."

"Okay, stay with Tabish. I'm almost at the crest," she said, huffing. "I'll call it in when I get there. Give me your GPS position."

Solberg checked his gadget. "Can't, not enough satellites. Bad PDOP. I'll have Bo make smoke so you can find us." He took two signal flares from his pack and handed them to Bo. "Make the ridge above us. Ignite one so Maile can find you."

"Got it."

"When Maile gets there, give the other flare to her and stay put. Clear?"

"Clear." Bo scrambled up the slope on all fours.

Matt returned his attention to Rob Tabish. The man wore an old smokejumper suit covered with ceremonial patches. His knuckles were slashed and crusted with blood. Matt dripped water on Tabish's lips. A faint twitch. He knew he shouldn't move the body—might be spinal damage. There was nothing to be done but wait for a helicopter, which could take a half hour or more. It might be in time.

All he could do was sit with this man who had sinned and tried to hang himself for it. Gently touch his hand to comfort him. Wonder why at the last moment Rob Tabish cut the cords that would free him from this angry Earth.

75

Bill Knight let the mist of Star Falls wet his face. Despite the official closure of the forests, he'd backpacked into the Pintler Wilderness and spent a week alone there. As he grew sicker, the lure of setting a fire to kill Michael Slaton became ever stronger. He'd come to the high mountains to try to pull back from death in all its guises.

Bill Knight leaned against a slender lodgepole pine. For the first time since it happened, he allowed himself to remember every detail of Molly's killing. To feel the loss in every cell. Cauterize the wound once and for all. He closed his eyes. He could swear he heard the collision.

On that bright morning three years ago, he'd kissed Molly good-bye, feeling the lovely lift that simple gesture always gave him. It was only ten minutes before sirens prompted him to get in his truck and speed down Bell Crossing Road. A column of smoke billowed up ahead. Bill Knight screeched to a stop at the scene of the accident on Highway 93.

Molly's car was a burning mass engulfed by the remains of a large SUV. Red flames and black smoke poured from the hulks. Fire equipment was on the scene with people spraying down the carnage. Cop cars were everywhere, lights flashing. Two ambulances blocked traffic. A bleeding man lay on a stretcher being treated by EMTs.

"That's my wife's car!" Knight had shouted. "Where's Molly? Has she been taken to the hospital?"

The cop swallowed hard. "Sir, I'm sorry, but due to the heat, we can't remove Molly yet."

Remove Molly yet. Those three words meant his wife was dead.

With an electric jolt, the world turned black and white. Knight tried to see inside the car through the smoke. White flames flared across his wife's black body.

"No!" Knight wailed. He rushed forward but was held back by cops. "Is that the son of a bitch who killed Molly?!" He broke loose and ran to the stretcher where a man lay covered with blood. "Motherfucker!" Knight screamed. He landed a heavy punch to the man's face, then cops tackled him to the ground.

Knight woke up in the hospital with a tube in his arm and sedatives in his brain. His vision was still black and white. The doctor said it would wear off. "A traumatic response."

The next day he saw colors again, but his soul stayed binary. Innocent or guilty. Alive or dead. The man who killed Molly was named Michael Slaton. He was guilty and he was still alive.

The following weeks were a blurry nightmare: a hastily arranged service, a wooden box full of ashes, distant family members, rare friends like Matt Solberg, words of condolence that meant nothing. No sleep, no food, no future. It didn't seem real. Molly was dead, the woman who had ended Bill Knight's isolation and given him a life.

Michael Slaton was only superficially injured. The investigation showed he wasn't drunk. There were no witnesses. Bill Knight had a lawyer push the cops to file vehicular manslaughter charges. At the hearing, one of the EMTs testified that Slaton said he was texting at the time of the crash. "The man said over and over. 'I'm sorry. It was my fault. I was sending a text.'"

Slaton's California lawyer had argued back: "My client was dazed after the crash. He suffered a concussion and has no memory of saying that." The case went nowhere and Michael Slaton went home to his wife, two kids, and a palace built in the Bitterroot trees.

Knight filed a civil suit that met the same fate. No settlement and no penalty. No justice for killing everything Bill Knight had.

One time, Michael Slaton apologized to Knight outside the courthouse. "I'm very sorry for your loss," he said, not making eye contact. That was it.

Slaton's apology was pointless. Molly was gone and his words were horseshit. Nothing would bring her back. Nothing would *ever* bring her back.

The whisper of Star Falls eased Knight into to the present. He opened his eyes and stretched. Despite its brutality, Molly's death felt more in the past now.

His rested his trembling hands on a mat of purple mountain heather. The shaking eased and stopped. His heart rate slowed and Bill Knight felt the Earth spinning patiently beneath him. A cow moose stood in willows beside a creek, watching him with curious eyes. "Is there a heaven for moose?" he asked her.

She went back to eating tender branches.

"You're already in heaven, aren't you?" Knight smiled.

Somehow he felt less tormented. His body and spirit were diseased, but the wilderness offered the prospect of relief. His rational mind knew that cancer scoffed at solitude as a cure. The same for grief and revenge. Bill Knight looked at his last picture of Molly, happy and smiling. She would want him to be kind. Molly would want him to live.

76

Linda Merchant was healing. Even on a Zoom call, Solberg could see her scars fading. She had time now—a life now.

"And you're sure those guys are the ones who set the fires?" Linda asked.

"Malcolm Fleming is dead and Rob Tabish will never hurt you again. I promise."

Linda smiled even as tears ran down her face. She carefully wiped them away with a cloth. "Thank you," she said softly.

"You're welcome," Solberg said.

No need to speak for a while.

"Oh," Linda said, smiling. "Blanca is taking me to Universal Studios tomorrow. We're going to the Jurassic Park exhibit, King Kong, and the Mummy. It's my first trip since the fire."

"That sounds great," Solberg said. "But aren't those monsters scary?"

"They used to be."

Solberg got her point. "I've never been."

"You should come down sometime. My dad can set up a VIP tour."

"Not sure I'm worthy of that."

"You are."

"So are you."

Linda smiled.

"Is your dad there?" Solberg asked.

"Yes. Just promise you'll come and see me," Linda whispered.

Solberg nodded. "I give you my word."

Linda beamed. "I'll get my dad." She walked away. A large living room with a high ceiling filled the screen.

Then Ed Merchant appeared. "Matt! Good to see you."

"Ed. I'm so glad Linda is doing better."

"Kid's tough. Lots more work ahead, but she's being treated by the best plastic surgeons in the world."

"Linda deserves it," Solberg said.

Merchant grew serious. "I really appreciated your call last night. The news that you caught the bastards pleased me no end. One dead and the other mangled sounds about right."

Solberg felt anger rise, then thought about his own daughter. "I suppose you're entitled to feel that way."

"Is there any other way to feel about it?" Merchant looked incredulous.

"Sorry we suspected you and Blanca. It wasn't personal."

"Wasn't personal?" Merchant said. "You try living with the FBI up your ass for months, then get back to me."

"You're right. I'm sorry. How's Blanca?"

"Pissed off, but focused on Linda. They've got a real bond. I can't believe you guys went after her."

"We got it wrong."

"In every way. Blanca is tough but not mean, despite the way we fight sometimes. We're both hot tempered is all. After we broke up, I really missed the woman. She's my best chance at being a better man. Sounds corny, I know. But that's why I crawled back to her."

Solberg was moved by the emotion of his words. "I guess from here, we just turn it over to the justice system."

Merchant reverted to form. "Justice would be this asshole Tabish dying of his injuries before he gets to court. Bastard had a chance to hang himself and make things right, but he didn't have the stones to go through with it. Pathetic."

"I've gotta go," Solberg said. His momentary gooey feelings for Merchant had vanished.

Merchant felt the brush-off. "Okay. I just want to thank you again for all you've done. Linda thinks the world of you."

"Likewise. She's a brave kid to put up with all the crap she's seen."

Merchant's face twitched from the shot. "Alright, Matt. Where are you going now?"

"The hospital to check on Rob Tabish."

Merchant scowled. "Pull the plug, will you?"

"Not likely," Solberg said.

"I know, but I want him to *pay!*"

Solberg exhaled. "He already has."

"How?"

"By living."

77

Bernie Katz waited at the door of St. Patrick's Hospital as Solberg strode up.

"Sorry to be late, I was Zooming with Merchant."

"Had that privilege earlier," Bernie said. "He still barking about payback?"

"Yup, but I gave him something to chew on."

Bernie shrugged. "Tabish is out of the ICU. Doc says we can talk to him briefly."

"He conscious?"

"Pretty boring if he wasn't."

The door to room 304 was closed. A uniformed cop sat in a chair out front.

"Why the guard?" Solberg asked Bernie.

"Death threats. More than a dozen."

Solberg nervously scanned the corridor.

They entered the hospital room. What was left of Rob Tabish lay on a bed. His right arm and left leg were encased in plaster casts. His throat was bandaged where the parachute cord had ripped in deep. His face was a mash of bruises and slashing cuts.

Solberg walked to the bedside. Bernie held a tape recorder.

Tabish's lashes fluttered open and he looked up at Solberg with bloodshot eyes. "Here to gloat?" he rasped. His voice was hoarse from the aborted hanging.

"Maybe," Solberg said. "You want a lawyer present?"

"Fuck, no. I already talked to the cops. Let Big Fed record me all he wants."

"Alright, why did you do it?" Solberg asked, zeroing right in.

"You know why."

"Protecting Mann Gulch," Solberg said. "Is that all it was about?"

"Mostly."

"What else?"

"I got old and ran out of memories. Wanted to leave a big one behind."

Solberg held back a curse. "But why did you set the fires in May? Why not wait until summer?"

"I didn't want anyone to be home, especially that girl."

"Honor among assholes," Solberg said.

Tabish gave him a fuck-you stare.

Solberg returned the favor. "You're note is clear about Fleming being part of this. Was he the only one?"

Tabish looked at FBI Agent Bernie Katz. "Could be."

"Did anyone help you locate where to set the fires?" Solberg asked. "Could be."

Solberg scowled. "Did Fleming set any other fires?"

Tabish shook his head. "That's your job to figure out. But I sure had you guys going with that Montana Tree Monkeys bit, didn't I?"

"We only chased that for a while," Bernie said.

"No, I yanked your chains pretty good." Tabish looked amused.

"What about the pyrometric cones at the site?" Matt asked. "How did you figure that out?"

Tabish relished the moment. "There's an old lady potter I know who hates the newcomers. She's damn good, right?"

"No, she's not good at all," Solberg said.

"Well, Boy Scout, you'll never catch her. Missoula is full of elder hippies with potter's wheels. The mother lode."

"Point is, we were on to *you*," Bernie said. "We just lacked the proof. And you were kind enough to provide it with that suicide note."

Tabish smirked.

Solberg ignored it. "If you wanted to leave behind a big memory, why did you cut yourself down?"

Tabish frowned. "Weakness."

"Can't argue with that. Do you feel remorse?"

"For surviving?"

"For Fleming's death and nearly killing an eleven-year-old girl."

Tabish nodded. "I suppose I do."

"You sounded a lot sorrier in your letter."

"Thought I was done for when I wrote it." He pointed to a copy of the *Missoulian* on the bedside stand. "Paper says a shitload of rich assholes are leaving the state because of all the fires. Maybe I just got the ball rolling. Who knows? History might call me a goddamn hero." He winked at Matt.

Solberg signaled to Bernie to leave them alone. Katz smiled and walked out, shutting the door behind him.

Solberg leaned over Tabish. "I know you're high on painkillers, but listen close. When you're healed enough to go on trial, they'll throw you in Deerlodge Prison for a stretch of years."

Tabish's smirk was back. "I'll pay for what I did. And after that, it's none of your fucking business."

Solberg leaned closer. "You said you wanted to create new memories, so here's a dandy. If you get out of prison and hurt Linda Merchant or anyone again, I will fuck you up."

Tabish huffed. "Big talk, college boy."

Solberg sighed. "Yes, it is, but I suspect it won't come to that."

"You think I'm afraid of you?"

Solberg smiled wickedly. "No, I'm sure you're not. That's why this college boy just posted photos of Linda Merchant on the prisoners' Internet site at Deerlodge. Photos with her ear and hair burned off. Ones with skin grafts looking like pork rinds on that sweet girl's face."

Tabish looked shocked.

Solberg nodded. "You'll have quite a welcoming committee in prison. Genuine badasses who will see you as a child abuser. You know what happens to child abusers in the joint?"

Tabish trembled.

Solberg whispered, "You shouldn't have cut the noose."

78

Bill Knight got home from his backpacking trip in the Pintlers and took a long shower. He felt more like himself again. Up in the mountains, with images of Molly fresh and fair, he'd decided to accept cancer treatments. Upon reflection, the science was plausible. He'd even try to pull back from vengeance against Michael Slaton.

Knight changed clothes and sat down at the dining room table, snacking on potato chips. He flipped on the laptop to check the news. A headline roared from the screen: ARSONIST KILLED IN BITTERROOT

FIRES. Knight gasped and read the story, including the FBI press release. The deceased was unidentified, but said to be of interest to the Feds for setting major forest fires. The perp had distinctive tattoos on his arms. He was found dead in the middle of what, Bill Knight feared, was one of his burns.

The Good Doctor couldn't catch his breath. He'd killed Fleming.

That cretin had tattoos, but then again, lots of cretins did—so maybe it wasn't him at all. But Knight's gut told him it was Fleming, especially considering all the coaxing he had given the sick guy. He thought of everything and nothing as the room spun and nausea filled his gut.

Murder.

Maybe Michael Slaton deserved to die for killing Molly, but until now violence had felt abstract to Knight. A crude theory. A fantasy algorithm. Besides, his plan was never supposed to harm anyone else.

Knight walked outside and paced, trying to calm his mind by working through the facts. The dead are more common than the living. That is a corporeal certainty. Fleming had simply been in the wrong place. Stupidly, lethally so. Most of the fire risk information Knight had shared with Fleming was available online so maybe he wasn't to blame for the guy setting burns. And even if he was, maybe the world was better off without him.

Knight exhaled heavily. He'd provided ample escape routes in his own fires; only houses were lost and no one was seriously injured. It was a seamless plan, but then the press said this Paladin imbecile had torched the Manor Vista development and killed three kids. Knight *knew* that place was too dangerous.

But whose fire had killed Fleming? His or Paladin's? Did it matter? Knight went inside and got a drink of water at the kitchen sink. A blue ceramic vase—Molly's favorite—sat empty on the windowsill as if she'd simply forgotten to put daisies in it. An oversight easily fixed when she got home. They'd walk over to the spring creek, pluck a handful, and make things sweet again.

Knight found brief respite in this illusion. Then reality rushed back. One way or another he'd killed Fleming. No rationalization could change that and no atonement would ever be enough.

Molly was finally gone in every measure. Extinct.

Lightning slashed and thunder pounded. The pull of gravity from a dying sun.

79

"Got time for scotch?" Solberg asked on the phone.

Hesitation on the other end of the line. "I'm in the lab, finalizing things," Bill Knight said. "What's on your mind?" He tried to sound casual.

"Tomorrow's the third anniversary of Molly's death," Solberg said. "Thought you could use some company."

"Kind of you," Knight said. He bit his lip.

"I'll be there in ten minutes." Solberg hung up and turned to Bo. "Alright, show me those maps again."

Bo displayed the current status of all fires in the Bitterroot Valley on her screen. "Here's the hole in the donut," she said, pointing. Northwest of Bell Crossing was a rough circle of unburned land about a mile in diameter. All the stands around it were torched. The presence of absence.

Bo clicked her mouse. "This GIS layer shows all new houses built inside the donut hole over the past decade. There are only five and the red star is Michael Slaton's."

Matt couldn't believe it. "The arsonist distracted us with fires in newcomer developments, didn't he? Except for Manor Vista, which confused things, right?"

"It did," Bo said. "But everywhere else has burned except this one area. Exactly where Slaton built his place in the middle of old-guard Bitterrooters. And while we were chasing clusters of Californians, Bill Knight bided his time."

"God, I hope you're wrong," Matt said. "I'm praying it's Paladin."

"Me too," Bo said. "But there's only one way to know. Stake out the place and wait."

"Make that two ways," Matt said. "If Knight shows up, it's him. If he doesn't, Paladin becomes the primary suspect."

"Or it's neither," Bo said. "Or it's the wrong night."

"I love your brain." Matt kissed her on the forehead and left.

The campus was eerily empty as Solberg moved across the grassy oval. Main Hall was dark. Even the university president stayed home during the firestorm. Solberg walked slowly up the steps to the Fire Ecology Research Center. This might be his last scotch with Bill Knight. He paused at the door, then entered.

Knight was staring into his microscope. "Tell me what you see."

Solberg took a chair beside the Good Doctor. Knight yielded the scope and Solberg peered in. "Looks like a classic sequence of rings with dry and wet years. The fire scars ended decades ago when the land was grazed and settled."

"Notice anything unusual?" Knight asked.

"No, I guess I don't." Solberg pulled back and looked at Knight. "That's the point, Matt. Despite all the work I do, nothing changes."

"Data don't make decisions," Solberg said. "Idiosyncratic human beings do."

"Tragic," Knight said, trying for a smile. He walked slowly over to his desk, pulled a bottle of Laphroaig from a drawer, and filled two shot glasses. His hands shook as he poured.

Solberg took his usual place, the student's chair in front of the teacher. The men lifted the whisky and toasted in the air. Decades of friendship hung suspended.

"You look exhausted, Bill. Are you okay?"

Knight blew by the question. "I heard about Rob Tabish. Guess we know why he took my fire seminar so many times."

Solberg shrugged. "It wasn't your fault, Bill. Guy surrendered to rage."

"Not my fault," Knight said under his breath.

Solberg took a sip of whisky. "It's hardly a shock that Tabish set the Mann Gulch fires. At least in hindsight. That MTM code was a stupid gimmick."

"That distracted us for a while," Knight said.

"Cover stories fall apart eventually," Solberg said. He stared at Knight until the man averted his eyes.

"Did Tabish work alone?" Knight asked, the usual power gone from his voice.

"We think an unknown potter came up with those fire cones." Tabish's suicide note about him and Fleming hadn't been released. Solberg wanted to see what Knight would reveal without that knowledge.

"As I suspected, he had a youngster helping him," Knight said, eyes back on Matt. "Mann Gulch is too big for a broken-down sixty-year-old to cover alone."

The men savored their whisky. The old clock ticked on the wall.

"Any idea who the guy was who died in the Bitterroot fires?" Knight asked, looking at his glass. He swirled the liquor around slowly, like the question meant nothing to him.

"Not yet," Solberg lied.

Knight stared at him. "But they figure he's the big arsonist in the valley?"

"It appears so," Solberg said.

"Appears or is?" Knight asked.

Solberg shrugged, giving nothing away.

"Was it this idiot Paladin?" Knight asked, looking right at Matt.

"We'll know if the fires stop."

Knight slowly refilled his glass, thinking. He looked ashen.

Solberg stared at the framed Aldo Leopold quote hanging crookedly behind Knight. A THING IS RIGHT WHEN IT TENDS TO PRESERVE THE INTEGRITY, STABILITY, AND BEAUTY OF THE BIOTIC COMMUNITY. IT IS WRONG WHEN IT TENDS OTHERWISE. "What would Leopold say about these fires?" Matt asked, trying for a smile.

"He *died fighting* a fire," Knight said with disgust. "What does that tell you?"

Solberg was stunned.

Knight shook his head. "It says that even great men make foolish choices."

Solberg set his whisky down. The Good Doctor was on the brink of honesty, but sorrow held him back. *But honesty about what?* Matt took a gamble. "Bill, it's not too late to put things right."

"What do you mean?" Knight's face hardened.

Solberg looked into his eyes. "In time, maybe a fresh start."

Knight help up one arm theatrically. "Time is a game played beautifully by children."

"Merle Haggard?"

"Heraclitus."

The men smiled like it was old times.

Solberg took a bigger leap. "Molly wouldn't approve of what you're doing."

Knight stiffened. "What are you talking about, Matt?"

Solberg poured himself more scotch, stalling, trying to conjure the right words to reach his friend. "Bill, if you're in trouble I can help you."

Knight almost smiled. "My words have forked no lightning."

"Dylan Thomas," Solberg said, sighing.

Bill Knight lifted his glass and finished it. The bottle was empty.

80

At midnight, Solberg parked his pickup in a gravel pit just off Red Crow Road. All the houses he'd passed were abandoned, porch lights left on. *Evacuation* means many things. Exodus, expulsion, flight.

Solberg staked out the "donut hole," as Bo called it. A curious circle of unburned ground with Michael Slaton's house in the center. Solberg flipped on a mini-Mag flashlight to check the map again. Bo had marked three locations she thought had the right combination of forest fuels, topography, and wind fetch to attract attention. Michael Slaton's house was in the damage path of all three.

Solberg got out of the truck, limped twenty feet away, and took a leak. His knee still hurt from the bashing it had taken in the scout plane. Back in the truck, he checked his pack. The usuals were there, except for a .357 that Bernie Katz insisted he carry. It felt ridiculous—except it wasn't. Solberg half heard his father Nels's voice. "Better to have and not need than to need and not have." Solberg checked the weapon. The .357 was loaded, a round in the chamber, safety on. He returned it to the pack.

His plan was to get some rest, then at 2 a.m. begin a slow, lights-off patrol of the three sites Bo recommended. Walking would be far better, but his banged-up knee made that difficult. Early morning also seemed less than ideal—that was when fires rested.

But in these tinder-dry conditions, 2 a.m. was perfect. Darkness, no traffic, and people sound asleep. And while humidity would be up and the winds down at that hour, this only made the arsonist's work easier. A fire they set might slumber until the first breath of sunlight awakened it. By then, the arsonist would be safely home when the destruction began. Solberg's goal was to stop all that from happening. His faint hope was that it wasn't Bill Knight after all. Maybe it was Paladin or some other lost soul.

Solberg lay down along the bench seat of the old Ford and tried to sleep.

81

Bill Knight woke up to the clang of an old alarm clock: 1:30 a.m. He sat on the edge of his bed, groggy, until a lightning flash jarred him awake. Thunder rumbled in twenty seconds later. The storm was only four miles away, likely the Bitterroot crest, just as the Weather Bureau predicted. A fine diversion. Knight looked at a calendar tacked to the wall. July 28. The date of Molly's death.

Knight got dressed, gulped a cup of reheated coffee, and double-checked his pack. Two bottles of water, cigar lighter, backup lighter, candy bar, and two gallons of gasoline in a metal can. No need for subtlety now. One last job to do. By dawn, he'd be frying eggs and bacon, taking a shower, then changing clothes and trajectory. He'd get treated for prostate cancer and head back to his lab cured and hearty. They'd be fires to analyze, articles to write, scotch to drink with Matt Solberg once all this died down. He'd fool everyone.

Bill Knight pretended all that was true.

82

Solberg waited on Kootenai Loop Road. Bo thought it was the most probable of the three locations her model predicted. Solberg had his doubts. The run-up to Slaton's mansion was the shortest, but there was a ravine in between.

He considered staking out Knight's house. Just wait for him to leave and bird-dog the man until he made his move. But Knight was far too intelligent not to notice someone trailing him, especially at night on the quiet roads of rural Montana. So it came down to this shell game.

There was nothing moving on Kootenai Loop except smoke, which drifted by like roasted fog. Even in the dark, the place looked fated to burn. Pines sagged from water stress. Snowberry bushes drooped under thick coats of cinders.

A lightning bolt ripped overhead and thunder rattled the truck windows. Solberg cringed. "Madness."

83

Bill Knight gathered his pack and checked the house. The day before, he'd removed the hard drive from his computer, wrapped it in a used burger bag, and tossed it in a trash barrel at the Conoco station in Victor. Then he burned his notebooks in a rock-ringed campfire.

Now all those precautions felt pointless. His experiment had taken on a grim life of its own. He paused at the kitchen door for one last look. It had been a loving home once. Molly's home. He felt like saying something, but there was no one left to hear. Even his last picture of Molly was thrown away with the hard drive. No trace of her left to see what he was about to do.

Knight got in the old GMC and eased onto Bell Crossing Road. The clock on the dash read 2:08 a.m. Nobody parked at the river access site. When the sun and temperatures rose, the beach would be mobbed with people seeking cool relief in the Bitterroot.

He stopped at the flashing light at Highway 93. Knight avoided looking at the cross commemorating where Molly had died. With gentle acceleration he went on, smoothly working the gears, barely pressing down on the gas. He steered through a bend below the old Curlew Mine, smoke obscuring the edges of things, barns and fields blurring together.

Knight moved forward, knowing his destination, fearing it. The attraction was impossible to resist. Finally, tonight, now.

84

Solberg coaxed the truck door open. He'd removed the bulb in the cab light. The world stayed dark except for the red glow of fires on the mountainsides. He paused to let his eyes adjust. Lightning flayed the sky and a crush of thunder pressed down. Solberg's arms rose in self-defense. "Shit," he whispered.

He collected himself and ate peanut M&Ms. Then he limped down a ranch road and stood vigil, leaning against a fencepost. Smoke sifted by, ebbing and rising. One moment he could see fifty yards, the next everything closed back in. People who spend a lifetime outdoors develop a sensory genius for negotiating the world in dim conditions. Something about millions of footfalls teaching the terrain to skin. The rise and fall of landforms, the pattern of trees, shrubs, and stones. The tactile signature of a physical world.

Matt Solberg was one of those people, but Bill Knight was too. It was a standoff at best, because if the Good Doctor was setting fires, he knew exactly where he was going.

Solberg could only wait.

85

Riddick Road. Bill Knight sat for ten minutes before getting out of his truck. He stepped into the red-fire night, moving slowly to mute the sound of cones and sticks crunching under his boots. Now and then, he stopped and listened for the alarm bark of a dog or the shout of a person. They never came. Most of the houses he passed were vacant, people wisely trading property for life. Besides, those modest structures were of no interest to him.

Knight took a meandering route around young pines until a pasture opened up ahead of him. The glowing firelight made Knight feel exposed, but there was no choice now. He made it to a rancher's outbuilding with a tractor and hay rake stored inside. The shed backed up to a stand of dry brome grass funneling toward a steel fence on the southern border of Michael Slaton's property. His mansion was just three hundred yards away in the trees.

A volley of lightning illuminated a row of dying pines along the margin. Knight stood back, observing. His St. Joseph fire still raged to the north and the Three Badger was wreaking havoc straight west. There would be no marriage of the two burns as he'd hoped, but perhaps there was no need; enough had already been destroyed on those faraway slopes.

He looked at the smoldering sky, willing down a lightning bolt to reprieve him. The branches of the half-dead pines stretched upward a hundred feet. They were perfect lures, the tallest trees around, with abundant fuel covering the ground.

Conditions were ideal. Knight would wait, but only so long.

86

Solberg checked his watched—3:18 a.m. Nothing happening at the Kootenai site. Bo was convinced this was the place, but Solberg's gut told him it wasn't. He made it back to the truck, swigged water, and checked his map, shielding the faint light of his mini-Mag with one hand. He'd bypass Bo's second choice and head directly to her third.

It was close by. So close that Solberg feared the sound of his truck would give him away. He slowly guided the Ford, headlamps off, through the turns of Old Schoolhouse Road. He knew the way by heart. He parked at the abandoned school building, where his grandfather had learned English and forgotten Norwegian.

Lightning jitterbugged across the sky, but thunder took longer to arrive. The storm was moving north. Solberg found his stride, pushing past the irritating throb in his knee. His instincts said the next site was it. Even odds the land was already on fire.

87

Knight shook his head in frustration. The lightning storm was headed north, so trees wouldn't be struck after all. He knew the odds of such a thing were low—really more of a wish. No time for hope anymore.

He lowered his pack and felt inside. The familiar shape of the cigar lighter filled his right hand. Then the angular steel of a can of gasoline. Both were blunt, reliable tools, and generic enough to be untraceable.

Bill Knight scanned in all directions. Safe. He eased past an oily shed. Setting the tractor on fire would be a pointless misdirection, so he felt the grasses. No moisture left. Knight unscrewed the can and sprinkled gasoline on the plants, then trailed a swath toward Slaton's million-dollar fence line. The useful breeze would take it from here. He resealed the sloshing can, returned it to his pack, and strapped it back on.

The power of the cigar lighter felt like overkill, but Knight was taking no chances. He gathered a handful of dry grass and touched it with a blast of blue-hot flame.

"Hey!" came a shout. "What are you doing?!"

Knight wheeled around, blinded by a wall of flames. He recognized Matt Solberg's voice, tossed the torch onto the gas-soaked ground, and ran into the trees toward his truck.

Solberg ran up, limping. "Bill!" he shouted. "I know it's you! Stop!"

The flames rose behind Knight, six feet high and spreading. Solberg kicked dirt on the fire with no effect. He raised his arms to shield his face from the heat. Tall flames lurched toward Michael Slaton's house. Solberg grabbed his cell and dialed.

"This is 911. What is your emergency?" the woman asked.

"There's a forest fire just off Riddick Road near the old school-house. It's heading north toward some houses."

"Who am I speaking with, please?"

"Matt Solberg from Search and Rescue. If you've got anybody left, send firefighters now!" He ran back to the truck, fueled by adrenaline, heedless now of his injured knee. He tossed his pack on the seat and started up the engine.

But where would Knight go? He'd never go home now—he was caught and knew it. There would be scandal, criminal charges, and jail. Solberg figured Knight was desperate and irrational, maybe suicidal. Where *would* Knight go? This was the anniversary of Molly's death, which led to only one answer—St. Mary's Peak. St. Molly's Peak, Knight called it. The forests north and south of it were ablaze, but somehow the mountain wasn't on fire. Knight might mistake it for a place of refuge. A castle to make a last stand.

Solberg raced down Indian Prairie Loop. He saw a contrail of dust up ahead and pressed the pedal down, trying to keep up. There was no way to know it was Knight, but no reason to think otherwise. Up ahead, the dust led left, up St. Mary's Peak Road. That cinched it. Knight was heading up the mountain on a long dead-end road. Crazy, but there it was. Solberg took a turn too fast and fishtailed in the gravel. Regaining control, he accelerated in pursuit.

Solberg had one idea—*catch Bill Knight*—but the switchbacks made this impossible. At each bend, dust rained down from above, nearly blinding Solberg, forcing him to slow down. There were nine major switchbacks in eleven miles to the top, each one tighter than the last. The dirt road was barely wide enough for one rig, let alone space for Solberg to pin Knight's truck against a slope.

It dawned on Solberg that this would play out on foot—and him with a banged-up knee. The end game wouldn't be a search, but it might be a rescue.

Dust poured down from a turn eight miles up St. Mary's Peak Road. Solberg braked to a dead stop. "Dammit!" He waited until the faintest visibility returned and raced ahead.

After the final bend, Solberg brought the Ford up to fifty, the truck rising above bumps on the washboard road. The trailhead parking lot appeared through the dust. Solberg laid on the brakes and barely avoided colliding with Bill Knight's abandoned rig.

He shut off the engine, yanked the parking brake, and jumped out of the cab. Solberg faced upslope and yelled. "Bill!" He turned his head to listen. Silence. "Come down! We can fix this!" Nothing.

Solberg gathered his pack. He needed water, possibly the first-aid kit, maybe the gun. He shook his right leg to loosen up the knee, strapped on his headlamp, and flipped the switch. No need to hide now. In fact, seeing a light gaining on him might convince Knight to give up. Solberg might still be able to save his lost friend.

The trail headed steeply up the mountain through lodgepole pines and Douglas firs. Solberg ascended fast, stopping once to cough and spit out smoke. Then he raged uphill at the limit of his capacity, slowed by a growling pain in his knee. Solberg made it to the spring a mile into the 3.8-mile hike, maybe a third of the twenty-five hundred vertical feet of gain behind him. From here the route would even out until the final steep section above the trees.

Still no sign of Bill Knight. Solberg looked down, his headlamp illuminating the dusty trail. Too many boot prints to tell. Even with the woods closed, people were climbing St. Mary's Peak.

Had Knight doubled back? Solberg rejected the idea. Unless the man bushwhacked downhill in the dark, this trail was the only way in or out.

SELWAY-BITTERROOT WILDERNESS. At the sign, trees thinned. Long avalanche chutes fell downhill to the left.

Solberg was crazed with frustration. Normally, he could out-hike anyone, but now... He pressed uphill, bullying past the pain in his leg. Reddish firelight revealed the lookout tower on the summit. He had climbed this mountain two hundred times for training and knew the tower was a mirage. Still forty-five minutes to the top. He vowed to make it in thirty.

Movement above him—someone was hiking with no flashlight. The figure made a bend through stunted pines. Bill Knight was heading for the summit. Beyond that, only cliffs.

Solberg put his head down and drove himself onward. Mouth open, breathing hard, then harder, heart punching against his chest. Death felt possible now, but Solberg knew his body and trusted it wouldn't be him. Faster, higher, no stopping.

Up ahead, Bill Knight had neared his limit. He panted and retched his way up the steep trail into the treeless alpine zone. Thick smoke rushed across the rock field and firebrands blew dangerously close. He cringed from a sharp pain in his ribcage. Needed more air. Knight grabbed a look downhill and saw the headlamp gaining on him. It was Solberg—no doubt about it. That familiar relentless gait. Besides, it couldn't really be anyone else. The trailhead parking lot was empty and the lookout tower was closed.

Through his fatigue, Bill Knight had a moment of clarity. *Is this how I want it to end?*

He pushed that thought away and crossed flat ground on the shoulder of the mountain. Knight tried to pull ahead, but couldn't. Legs heavy, spent. He swayed from side to side as he hiked, gasoline sloshing in the can digging into his sweating back. Knight struggled up the last switchbacks, pausing to pull breaths into his quaking lungs. Glowing fires spread as far as he could see, like a chain of erupting volcanoes: St. Joseph to the north, then Three Badger, then a string of burns leading across the world. All this was far beyond Bill Knight's expectations.

But Matt Solberg was catching up.

Two hundred yards back, Solberg made the flat and raced forward. Somehow his knee wasn't caving. At the switchbacks, he willed his body up the last pitch and saw Knight just ahead, bent over at the waist. "Bill," he gasped. Too soft to be heard. Solberg pushed forward, breathing loudly, groaning, refusing the pain permission to take over. Just a bit farther.

Knight struggled past the fire lookout tower, his body yanking in breaths. He tripped on a guy wire and fell hard against the rocks, cutting his wrist. Knight struggled to his feet and weaved toward a rise of granite boulders that marked the true summit. Beyond it was a cliff—one thousand feet of open air.

Solberg crested as dawn arrived through the smoke. To the west he saw the outline of Bill Knight, backlit by firelight. Solberg moved slowly, letting his brain gain oxygen. He pulled one arm from his pack and eased forward.

Knight stood looking over the cliff, holding something angular in his right hand. Orange and red flickered off its metallic sides.

"It's me, Bill," Solberg said, stopping thirty feet away.

"I'm glad it's you," Knight panted, turning toward Solberg. He held a lighter in his hand.

Solberg smelled gasoline. He fell back on his search and rescue training. Calm the person down. "Quite a hike. Might be my personal best. How about you?"

Knight didn't respond. He rocked back and forth, clasping the gas can against his chest. The sound of fluid splashing against metal.

Solberg barely recognized the man in front of him. "You can have a life after all this, you know."

"In prison?" Knight said.

"It's better than dying."

Knight rocked faster. "I'm dying of cancer, Matt."

"What? I had no idea you..."

"But cancer doesn't matter now. My fires killed someone." Knight lifted the lighter to the can.

"We don't know that," Solberg said, trying to stay calm. "There are so many fires."

Solberg thought of the .357 in his pack, but Knight was holding gasoline. Solberg pulled a water bottle out of his pack, casually took a drink, then held it out in front of him. "It's not Laphroaig, but it'll do."

Knight eyed the cliff, teetering at the edge.

Solberg spoke evenly. "The man who died was hiding from the law. He set fires at Taylor Creek and Lolo. He was involved with the burn at Cyr and helped start the Mann Gulch fire that almost killed Linda Merchant. The guy was a troubled soul with a criminal record, so..."

"Fleming," Knight said.

Solberg was stunned. "How did you know that?"

"I poisoned his mind with knowledge." Knight said, sloshing the gas back and forth, handling the lighter.

Solberg resisted asking what that meant.

"Tell me why I set these fires?" Knight asked. A hint of the Good Doctor remained.

Solberg played along to buy time. "You teach that fire heals forests," he said. "We've forgotten that and maybe this year you reminded us. Just in a way that..."

"Don't pander!" Knight yelled. He reeled along the brink of the cliff.

"Alright, you set the fires because Slaton killed Molly, the Earth is fucked, and your heart is broken."

Knight nodded approvingly. "*Quod erat demonstrandum.*"

Ashy wind blew across the summit and Solberg rubbed soot out of his eyes. When he looked back, Knight stood on the edge of the cliff, emptying the gas can over his chest.

Solberg yelled, "No! Bill, don't!"

Knight looked back. "I'm sorry."

He flicked the lighter and flames exploded over his chest and head. Knight ran three strides and dove off the cliff, trailing bolts of fire behind him. No screams, just a human fireball plummeting through the air.

Solberg rushed to the edge and watched Knight's still-living body light up the canyon until it crashed against a spire and rag-dolled into the forest far below. "Oh, my God," Solberg whispered. He pulled back from the cliff and fell to the ground, arms covering his eyes, breathing in gasps.

When the world stopped spinning, Solberg got to his feet and looked below. A fire was spreading from Bill Knight's corpse into the loyal wilderness.

88

"Knight set himself on fire?" Bernie Katz sat back in disbelief.

"Yes," Solberg said. He slumped in a chair at the FBI office.

"When you called from the mountain, I thought you'd lost it," Bernie said.

"I had." Shock covered Solberg's soot-covered face.

Bernie sighed. "Revenge for his dead wife, cancer, too many trees, too many houses. I get the revenge part, but the rest..." He paused. "I guess a scientist rubbed two sticks together and came up with crazy."

"It's not that simple, Bernie."

Katz accepted that. "We'll send someone up for the body once the Forest Service gives the green light. The woods are still closed, even to the Bureau, unless we push it, which I'm in no mood to do."

Solberg's hands trembled.

"Are you alright?" Bernie asked.

"No, I'm far from alright. But there's someone who can help."

Solberg drove across the Beartracks Bridge to Bo Xiong's blue house beside the Clark Fork River. He stood for a moment on the porch, unsure what to say to her.

Bo opened the door, her face stricken.

Matt couldn't speak.

She reached out to hug him, but he walked inside in a daze. Bo brought him a glass of orange juice and Matt drained it. They sat close together on the couch.

Bo rubbed his back. "Like I said on the phone, maybe if I hadn't pushed, you wouldn't have gone out there and..."

"...maybe Michael Slaton and a lot of other people would have been killed. A rural volunteer company put out Knight's fire before it caused much damage. That wouldn't have happened if you hadn't solved this. And who knows how many more fires Bill would have set?"

"I just wish you hadn't seen him die so horribly."

Matt embraced Bo and whispered, "Bill died in that crash with Molly. It just took him three years to burn."

89

Solberg was in the kitchen when Becky showed up at the open door. "Are you alright?" she asked, eyes wide. "I read what happened on the Internet and drove right over."

"I'm okay, but why did you...?"

"A text wasn't enough." Becky picked at the sleeve of her checked shirt.

"You want some tea?" Solberg asked.

"No, thanks." She sat across the table from him. "The way that man died sounds awful. I can't imagine."

"It's good that you can't imagine, but it's over now."

"Dr. Knight was your friend, right? I sort of remember him."

"Yes, he was my friend."

"Why did he set those fires? It sounds nuts." She looked much too thin.

Solberg sighed. "His wife died and grief poisoned him."

Becky nodded her understanding. Her green eyes were unguarded and adult. "By the way, my relationship with Brace is over."

"What happened? Did he hurt you?"

She shrugged. "Brace lacks the commitment to be a bully. My girlfriends said I deserved better than that lying scumbag. I finally wised up and gave him the boot."

"Good," Solberg said. "You *do* deserve better."

"I'll live by myself for a while. Got some things to figure out."

A long silence as they stared at each other. Matt's eyes welled up.

"You mind if I come home for Thanksgiving?" Becky whispered.

"I'd love that."

"I miss your stupid sweet-potato pie." A hint of his little girl.

"But please make the cranberry sauce. I'm sick of that canned stuff."

"And I'll bake some gluten-free bread," Becky said, grinning.

"Imagine my joy." Matt rolled his eyes.

They laughed together for the first time in forever. It felt like oxygen to Solberg.

"Oh," Becky said, "let me get something." She walked outside and returned carrying a canvas. "Mom would want her painting of

234

Totem Mountain to live here. I could never bring myself to take it out of the closet."

Solberg fought back emotion.

"I still miss Mom every day," Becky said.

"I know, sweetie. I'm so sorry I wasn't there when she died."

"Me too." Becky cried for a while.

Solberg did too.

Becky finally wiped her eyes and asked, "Are you still with Bo?"

"Yes."

"Do you love her?"

"I do."

Becky nodded. "Maybe at Thanksgiving I can get to know her a little."

Solberg smiled. "Bo would enjoy that."

They ate stir-fry veggies for dinner, then played cribbage like they used to. Neither of them said much except "15-2, 15-4, a pair for 6." When she got tired, Becky slept in her old room under a blue and beige bedspread her mother had knitted years before. Solberg lay awake for hours, his mind filled with memories and regrets.

The next morning, he made Becky huckleberry pancakes. They talked in spurts over breakfast: struggling, then at ease, back and forth, feeling each other out. There was time now to learn to do better. After washing the dishes together, they hugged with stiff, familiar arms.

"I'll fly out to see you in a few weeks, if that's okay," Solberg said.

"Okay, Dad," Becky said picking up her purse.

She had finally spoken that word again. Solberg swallowed hard. "I'm heading to L.A. to see a kid I helped, so I'll make a stopover."

"Is it the girl you saved at Mann Gulch?" Becky asked.

"Linda Merchant."

"Is she alright?" Becky looked into her father's eyes.

Matt gazed back at his daughter. "In time she will be."

90

A month later, the weather turned cool and rainy. This blessing often came around County Fair Week; it was an event meteorologists call the Singularity. It brought wet chilly days in the valleys and cold downpours in the mountains. A message to have faith in the salvation of snow.

Matt Solberg led a mule through a steady rain up Kootenai Creek Canyon in the Bitterroot Mountains. He wouldn't dream of riding the sweet animal; he had too much pride in his own two legs. But there was work to do that was beyond his strength, and the mule seemed willing. Her name was Sarah, and she was burlap brown.

After Knight died, Michael Slaton publicly thanked Matt and Bo in the *Missoulian* for saving him and his property. "But we're putting the house on the market and leaving Montana for good." He'd even called and offered to buy Matt and Bo dinner.

They declined ungraciously.

Solberg moved forward in the rain. The canyon walls were made of cooked granite—border gneiss—the transformed underbelly of a former world. The divide between a colony of people and an empire of elk.

A mile later, Solberg walked into the pure granitic core. The Bitterroots were born of fire, a molten mass that intruded and sloughed off a thick block of mudstone that slid twenty miles east and came to rest as the Sapphire Mountains. A gravity slide block. An irresistible force of change. Steep canyon faces rose up, smoothed by the rough caress of glacial ice thousands of years ago. Solberg knew the geology well, like the biography of an essential friend.

After five miles, he turned south into a side canyon with no particular name. Sarah paused to drink in the creek, then looked at Solberg with huge womanly eyes. "Another hour or so," he told her.

It was slow going: dead-fallen trees, soaked bushes, and minimal trail. Hard to go wrong, though, just head uphill and follow the sound of water. And there was lots of water now, replenished by days of prayed-for rain.

The forest fires were mostly out, but weeks of summer remained, and you never knew when an injured blaze might heal and flare up again. For now, though, a corner had been turned. The Missoula Smokejumpers were finally getting days off to sleep in their own beds and eat anything but MREs or Spam. Hotshot crews were also catching up on desperately needed rest. Slurry bombers, choppers, and scout planes were flown back to their bases and serviced. Jokes were heard and T-shirts made: "I Didn't Burn out in Montana." There was talk of school beginning and football games.

But the fires had inflicted a body count. Forty-seven people had died in Montana—including Malcolm Fleming and Dr. Bill Knight. More than eleven thousand homes had been destroyed—half of those in fires set by Knight himself.

Knight had been excoriated in the press and made the sole scapegoat. Not climate change, not lightning strikes, not Tabish, Fleming, Paladin, or any of the other arsonists. Bill Knight alone was responsible for the losses. It was easier for people that way: a dead lunatic—a liberal scientist, no less. It'll never happen again.

Paladin had vanished except for a signed post to the *Missoulian* website. "I'm totally sorry. Never meant to kill those kids. Game over." But a day later another signed message read: "See you next summer, Monsters."

People called it fake news or believed a copycat had claimed Paladin's name. Memes filled the Internet: Paladin as hero, villain, anarchist, saint. Viral irrational America.

But realtors still reported slim sales and quiet telephones. Solberg knew this fear would fade in time. Montana history shows that memories are weak and myths are incurably strong. In a few years, those dream houses would be rebuilt even bigger than before. The forests would be reborn too, but as diminished versions of themselves in a rapidly warming world. Ironically, Knight's vengeful fires had sped up climate change by unleashing vast amounts of carbon dioxide. A feedback loop of loss. Turns out the Good Doctor was wrong in every way.

Solberg went back to the task at hand, picking up his pace. He entered the basin below St. Mary's Peak and stopped beside a small lake. The air smelled wet and lonely. His friend had chosen to die up here in a horrifying way. That mystery was tragically easy to solve.

Bill Knight got lost.

Solberg still hadn't figured out what Bill meant about poisoning Fleming's mind with knowledge. He might never know since Rob Tabish had lawyered up and quit talking. Perhaps there was no need anymore.

Solberg looked up at St. Mary's Peak. Despite the summer's record heat, a small patch of snow survived on a north-facing headwall. A reason for hope.

Getting closer. He moved forward by intuition, then stopped in an area of low, burned trees. He tied Sarah to the black remains of a whitebark pine. She shook water from her body and eased into a nap. There was no sign of the lookout tower from this angle, and no hikers were visible on the summit. He was alone.

The rain fell harder. Solberg walked hundred-foot transects through a charred area. He pulled his jacket close and snugged his wool cap, searching back and forth in a grid pattern. It was the only rational way to find a body, or what remained of it, after a month exposed to the elements. A burned body—after bears, lions, and ravens had eaten their fill and scattered the rest.

The Forest Service had forbidden this recovery until the fires receded and the weather broke. A concession to good sense and rough politics. It was the now-infamous Bill Knight after all, and no one was in a big hurry to bring his carcass out.

Solberg wasn't either. He was alone in this faraway canyon spending his last time with a forever-gone friend.

The trees around him had burned in a mosaic. Some died, while others, for no obvious reason, survived. Just as Knight said, fire is a lovely monster. Solberg completed ten transects without finding any sign. He disturbed Sarah by retrieving jerky from a saddlebag, and felt refreshed by the savory salt.

On the south edge of the grid, Solberg found a charred femur. He exhaled hard. Within three strides he found a ribcage with tatters of fascia dripping water onto the spine. Solberg fought back vomit and withdrew a GPS unit from his pocket. He hesitated, then put it away. There would be no record. The skull was lodged under a Labrador tea bush. There were bite marks on the blackened temples and strips of flesh on the crown. The skull had Bill Knight's gap-toothed smile.

Solberg went numb.

He searched steadily, recovering arm bones, legs, the pelvis, shoulder blades: the big parts. Solberg was a grim collector of what remained. He searched until he'd done his best, then he searched again.

Cold rain turned to snow. Large flakes drifted down, melting when they hit the ground. Solberg went over to Sarah, pushed aside the body bag, and slid a shovel from a cinch. He walked back and dug a hole in the sopping ground. Took an hour. The air got colder and flakes began to stick.

He gathered Bill Knight's bones and laid them in the grave, placing the skull at the far end facing him. Solberg touched a cheekbone, then shoveled wet earth until his friend was safely home. There would be no marker. He lifted a flask of Laphroaig toward the remains, took a sip, and stood awhile.

Snow would cover any trace of his passing.

About the Author

JOHN B. WRIGHT is a former land use planning director in Montana and has forty-five years of experience in designing conservation easements in Montana and across the West. He is a founder of the New Mexico Land Conservancy, an NGO that has conserved over seven hundred thousand acres. Wright taught Geography for twenty-seven years at New Mexico State University, where he was named a Regents Professor. He is the author of over one hundred scholarly articles and four award-winning books, including *Saving the Ranch: Conservation Easement Design in the American West, Montana Ghost Dance: Essays on Land and Life,* and *Rocky Mountain Divide: Selling and Saving the West. Fire Scars* is his first novel.